THE ONES WE'RE MEANT TO FIND

ALSO BY JOAN HE

Descendant of the Crane

THE ONES WE'RE MEANT TO FIND

JOAN HE

ROARING BROOK PRESS
NEW YORK

Published by Roaring Brook Press
Roaring Brook Press is a division of Holtzbrinck Publishing Holdings Limited Partnership
120 Broadway, New York, NY 10271 • fiercereads.com

Library of Congress Cataloging-in-Publication Data is available.

Our books may be purchased in bulk for promotional, educational, or business use. Please
contact your local bookseller or the Macmillan Corporate and Premium Sales Department
at (800) 221-7945 ext. 5442 or by email at MacmillanSpecialMarkets@macmillan.com.

First edition, 2021 • Book design by Aurora Parlagreco
Printed in the United States of America

ISBN 978-1-250-25856-4 (hardcover)
10 9 8 7 6 5 4 3 2

ISBN 978-1-250-83063-0 (special edition)
10 9 8 7 6 5 4 3 2 1

ISBN 978-1-250-83338-9 (special edition)
10 9 8 7 6 5 4 3 2 1

For my mom, a sister in spirit.

And for Leigh. Thanks for loving Kasey most.

For whatever we lose (like a you or a me),
it's always ourselves we find in the sea

—e. e. cummings
"maggie and milly and molly and may"

1

I WAKE ON MY FEET, wind tangled in my hair. The sand is cold beneath my arches and the tide is rising, white foam and gray water frothing around my ankles before fizzing through my toes.

My *bare* toes.

That alone wouldn't be a problem. But I'm also in M.M.'s cargo pants, the softest pair in her moth-eaten closet. I wore them to bed last night, the same night, apparently, I sleep-walked to the shore. Again.

"Shit."

"Shit," repeats a voice—monotone, compared to the wave-forms rising from the sea before me. My sleep-soaked eyes swivel over my shoulder and spot U-me as she rolls through the morning mist enshrouding the beach. Her belted wheels leave behind triangles like paw prints. Her boxy head, perched atop a canister body, comes halfway up my thigh when she reaches my side. "Shit: fecal matter, noun; to expel feces from the body, verb; to deceive—"

"I locked the door."

U-me switches gears at the declarative. "Strongly agree."

"You hid the key in the house."

"Strongly agree."

The surf surges forward, forcing me back onto the beach. As I retreat, a glint on the ground snags my eye.

The house key, embedded like a shell in the gray sand.

I scoop it up. *"Shit."*

The one-worder sends U-me down dictionary lane a second time. I barely hear her over the sea's drone.

Every other sleep, I dream of swimming to the horizon and finding my sister at the edge of the world. She takes me by the hand and leads us home. Home means a city in the sky, sometimes. Or another island. Home could be here, for all I care, if she were with me. She's not. I don't know what separated us, just that waking up really sucks, especially when my body is hell-bent on miming the dreams no matter how many doors I lock. My solution? Turn dreams into reality. Find my sister, sooner preferably to later.

"Come on, love," I say to U-me, turning my back to the tide. "Let's try to beat the sun."

I stalk up the beach. My shoulders still ache from the last trip inland, but recovery can wait. The first of my nighttime escapades never took me into the water. Today, I'm ankle-deep. Tomorrow? Finish Hubert today, and I won't stick around to find out.

In fifty strides, I'm upon M.M.'s house. It sits daredevil-ishly close to the coastline, a squat little shack overlooking the ocean from atop a bed of rocks, half-sunken into the sand. Stuff's everywhere. On the porch steps. The deck. Prized possessions, like M.M.'s fanny pack, must be stored above sand level. I tear the pack off the porch rail, then loop to the house side, where Hubert is lounging.

"Morning, Bert." I shoulder the pack. "Feeling lucky today?"

No reply. Hubert's not very chatty, which is fine by me. I make the small talk; he keeps me sane by existing.

You see, I've divided my time on this island into life-before-Hubert and life after. Life-before-Hubert . . . Joules, I hardly remember what I did to pass the days. Probably planting taro, fixing M.M.'s water pipes. Standard survival stuff.

Then I successfully completed my first journey inland and met Hubert. He was in pieces. Now he's one propeller short of his normal self, and I have to say, I'm proud of how far we've come. Sure, bringing back his body almost broke mine, and a freaky situation involving his hull, some rope, and gravity nearly tourniqueted off my leg, but he's relying on me and that gives me strength. I'm relying on him, too. I *wish* I could swim to my sister like I do in my dreams. The problem with oceans? They always seem smaller from the shore.

"Just you wait, love," I say to Hubert, nudging him with my foot. "You. Me. The sea. This evening."

One propeller.

I won't return without it.

U-me rolls over and together we set off inland. We outstrip the sounds of the sea and gulls, until it's just the crunch of rock under U-me's wheels, the squish of gray mud under my rubber clogs—compliments of M.M.—and foggy silence for kilometers on end. Eventually, the mud calcifies to shale. Pools of rainwater form little shallow, sterile ponds. Shrubs lean in the direction of the wind, their roots crawling like veins along the rock. This side of the island—shore side—is mostly flat in elevation. If not for the fog, you'd be able to see straight to the ridge. It bisects the island, a wall of stone that can't be circumnavigated, only climbed.

In the shadow of the towering ridge face, I unzip my pack, remove the coil of nylon rope, and drape it around U-me's neck. "You know what to do."

"Strongly agree." She rolls over the ridge's crumbling base and up, shrinking to a speck. At the top, she sends the now-fastened rope back to me. All one hundred meters tumble down.

I catch the end and yank, checking that it's secure before knotting it around my waist. I get as good a grip as I can around the slick nylon, breathe in, and push off the ground.

Foothold. Handhold. Repeat. The rising sun warms my shoulders as I hit the final stretch. I heave myself onto the narrow ridgetop, drenched beneath M.M.'s sweater, and catch my breath while surveying the land on the other side. Meadowside. Grayscale like the rest of the island, trees growing in scraggly bunches. Brick mounds swell through the waist-high grass like tumors. I have yet to figure out what they are. Shrines, maybe. Very mossy, neglected shrines.

Shaking out my arms, I start the descent. U-me rolls beside me, occasionally beeping out a "Strongly disagree" in response to my foothold choices. But I've memorized most of the soft spots in the ridge, and I order her back up top when I'm half-way down.

The untied rope drops just as my feet hit the ground. I stuff it into my pack and pat U-me's head when she rejoins me. "Good work, love."

Aside from us, the mist is the only moving thing in the meadow this morning. I try my best to ignore the shrines and attribute my goose bumps to the sweat cooling on my back. Hunger stabs my stomach, but I don't stop for a taro biscuit. Not here. Doesn't feel right to eat here.

The meadow ends with a sparse forest of pines. Several are fused along the trunk like conjoined twins. Infiltrating the pines are eight-point-leaf trees. They dominate the forest deeper in. Branches clasp above our heads, leaves strewing the path with rotting mulch. A beetle darts in front of us—and ends up under U-me's wheels.

Crunch.

I flinch. The taking of a life—however small—seems bigger when there's so little of it on this island already. "Heartless."

"Heartless: without feeling, adjective; cruel, adjective."

"Or literally without a heart."

"Neutral."

"Okay, what do you even mean by that? Neutral to the def-inition? Or to the idea of not having a heart?"

U-me's fans whir.

I duck under a low-hanging branch. "Right. Sorry, love.

Forgot you don't do direct questions." *Along with a bajillion other things.*

When I first found U-me in the cupboard under M.M.'s sink, in need of some sun juice, I'd danced around the house. A bot could help me build the boat. Or map out the waters in my vicinity. Or simply provide me critical intel, like where I'm from and how to find my sister.

Except U-me isn't your average bot. She's a mash-up of a dictionary and a questionnaire rating scale, about as useful to me as . . . well, a dictionary or questionnaire rating scale. It helps that she can tie ropes, dig holes, and follow my lead, like roll over in the general direction of the junk piles when we finally arrive at the Shipyard, my name for the clearing in the forest, where there's another little shrine and something that looks a lot like a swimming pool. The rim is overgrown with moss and surrounded by heaps of scrap metal. Most of the scraps are oxidized, deformed, and unsalvageable, especially now that I've used what was salvageable on Hubert.

Still, I crouch and go through the piles, methodically at first, then less so. The odds of finding a propeller are slim. But so were the odds of finding *any* boat parts and yet, here we are: hull, rudder, tiller, motor, bolt, all accounted for. Just when I think, *That's it, my luck's run out,* I find another piece. What's more, each piece seems to come from the same boat. It's kind of magical. Everything about Hubert is. He came to me at a time when I needed him most. *Don't give up,* the universe seemed to be saying on the day I met him. And I haven't. I'm so close to finding Kay. My breath shortens as I think of her. A flash of sequins. A shriek of a laugh. A cherry-ice pop stained smile, the color red fleeting. Two hands joined, mine and hers. An impossibly white ladder, connecting sky to sea. We splash in and float for days.

When I linger in the memory, though, the water around us trembles. I see a boat, carried away by the waves. I hear a whisper—*I'm sorry*—laced with the sorrow of a goodbye.

Positive thoughts. It's better to focus on the present. To break things down into manageable tasks. Build Hubert. Find Kay.

Build.

Find.

Build.

Find.

But dread poisons my thoughts anyway.

I drop the scrap in my hands. My knees crack as I rise. Pins needle my toes as I walk to the edge of the pool. It brims with rainwater, reflecting a wobbly image of me: a girl with straight, dark hair just past shoulder-length, face too pale and eyes black, if I have to guess. Along with my memories, I've lost my ability to see in color. Weird, I know. Weirder is what happens next. The image in the water shifts, and I'm looking at a reflection of Kay.

"Where are you?" she asks, her voice a quieter, deeper version of mine.

"I'm coming, love."

"You're forgetting." I shake my head vehemently, but Kay goes on. "Look again," she says. "You're just seeing yourself."

And I am.

The girl in the water isn't Kay.

It's me.

My pulse drums in my ears. Obviously, my sister isn't here. But the Kay-of-my-mind is right: I *am* forgetting. When I dream of her, it's in vibrant color, unlike the gradients of gray of my monochrome days. But everything is hazy when I wake. The details merge. The colors fade.

I screw my eyes shut as if to wring them out. Reopen them. The tiles at the bottom of the pool shimmer. The water seems to be calling my name.

Cee.

My feet move to the rim before I realize what I'm doing. I slap my cheeks. I'm awake. Not dreaming. Not sleepwalking. Definitely *not* going to end up in microbe soup.

One step after another, I back up. My chest tenses, like there's a rubber band slung between it and the water. I'm half afraid my heart's going to snap out when I tear myself away from the pool, but it remains firmly behind my ribs, pounding hard as I kneel back beside the junk pile.

Sometimes the need to find Kay overwhelms me, so I don't think about Kay. I think about Hubert, who's depending on me. I think about the sea and how impossible-to-swim big it is. I think about all the restless nights I've spent in M.M.'s house, dressed in her sweaters and cargo pants, living a hand-me-down life. Nothing here is truly mine. Not even U-me. My real home waits for me across the sea.

First things first: Get off the island.

I dig deeper—and yank my hand away, hissing. Then the

pain recedes, because I see the blade. It protrudes from the dirt, glistening with some gray liquid—my blood, I think. I also think . . .

Don't jinx it.

Carefully, I ease the blade free. Two more emerge, all three spiraling around a hub. I hold it up to the light streaming through the trees. The three metal petals wink, slightly dented but otherwise very propeller-shaped to my amateur eye.

"Joules." *Am I dreaming?*

Nope, still bleeding. Still holding on to the tarnished propeller like it's some exotic flower.

U-me rolls to me. "Joules: a unit of work energy, noun—"

"Fucking megajoules! We did it, U-me!" I tackle-hug her, then let out a whoop that echoes across the island. U-me blinks, probably wondering if the sound counts as a translatable word. Whatever her verdict, I don't hear it. I'm already rushing back to the ridge, not sure if I should cry or laugh or shout some more.

So I do all three.

Goodbye, meadow. I dash through the too-tall grass. *Goodbye, shrines.*

Goodbye, ridge. I scale it in record time, my arms numbed by adrenaline. *Goodbye, M.M. Thank you for sharing your house. Sorry the moths got to your sweaters before I did.*

I save the last goodbye for myself, the only soul on this Joules-forsaken place. Trust me, I've searched. Everywhere. Whittled my situation down to the disheartening facts:

#1 I'm on an abandoned island.

#2 I have no idea how or why, because (see #3)

#3 I quite possibly have a case of amnesia that worsens by the day.

Not-so-disheartening fact #4?

I'm out of here.

2

FROM A DISTANCE, THE CITY in the sky appeared as life-less as the ocean below it.

Beneath the surface was a different story.

Inside stratum-99, the penultimate level of the eco-city, the party had left Kasey Mizuhara marooned at her own kitchen island. As everyone else jumped to the beat, bodies shimmering under the blacklight, Kasey stood behind a facade of drinks and cups, watching like one might watch animals at a zoo, except she didn't feel quite human. Alien was more like it. Or ghost.

About time. Kasey had missed her invisibility. She'd been recognized twice in the last week alone, and when the first wave of partiers had logged in, she'd almost logged out.

But the universe had a way of balancing itself. Within fifteen minutes, a group of Kasey's classmates mistook her for the hired bartender. Then, while Kasey was winging the mixed drinks, Meridian messaged to say she could no longer make it. *That's fine*, Kasey sent back. Better than fine, actually, that the mastermind of Kasey's so-called "moving on" party wasn't present for it. Because no one was here for Kasey, to her great relief.

To her equally great consternation, everyone was here for her sister, Celia.

Case in point: "Fifty bytes she shows up tonight," a girl on the dance floor said to her partner, her words captioned in Kasey's mind's eye thanks to her Intraface. The most portable computer yet, the Intraface was an interface within the brain capable of capturing memories, transmitting thought-to-speech messages, and—in this instance—lip-reading sentiments Kasey found ludicrous but forgivable. Crashing her own party would be a Celia thing to do. She'd show up fashionably late, bedecked in sequins, and everyone would stare, the fear of missing out on a laugh, a kiss, a whispered confidence written over their faces.

Even then, they missed things.

Like the way Celia never failed to find Kasey among a crowd.

The way Celia found her now.

A pulse went through Kasey. She tore her gaze from the sea of bobbing heads and focused on the city she was modeling out of cups. It was the lights. The music. Too dark, too loud, messing with her senses. Withdrawing inward, she tended to the slew of log-in requests cluttering her mind's eye. ACCEPT GUEST. ACCEPT GUEST. ACCEPT GUEST. More people appeared on the dance floor. None, however, could outclass

THE ONES WE'RE MEANT TO FIND • 13

her sister, and Celia was still there when Kasey dared another glance. She was dancing with a boy. Their gazes met, and Celia lifted her perfectly lasered brow as if to say: *This one's a catch. Want to try your luck, love?*

Kasey tried to shake her head. Couldn't. Was transfixed as her sister abandoned the boy and slipped through the partiers with ease. She joined Kasey by the island, dispersing the group that was blowing rings of hallucinogenic smoke in Kasey's direction.

The smoke cleared.

Celia disappeared.

In her place was a girl with electric-blue hair and Newton's cradles for earrings. *Gimmicky*, Celia would have said, whereas Kasey might have actually found the earrings pretty cool if her mind hadn't flatlined, deleting all opinions, fashion or otherwise, her heart racing 100 bpm as the girl seized a cup and filled it. "Quick, talk to me."

Was she still hallucinating? "Me?" Kasey asked, checking to see that the kitchen island had, in fact, been deserted.

"Yes, you," said the girl, prompting Kasey's Intraface to launch SILVERTONGUE, a conversation aid recommended by Celia. *It'll make things easier*, her sister had promised.

Mostly, its rapid-fire tips just made Kasey dizzy. She blinked, popping the bubbles lathering her vision. "Talk to you about . . . ?"

"Anything."

Insufficient parameters. Annoyed, Kasey surveyed her surroundings for inspiration. "The entire human population fits into a one cubic kilometer cube?" The fact came out sounding like a question; she corrected her inflection. "The entire human population fits into a one cubic kilometer cube."

"**REPETITION DETECTED!**" chimed SILVERTONGUE in disapproval.

"Really?" said the girl, peering at the dance floor over the rim of her cup. "Go on."

"About the homo sapiens volume?"

The girl laughed, as if Kasey had told a joke. Had she? Jokes were good. Humor was a core trait on the Coles Humanness Scale. It was just . . . Kasey hadn't been expecting laughter as a reaction. This wasn't going well, by standards of an experiment. She had half a mind to ask the girl what was so funny, but was outpaced by the conversation.

"Thanks a million," said the girl, looking away from the dance floor and finally facing Kasey. "Some people can't take a 'not interested' hint to save their life. So, you here to see her too?"

Questions were straightforward. Questions, Kasey could handle, especially when she knew the anticipated answer. "Her?" she asked, only because she didn't want to encourage it.

She waited for Celia's name. Braced herself for it.

"Yeah, Kasey? Party host?" The girl nodded at the city Kasey had built out of cups when she failed to reply. "Guessing you aren't here to mingle. Gets old fast, once you get over how real it feels. The younger sister, though . . ."

Don't ask. Nothing good could come of it.

"What about her?" Kasey asked, caving to her curiosity.

"I don't know." The girl sipped her drink, eyes veiled. "That's the lure, isn't it? One minute, she's dodging the press. The next, she's e-viting everyone within a twenty-stratum radius to her party. The disconnect is disturbing, don't you think? Like, I have a sister too, and I don't know what I'd do if she went missing." A new song came on, heavy on the delta-synth. "But sure as hell wouldn't be jamming it up to Zika Tu."

Fair. All solid points. "Maybe it's her moving-on party," Kasey offered, rather wishing now Meridian hadn't flaked. Meridian would've been able to explain, in the same way she'd explained to Kasey, why this party made perfect sense, for reasons Kasey was blanking on.

Oh well. She'd tried. She added another cup to her city—and almost knocked the whole thing over when the girl said, "Hard to move on when they still haven't found a body. Too morbid?" she asked as Kasey steadied her model. One cup rolled out of her reach. The girl caught it. "Sorry." She placed the cup atop two others, where it wobbled. Kasey fixed it. "I keep forgetting it's different here. Where I'm from, bodies are every . . . okay, yeah, I'll stop." She bobbed her drink at Kasey. "That's me for you. Yvone, queen of gaffes."

Silence followed.

The girl was waiting, Kasey realized after a delay, for Kasey to introduce herself as well.

Was it too late to come clean about her identity? Probably. "Meridian."

"Sorry?"

"Meridian." How did people talk at parties? *Did* people

talk at parties? Why couldn't this girl have ordered a drink like everyone else and been on her merry way? *"Meridian,"* Kasey repeated as the music turned up.

"What?"

"Meridian." Was it condescending to spell out a name? Or overkill, when the name was as long as Meridian? She should've picked something shorter, in hindsight. *"M-E-R—"*

"Wait, I got it." The girl blinked at Kasey three times, causing Kasey's Intraface to emit a cheery little *ding* as it projected Kasey's ID over her head.

MIZUHARA, KASEY

Rank: 2

Crap.

Kasey canceled the projection, then checked to see if anyone had noticed. Outside, in streets, schools, shops, or any public domain, rank was auto-displayed, the number over your head dogging you wherever you went. Private domains were the only respite. As such, it was considered bad form to swagger around with your rank when it wasn't required.

It was also bad form to lie about your name.

"You're . . ." A frown spread across Yvone's face. "Celia's . . ."

Abort. The LOG OUT screen, already up on Kasey's Intraface, was just a CONFIRM button away when something clapped onto her shoulder.

A hand.

"Kasey?"

She turned—

—and knew, the second she saw the boy, that he was one

of Celia's. Tristan, his name must have been. Or Dmitri. One of the two.

Which?

"Kasey," repeated Tristan/Dmitri, blinking as if he didn't quite believe his eyes. Behind him, the crowd danced on. Kasey would've given anything to be in the thick of it right now. "Thank Joules. I've been trying to reach you for months."

As had everyone else. Spam and malware had flooded her Intraface. All unknown contacts, she'd had to filter out.

"I need to know if it was my fault," Tristan/Dmitri said, voice rising when Kasey shook her head. *"I need to know!"*

Yvone's gaze darted between the two of them, sponging up the exchange.

"I can't sleep at night." Tristan/Dmitri's chest heaved. He took a wet-sounding breath. Kasey's mouth was dry as dust. "Haven't been able to, ever since . . . I thought we were cool, after the breakup, I thought—but now I wonder—was it something I said? Something I did?"

Dmitri, Kasey wanted to say; she did, after all, have a fifty-fifty chance at guessing right. *It's not your fault.* Not anyone's fault. Sometimes there were no answers. No cause and effect, no perpetrators and victims. Only accidents.

But those weren't the words of a loving sister, Kasey knew. Just didn't know how to act like one. A loving sister wouldn't let statistics guide her decisions. *Tristan or Dmitri?* Wouldn't be throwing a party without knowing why, motive left open to interpretation. *Tristan or Dmitri?*

How could she be okay with fifty-fifty?

How could she be *okay* when no one else was?

The bass gobbled up Kasey's heartbeat. Her chest felt weak. She fumbled for the kitchen island behind her, clutching it like the rim of a pool. "Hey, buddy," she heard Yvone saying to Tristan/Dmitri, her voice murky as if buffered by water. "You've got the wrong person."

"I saw her ID just now."

"Well, you saw wrong."

It was nice of Yvone to cover for Kasey. Kasey should have thanked her. Celia would have, not that she'd ever be in Kasey's situation, but *if*, hypothetically.

Celia would have done a thousand things differently from Kasey, who pressed CONFIRM LOG OUT.

The kitchen island vanished. The dance floor, the lights, the drinks and cups, consumables that would turn into carbon emissions at the end of their life cycles if they existed, disappeared, only ever strings of code. Over in the virtual domain, the party went on for everyone still logged in. No one would miss Kasey.

Just as well.

Kasey opened her eyes to the blue-dark of her stasis pod. Its sarcophagus-like interior glowed faintly with data arrays transmitted from her Intraface's biomonitor app, which tracked her vitals whenever she holo-ed. Her heartbeat, while high, fell within the normal range. Her peripheral vision displayed the time—00:15—and the current number of residents still traversing the eco-city as holographic versions of themselves: 36.2%.

Holoing, as it was called, was less of a green alternative and more of a last resort. To live sustainably, people had to live less. Conduct nonessential activities ("essentials" being eating, sleeping, and exercising) in the holographic mode. Fine-dine and jet-set virtually, without trace or footprint. Reduce transportation needs and shrink infrastructure, energy and materials conserved. Concede these things and only then could architects build eco-friendly cities in the skies, safe from rising sea levels. The trade-offs were worth it, in Kasey's opinion. A minority one. Most people rejected living like bento-packed vegetables—be it for their own good or the planet's—and stayed in their land-bound territories. The weather was more extreme, yes, but sufferable. The arctic melt, while lamentable, didn't affect them like it did island and coastal populations.

But the wildfires did. The hurricanes and monsoons. Earthquakes rose in magnitude, exacerbated by decades of deep-crust mining. Natural disasters catalyzed man-made ones: chemical factories and fission plants compromised, meltdowns disseminating radioaxons, nanoparticles, and microcinogens across the land and sea. Global opinion flipped overnight. Eco-cities came to be viewed as utopias, so removed from disaster epicenters. And holoing from one's stasis pod, once seen as restrictive, came to represent freedom and safety. Why experience something in real life when real life had become so volatile?

Why? Kasey wondered now to her sister, even though she knew. Boundaries existed so that Celia could push them.

Nothing was off-limits, no trouble too deep. Her sister was *alive* in a world increasingly removed from life. It was why people found it difficult to cope with the news of her disappearance, with some going as far as to straight-up deny it.

Fifty bytes she shows up tonight.

Others grieved.

I have a sister too.

Still others blamed themselves.

I need to know if it was my fault.

This, Kasey found to be the most nonsensical reaction of all. Her sister was gone. No amount of lost sleep could reverse that. Guilt was irrelevant. Irrational.

Kasey wished she felt less of it.

III

WAIT FOR ME, KAY. I'M coming for you.

My blood swirls down the drain as I rinse the propeller in M.M.'s sink. I dry it with a fistful of sweater. Then I start hammering at the dents. My hands shake so badly, it's a miracle I keep my thumbs. My heart feels like it might detonate, and back outside, I drop the bolt into the sand twice before finally twisting it onto the drive shaft, screwing the propeller in place.

At last, it's done. As the sun sinks, I drag Hubert out on his first test run with M.M.'s solar-cells repurposed as boat motors. I crank on the engine once we're in the water and crab-crawl to his stern.

"Come on, Bert." I grip his sides. "Make me proud."

Hubert groans.

"Come on, *come on*."

A wave rolls under us, pitching me stomach-first into the stern. I brace myself for the next lurch.

It never comes.

Because Hubert moves. He *moves*, skimming over the waves, foam pluming in his wake, and I could kiss him. I really could. I adjust his trim, test his tiller, then steer him back toward the shore. I leave him on the beach and run to the house for my stockpiled supplies. Some of the taro biscuits have gone moldy. I toss them onto the kitchen floor and replace them with fresh ones from M.M.'s glass jar. On a whim, I pour in the entire jar. Gotta go big to go home.

"Strongly disagree," U-me says, following me as I carry the supplies to Hubert.

I stash them in the locker under his stern. "You knew my endgame all along."

"Agree."

"This shouldn't be coming as a surprise."

"Disagree."

"You're contradicting yourself," I complain, but she's not looking at me anymore.

She's looking to the sea.

I look too. In my dreams, there are other islands out there, even floating cities. But in my dreams, I can also see in color and swim for days. Dreams are dreams. I know better than to rely on them.

Truth is, I haven't a clue where Kay is. Joules, I don't know where *I* am. I used to row Hubert as far out as I dared, hoping to find land, or at least something to orient myself. But I never discovered anything, just kilometers of choppy sea.

And now I'm reminded of how it felt out there. How quiet, on the best of days. How stormy on the worst. The *muchness* of things, solid water all around. The *littleness* of things, silence and sunlight to spectate if I drown.

Shivering, I trudge back to the house. The sand-carpeted steps whisper beneath my feet as I climb onto the porch. The kitchen greets me from behind the door. The windows above the sink are open, facing the sea and inviting in its breeze. On windy days, one gust can travel through the half door separating the kitchen from the living room and into the modest hall, breathing life into every nook and cranny, teasing the tattered lace curtains into a dance and animating the rocking chair in the bedroom.

But even without the sea's spell, the place is alive. The furniture is minimal but mismatched, as if collected over time, and the floor plan, while straightforward, springs the occasional oddity, alcoves indenting the walls like sealed-off entryways to other worlds. The house must be an heirloom, cherished and passed down, and as I pull on a sweater from M.M.'s closet, I'm almost tempted to stay. It's possible I'll go mad in isolation, or lose my vision entirely, or the taro plants will catch blight and die. But the future is too abstract. In the here and now, I'm safe. We take care of each other, M.M.'s home and I.

The bedroom door behind me sighs open. I don't turn because it can be no one else, and sure enough, U-me rolls next to me, something in her arms.

A purl-knit sweater embellished with iron-on pugs.

My heart catches in my throat as I remember my first days here. Waking up on the shore, naked as a newborn, drawing air into my deflated lungs. The water has never been warm, but that day, it must have been freezing. My teeth chattered so hard that my vision flickered as I crawled toward the house on the sand-submerged rocks.

M.M. saved my life. Well, her sweaters did. I yanked the pug one from her closet, right after the moths flew out. It was thick and warm, and all I cared about.

It took a full day for the shivering to stop. A week to remember my name. Then the other pieces came back. Memories of colors I can no longer perceive. A sister back at home, wherever home was. We were close—I knew that in my blood. She must have been worried sick when I disappeared. Maybe I'm forgetting her, but what if she's also forgetting *me*?

My heart hardens as I stare at the sweater. I thought my enemy was the sea. But it's this house. These sweaters. Even U-me. They've let me grow comfortable.

I can't grow comfortable.

I leave the bedroom. The living room. I ignore the mess of taros I've made in the kitchen and head out to the porch again. U-me trails me. She watches as I use a piece of metal scrap, foraged from the Shipyard, to etch one more line onto M.M.'s porch rail. It's striped with tally marks of all the days that have passed since I first washed up.

With any luck, this will be the final mark.

"Stay," I order U-me, dropping the scrap metal. "Good," I say, backing down the porch steps as U-me blinks from the deck, sweater still draped in her metal arms. "Just . . . stay."

I swallow, turn, and jog to Hubert. I push him into the water, clamber aboard, and switch on his motor.

I don't look back.

The sun sinks into the horizon as we zoom toward it. It's beautiful, I recall. Sunset. Honey-hued and apple-skinned. But it's hard to retrieve images from the past without feeling like I'm running through dry sand, and soon, the charcoal skies dim to black. The moon brightens slowly, like an antique filament lamp. We hit a calm patch of sea a couple hours later, and I turn off Hubert's motor to save some battery before resting against the supply locker, a spare sweater folded beneath my head. The stars in the sky are the last things I see, and then the sun is rising, rinsing the waters around me to a powder gray. I start the motor again.

I mark the days on Hubert's gunwale. I drink some water, confident it'll rain soon. I nibble on taro biscuits and try to keep up the conversation.

"Bert, love. Do you think we're going the right way?"

"Want a hear a joke? Okay . . . guess not."

"Want to hear it anyway? Why don't oysters give to charity? Because they're shellfish. Get it? Shellfish? Selfish? Okay, I'll stop now."

"Why don't you ever define my curse words?"

"Joules, you're worse than U-me. Why can't you say something?"

I stop talking to Hubert after a week, because I run out of water.

I had to make a choice: Pack enough water that it'd slow Hubert down or hope for rain. I'd hoped for rain. On the island, it rains at least twice a week.

But there's no rain.

Until there is.

I'm trying to nap—the only way I can ignore the desert growing in my mouth—when something plops onto my head. At first I think it's gull poop, but the skies are quiet. I sit up. Another plop, and I almost weep with joy.

Rain. Fat droplets falling out of the gray heavens.

My face tilts back and I part my lips, catching the cold, sweet drops on my tongue. Then I dive for Hubert's locker and wrestle out the empty water bin—not so empty when the first wave crashes into us.

For a stomach-dropping moment, we're shoved under. Bubbles burst before my eyes—I think I scream—and then I'm coughing, eyes stinging with salt and rain, pelting down, because we've resurfaced, thank Joules, and I'm clutching to Hubert's gunwale as the ocean thrashes, waves blacker than ever, and among all that black is a speck of white.

My water bin. Washed overboard, quickly swirling away from us. My taro biscuits, too, dusting the waves like dandruff. The door to Hubert's locker is gone. Torn off. My supply pack is nowhere in sight and I'm sitting in more seawater than not.

"Fuck."

I almost expect to hear U-me, defining my word in response. But she's not here. It's just me and Hubert, volleyed from wave to wave, a toy to the sea. I turn off his motor, hoping it'll help. It doesn't. *Think.* Lightning splits the sky and rain lashes into my face and a wave looms over us out of nowhere, casting us in the shadow of its maw.

Thinking time is over. I start the motor and seize the backup oar, rowing with all my might.

Slowly, we move.

In the wrong direction.

The wave curls us into its grasp. Crushes us.

My ears pop as we plunge. But I still hear it: the scream of tearing metal.

4

THE NEWS HAD RIPPED THROUGH the city like an explosion. The fallout lingered for weeks.

Celia Mizuhara, elder daughter of eco-city architect David Mizuhara, lost at sea.

It was a missing-persons case from pre-Intraface times, when holoing *wasn't* a way of life, biomonitors *didn't* correct neurotransmitter imbalance–driven behaviors, and a person's whereabouts *wasn't* a geolocation query away. And yet, authorities verified the authenticity of the public cambot footage. Prior to sunrise, Celia had indeed taken a duct down to the boat rental below the eco-city. Now both boat and body had vanished, leaving behind a ready-made news story. Friends and exes emerged from the woodwork, eager to fill in Celia's blanks.

Only one relation was absent.

"Kasey Mizuhara!" She evaded the reporters; they holo-ed to her location whenever they could track her down in the public domain. "How are you coping in the days since city authorities declared your sister missing?"

"Presumed dead," Kasey supplied, thinking they'd go away if she kept it concise. Instead, the sound bite went viral. People lambasted the monotone of her voice. Others defended Kasey, explaining her stoicism as if it were a mask concealing her grief. That disturbed Kasey more than the vitriol. Hope was a drug. Why self-medicate when the numbers were right there, time-stamped on the cambot footage? Three months and twelve days, her sister had been lost at sea. Celia was many things, but still mortal. Dehydration would have killed her first, given that she'd taken the boat as is, packing no additional supplies. Who did when going on a recreational spin?

Unless recreation wasn't the intention.

"Attempts to geolocate your sister have failed," reporters were always quick to mention. "Her Intraface seems to have gone completely off-grid. Kasey, would you like to comment?"

"No. No comment."

"Might this be deliberate?" they'd press, and that would stop Kasey, wherever she was—usually at the ducts, waiting for an up-ride home after school, commercials blaring in the background, but even they couldn't drown out the unspoken question.

Might your sister not want to be found?

What could she say? The Intraface was more likely out of range. The boat and body could very well be at the bottom of the seafloor. Possibility didn't equate high probability, and anything was more probable than a conspiracy theory.

But sharing what she really thought would only appall

people, so Kasey would simply shake her head at the reporters and step into the duct when it finally came.

Now, as her moving-on party continued in the virtual domain, she stepped out of her stasis pod, closed the door behind her, and left the room she was fortunate to call her own. Make no mistake: The Mizuharas practiced what they preached. Their unit, like most designed by David for a family of four, was only thirty-five square meters. But at least they had individual rooms connected by a narrow hall, and a window at the hall-end. Everyone else had filled in their walls to boost their units' thermal efficiency scores, causing voice support for windows to be discontinued across the board.

Undeterred, Celia would manually open theirs after sundown. She'd made the task look easy; it was anything but. Kasey had calluses as proof. Tonight, as she had the night before, she grasped the handle beneath the sill and cranked. Turn by turn, the sheet of polyglass opened like a protractor's arm.

On the tiny balcony outside, a ladder was bolted to the wall. Kasey gripped the rungs and climbed until her head met the stratum overhanging theirs. The ceiling—or rather, the stratum's ground floor, *was* still voice-supported, thankfully, and at Kasey's command, a circular entryway opened like an eye.

She hoisted herself through, into the moonlit unit above. It was devoid of life, unless you counted the cleaningbot, to whom Kasey was indebted. She wouldn't last a minute here without it, for the Coles had been avid collectors, and aside from their stasis pods (lofted), they'd furnished the unit with a coffee table crafted from driftwood and armchairs upholstered in turquoise velvet, the degradable materials a magnet for particulates. The first time her parents had taken her to visit their upstairs neighbors, colleagues, and friends, Kasey had sneezed nonstop. She'd sneezed again, years later, when Celia dragged her back up the ladder even though Kasey said they shouldn't. They were no longer invited. This wasn't their home.

But Celia couldn't resist the call of the windows. And what windows they were: 360 degrees drawn from floor to ceiling, the unit on stratum-100 a gleaming cone at the pinnacle of their teardrop-shaped city. Celia would sit on the chaise by the glass like their parents once had, their mother and Ester Cole, both policymakers, discussing the latest humanitarian crises while their father and Frain Cole compared microhousing blueprints. The two most influential families of the planetary protection movement, bathed in light.

In the dark, Kasey now sat and looked out beyond the glass, to the panorama of sea and air surrounding their eco-city and seven others around the world. The eight, collectively, housed about 25% of the human population. Seventy-five percent still lived in the land-bound territories—and not all by choice. Sky-bound immigration had risen to unsustainable levels; admission was now limited by rank. Rank was calculated from the planetary impact of an individual's Intraface-tracked behaviors—and the behaviors of their ancestors. Territory denizens, many with family histories in carbon-heavy industries, decried the system as stacked against them. Was it? Kasey supposed it was hard for people to accept their own insignificance, their actions like droplets in a sea created by their antecedents.

But even in a sea, every life rippled far beyond its end. Rather than blame systems or ancestors, Kasey blamed human nature. People weren't hardwired to think generations ahead. Entities like Mizuhara Corporation, who'd sponsored the first eco-cities for communities displaced by the arctic melt, were few and far between. So were the Coles, ranked number one for curing diseases such as the common cancer to curtail the effects of pharmaceutical production on the biosphere. More than doctors, they were humanists. To give people more agency over their lives, the Coles had invented the biomonitor, an Intraface app that put health in the hands of individuals, alerting them when corrective action was needed.

Like now.

Ding. The notification rung in Kasey's head. She opened her biomonitor app and found her neurotransmitters reading in the **MILDLY DEBILITATED** range.

Odd. She didn't feel debilitated. Functioned more or less fine. She stared at the corrective option in her mind's eye.

ADJUST SEROTONIN LEVELS

Blinked it away, only to have it replaced by another.

COGNICISE RELEVANT* MEMORIES

*memories of SISTER, CELIA MIZUHARA

Cognicision therapy embargoed memories that triggered the body's stress response, then reintroduced them gradually. But memories didn't distress Kasey. They were unreliable and degradable, subject to the wear and tear of time unless you recorded them religiously like Celia, which Kasey didn't. History was her least favorite subject for a reason. Even her memories of their mother, Genevie, were piecemeal at best. A manicured hand, reaching to fix Kasey's bangs. An authoritative voice, telling her to go play with the Coles' only child, a boy as silent as his pet rabbit. Too-loud laughter, from Genevie and Ester, when Kasey refused to, hiding behind Celia.

What she did remember: the weather—25°C, humidity at 38%—that day David Mizuhara had taken the girls to see Genevie and the Coles off on their disaster relief trip to an outside territory. In a show of solidarity, they opted to travel in the flesh—a choice that proved fatal when the autopilot malfunctioned and sent the copterbot into a mountain face.

After the funeral (four urns of sea salt: three for the Coles and their boy, one for Genevie), David had disappeared into his room, where Kasey assumed he'd stay for a few days, like he usually did while working on his blueprints. It was to her surprise, then, when he emerged the next morning, clean-shaven and suited, leaving for the eco-city's HQ as Genevie would have. But David wasn't Genevie, and Celia wasn't David, and Kasey's confusion grew when her sister *did* stay in her room. For hours. Sobs came through the wall between them, and Kasey listened, helpless, unable to understand why her sister and dad were acting so out of character.

Finally, at noon, she hacked into Celia's Intraface. Found files of her sister's unfinished homework. Completed it for her. Saw a biomonitor recommendation to restore falling neurotransmitter levels.

That had to be the answer to her sister's strange behavior, thought Kasey, selecting YES.

Her door flung open shortly afterward. "What the hell, Kay?"

"You're in pain." And pain was an objectively undesirable sensation and emotion.

But Celia had looked at Kasey as if *she* was one with bloodshot eyes. "What's wrong with you?"

Her sister would take back the words two days later. Two years later, they'd mend their rift.

But immediately after their mother's death, a nine-year-old Kasey would ask her biomonitor Celia's very question, and be disappointed to learn there was nothing biologically or psychologically wrong with her. Nothing to cure, nothing to fix. Kasey had a hard time buying it. Something inside her had to have been misinstalled. Why else hadn't she reacted like Celia to the death of the woman who'd birthed them, or like the public to Celia's disappearance?

Why else, now, when she blinked away the option to cognicise her memories of Celia, would she be faced with the following field?

INVALID REQUEST

more details

more details [x]

All citizens must maintain minimum mood level above SEVERE_DEBILITATION [value ≥-50]

However, your minimum mood setting requires corrective action at MILD_DEBILITATION [≥-10] due to court override[†].

† P2C court records: see past felony.
Failure to take corrective action will result in eviction.

She wasn't as good as Celia, Kasey thought as she returned to the previous field and selected neurotransmitter adjustment instead. If Kasey had gone missing, Celia would've traveled to the ends of the earth looking for her. If *Kasey* had died, Celia would have been more than *mildly* debilitated. She would've stared into the reporter's cams with tears in her eyes and spoken her mind, not lied as Kasey had.

Might your sister not want to be found?

To be honest, Kasey didn't know. Didn't deserve to dissect Celia. Present her with any other problem and she wouldn't rest until it was solved. Her sister was the exception. When Celia insisted on seeing the sea in person, as if that was somehow different from holoing to it, Kasey had followed along, trying to understand. When Celia snuck out at night to go Joules knew where, Kasey let her, resisting the urge to track her geolocation. Had she, she could have prevented this. Celia wouldn't be dead. Instead, she'd respected the sanctity of what went on in her sister's head. Surely that had to count for something.

Yet here Kasey was.

Unable to sleep at night, as if she might stop her sister from sneaking out one last time.

Running a search for Celia's Intraface, long after authorities had deemed it off-grid.

Staring at the sea from the highest stratum, as if she might be the first to spot the boat's return.

Three months, twelve days.

Her actions made no sense. Logic couldn't explain them. Only hope. It'd leaked into her system, despite her best efforts to keep it out, and in the morning, when Kasey woke to an alert flashing in her mind's eye, she got her first taste of its addictive rush.

[CELIA MIZUHARA] INTRAFACE LOCATED

||||

WHERE AM I?

Who am I?

What's my name?

Cee. I smile in relief when I remember, eyes shuttering against the sun, white overhead.

Then I roll onto my stomach and vomit onto the sand.

My relief sours to panic. *No. No, no, no.* I can't have my taro and chuck it up too. I need to hold it in. But the only thing coming out of me is a cocktail of seawater and bile. No taro. Not in me. All in the ocean, dissolved to slime. Months' worth of taro, food for the fish.

And Hubert . . .

I wobble to my feet. My legs are already weakening, my vision zooming in and out of focus before finally stabilizing on an object farther down the shore.

A hull.

Or half of one, resting on a crescent of wet sand.

Hubert.

I thump to my knees and crawl to his remains. "Morning, Bert," I manage.

And lose it.

I bawl until the tide rises, then, as I hold Hubert down so the sea won't wash him away, I form my first truly coherent thought: *I need to bury him. Give him a proper goodbye.*

I drag him onto safe, dry sand, and stagger around to face whatever lies behind me.

And what do you know.

There's a house on the rocks that looks suspiciously like M.M.'s.

Then there's me. Standing. On a shore. *The* shore. After sailing Hubert seven days out into the sea, plus however much time has passed since, I'm back. Waterlogged but alive.

Which begs the question: *How in the fucking world?*

Did I swim? Did I cling to Hubert and drift on some lucky waves? And even then, shouldn't I have thirsted to death?

I rack my brains, trying to remember something, anything, but all I've got are muggy memories of drowning.

Chasing after the *hows* drains me, so I focus on the *shoulds.* I *should* be ecstatic. I *should* be grateful I'm not a bloated body in the sea. I *should* rebuild Hubert. Try finding Kay again.

Instead, I feel nothing.

I'm back.

I'm *fucking back.*

I failed the greatest mission of my life, the one goal that kept me going day after day, and I couldn't even die in peace.

I'm back to exactly where I started: marooned, color-blind, memory-less. I'd be furious if I weren't so fatigued.

"All right, Cee," I mutter as the clouds move in—not enough to visibly dim the beach but enough to chill me. "So what if you're back? You're a pro. You know what to do. Climb the ridge. Find the pieces. Build. It'll be easier than before. Trust me."

The pep talk fails. I let out a strangled chuckle, self-pity tears leaking from my eyes. Who am I kidding? I spent *months* digging through rusted piles of junk, looking for a single propeller. There's no workable metal left. Not enough for a whole boat.

Wiping my eyes, I look up, in the direction of the house.

No metal?

No problem.

"Strongly disagree," intones U-me when she finds me crouched by the porch, prying at the wooden steps with my bare hands. "Strongly disagree. Strongly disagree."

"For Joules' sake, *shut up.*"

U-me goes silent.

I cover my face and exhale into my palms. "Sorry." It's an apology to U-me and to the porch. After everything M.M. has given me, this can't be how I repay her. "I'm sorry."

U-me doesn't say anything, just rolls close.

Uncovering my face, I rise. "Stay," I order, heading across the beach. U-me follows. "Really, stay! I'll be back this time."

But when I make it to the end of the sunken pier on the

west side of the coast, I'm not so sure if I want to go back. Everything's still gray, including the water lapping over the pier planks. I've stepped off the end before to swim. I don't want to swim anymore. I want to sink. The memory of pain returns to my lungs, and I can almost feel them filling again. It'll suck. A lot. But then things will go still. Tranquil. Easier than this.

Megajoules. What am I thinking?

I get to my knees and dunk my head into the water. The salt stings my lips. I part them to scream.

Nothing comes out.

No point in screaming if there's no one to hear.

I say her name instead. *Kay.* I ask if she's out there. If she knows I tried—really, really tried—to find her.

And if she'd forgive me if I don't try again.

• • •

In the end, I don't bury Hubert. Feels wrong to trap a part of him on this island when at least one of us can be free.

"Goodbye, Bert," I say, releasing him.

The waves carry him out. For a second, regret fills me like wind in a sail. It blows me deeper into the water, after Hubert. I've changed my mind. I want to bury him. Keep him near, in case his other pieces wash up.

The ocean reclaims him before I can.

I stumble to a stop. Foam rises around my knees, pulls away. Sand slips out from under my feet. I keep my footing. I stay until the gulls circling me lose interest. They go home and I do too.

The fifty strides from shore to house feel closer to a hundred. My calves burn as I climb the sandy steps to M.M.'s porch, and as I clutch the rail for support, I find myself eye level with the tally marks, all 1,112 of them.

Now 1,113. I gouge it in with the metal scrap, drop it. It plinks onto the porch.

1,113 days.

Three years, and then some, on this island.

Now back to square one.

"This calls for a renaming of an era," I say as U-me joins me. But life-after-life-after-Hubert sounds uninspiring, and frankly, not much has changed. The kitchen is the way I left it: empty jar on the counter, broken taro biscuits on the scuffed floor. I pick up the pieces, de-fluff them of mold, and begin refilling the jar. Don't know why—pretty sure I can sicken and die from eating mold just as easily as *not* eating, but it's something to do, and when I'm done refilling the jar, I wipe down the dust covering the countertops and check the water tank. The pipes run under the house and draw salt water from the sea, which is then passed through a solar-powered boiler that traps the steam and condenses it to fresh water. The system failing would seriously throw a wrench in my whole I-will-survive thing, so I'm relieved, as always, to find it still working. I turn on the valves and head to the bathroom to run a bath, shrug out of my sand-caked sweater and cargos as I wait for the porcelain tub to fill.

The water isn't hot, but it's warmer than the sea. Sighing, I slide under. My hair lifts from my scalp, buoyed. My thoughts jellify, and in the clear, semisolid silence, I find a memory.

"We shouldn't," Kay says under her breath. We're standing in a glass elevator, facing forward, sandwiched between six other people. Light—dark—light—it flickers over our faces as we sink through the ground of one neighborhood and into the sky of the next. At each level, we stop, the curved doors hiss open, and people trickle off.

After a certain point, no one gets on.

People don't know what they're missing. As for the ones still on the elevator, I bet they're all in their heads, reading the news in their minds' eye or messaging colleagues. What's the point of traveling somewhere in person if your brain is elsewhere?

But I shouldn't judge so harshly. I know Kay would be devastated without her Intraface. I turn to her now that the elevator is emptier. "You've got to see it, love."

She's still in her school uniform, hair bobbed and unstyled. Freckles spangle her cheeks. Her mind is a diamond—unbreakable, and dazzling from every angle. Unlike me, she doesn't need sequins to shine. Doesn't need people or places to entertain her.

And now I can tell, from the slight wrinkle of her nose, that she doesn't need this adventure, either. "I've seen the stratum," she says.

"No, the ocean," I quickly correct, then add, "Up close. It makes a world of difference."

I'm worried Kay will think the idea is vapid.

The elevator comes to a stop.

Kay sighs. "All right. Just this once."

• • •

I come up gasping for air.

Water streams down my temples. I squeeze my eyes shut and hold on to the image of Kay's face, her mouth set straight like her bangs, her eyes black like coffee. I'd forgotten that.

Forgotten she had black-brown eyes.

And the ocean. In the memory, it felt like it was a stone's throw away. Maybe it was right outside our door. Or city, floating above the sea like it does in my dreams.

I might be closer to Kay than I think.

My jaw tightens, my determination renewed. Tonight, I'll rest. I'll regroup. But tomorrow at the crack of dawn, we resume. Whatever it takes—another boat, another year—I'm going to find my sister. I can't fail until I give up.

Water sloshes off me as I rise from the tub. I dry off with one of M.M.'s threadbare towels, monogrammed like so many other items in the house, and put on a chunky sweater with just *two* moth holes in the right sleeve. My stomach growling, I start for the kitchen before remembering I probably shouldn't risk my second-chance-life on a moldy biscuit.

"Sorry, U-me." She follows me into the living room. I tuck up onto the lumpy gingham couch beside the window, the carpet beneath it repurposed as my throw blanket. "We'll have to make do without dinner tonight," I say, swaddling myself in the coarse fabric. "I know it's your favorite meal to watch me eat."

"Agree."

There might still be a couple of taro plants out back. Will have to check on them tomorrow, when I have the energy to worry about starving.

I settle in as night falls, resting my head against the couch arm with the window for a headboard. The blanket reeks of feet. Gross, but it reminds me of people, and when I'm lulled to sleep, I dream of them. Their voices fill the house, their laughter ringing, and over all the noise comes a knock. I open the front door.

Kay stands on the porch.

The dream is more vivid than usual. It's like my brain knows I need the pick-me-up, and I curse when I'm jerked out of it—by what, I'm not sure, until lightning blinds the room. Thunder follows, rattling the house. Shadows, as if shaken loose, unfurl back over the walls.

I sit up in the darkness and wipe the drool off my chin. Can't sleep anymore—can't risk sleepwalking out into a storm. It's pummeling the roof and pouring down outside when I look. The sea seethes, swollen and reaching for us. But we won't be touched. I send my grateful regards to whoever designed M.M.'s house as thunder booms and my hand trembles, planted on the window. I lift it, palm chilled, and rub at my handprint with a sweater sleeve.

Freeze.

Bringing my nose to the glass, I squint through the smudge, and recoil at the next flash of lightning—not because of it, but because of what I've seen. It's still there, even when the beach plunges back to black.

A body on the sand.

6

SOMETIMES KASEY FELT LIKE A stranger in her own skin. Holoing as much as she did could do that to a person. The full spectrum of bodily discomforts *was* available to all holographs. Kasey simply opted out. She derived no pleasure from getting pins and needles in her feet, or desiccating her eyes under the glare of conference room lighting, an effect she couldn't escape even after toggling on the tear production setting in her biomonitor.

At least her mind was free to wander out of its flesh prison. Except today, it'd caged itself within an endless thought loop, consisting of two words:

INTRAFACE LOCATED

The signal had lasted for only a second before it was lost. The hope-induced high was just as fleeting. The geolocation coordinates corresponded with a residential unit. Private domain. Breaking in—virtually or physically—was a felony and one was plenty for Kasey. Besides, what were the chances of Celia sneaking back in under the nose of every eco-city cambot? Minuscule.

THE ONES WE'RE MEANT TO FIND · 47

Possible, yes, but improbable that the signal had come from Celia's Intraface. More probable (and thereby possible) that a hacker or spambot was trying to prank Kasey. Or her search program had sent back a false positive. That was also possible. Probable?

Not if this was Kasey's own program, coded by her own two hands.

But it wasn't. She wasn't allowed to code—or to touch anything related to science.

These were the P2C restrictions on her, monitored as strictly as her mood levels.

"And that's a wrap." An earsplitting clap returned Kasey to her body, half-asleep in its chair. She blinked and looked up at the woman at the head of the oval table.

Ekaterina Trukhin. Specifically, her holograph, semi-transparent to Kasey; it was how her Intraface delineated those in holo when she herself was in the physical mode.

Ekaterina at 50% opacity was no less of a commanding presence, though, and her heels clicked against the floor as she made her rounds, the room configured to react to virtual stimuli. "It's six p.m.," she said to the seated mix of solid and transparent people, faces lit by the screens floating before them. "You know what that means." She stopped beside Kasey and bore her weightless palms against the tabletop. "Scat."

The holographs evaporated—screens followed by people. The rest of them pushed in chairs and gathered their briefcases. Everyone would be back tomorrow. The Planetary Protection Committee spurned inefficiency, and P2C officers wore too many hats to take weekends off. They ran the

government within the eco-cities and served as their delegates
outside of them. They were stewards of the planet above all,
and in response to the mounting environmental crises (as
well as pressure from the Worldwide Union, which over-
saw both territory and eco-city polities), P2C officers had
recently taken on one more role: as a judging committee for
doomsday solutions. Thousands of submissions had flooded
in from around the globe, now awaiting review. It was exactly
the kind of grunt work Kasey didn't mind being assigned to,
requiring limited effort and investment. Policy wasn't her
passion. She wasn't like senior officer Barry Tran, who took
personal offense at every unworkable solution that crossed
his path.

"Do they even teach reading comprehension in schools anymore?" he ranted, and Kasey remembered a time when Barry
would've looked to *her*, a sixteen-year-old who spent her weekends at P2C headquarters, as the expert on all matters adolescent.

Thankfully, Barry knew better now and addressed his griev-
ances to anyone willing to listen, which, more often than not,
still made Kasey his audience of one.

"What does it say here?" He swiped the competition
guidelines to the front of his screen. "A solution for *all*!
Is fifty percent of the pop the same as all? And this one!"
Another swipe—this time a submission's abstract. Looked
like extraterrestrial migration. Kasey had rejected several of
those herself. Whether the public accepted it or not, all missions to colonize Earth-like planets had failed.

"Have they no regard for the budget?" *No*, thought Kasey, recalling the proposal that they all travel back in time to a more habitable Earth. "Did the bots even *screen*?" Yes, but bots weren't the ones depending on the final solution.

"Any luck with your batch, Kasey?" asked Ekaterina, ignoring Barry.

Yes, she could say. Telling the truth was thankless and tiring and very Kasey, who couldn't rewire her brain to give the people what they wanted. "No."

"Why not?" Meridian had whined earlier over their call, when Kasey had also said no to submitting their own solution— theirs, insofar as Kasey had conceived it while still on the school science team with Meridian. "Please, Kasey? College apps are due next week and it'd be great if I could list this. Just imagine: coauthor of proposal under P2C consideration. Legit, am I right?"

Kasey, feeling sleepy and itchy but not one bit legit in her school blazer (the other option was sleepwear), left that judgment call up to Meridian. "It's not ready."

"It was the winning idea!"

"At an eighth-grade competition. It's not ready for the world." Never would be. It was missing its final piece, which Kasey couldn't complete without breaking the very law that'd taken science from her.

Still, she hated denying Meridian. Ask Kasey to throw another party or to dye her hair red, and she'd have gone along. There were few things in this world she was protective about. What to do? SILVERTONGUE suggested changing the topic. To what? *Intraface located*, her mind volunteered. No. Out of the question. Again: private domain. Long gone were the days when strangers could visit you for tasks as mundane as delivering food. Every job below a three on the Coles Humanness Scale was automated, eliminating resource waste as well as anything Kasey could reasonably impersonate.

She couldn't go. She couldn't. She—

"How would you go about accessing someone's unit?"

"Excuse me?" asked Meridian.

"Someone's unit," Kasey repeated.

"Yeah, I heard you the first time, but, uh . . . why?"

To change the topic. To make Meridian forget about submitting their solution.

Not, most definitely, because Kasey needed any suggestions.

"Hypothetical," she said, and if she hadn't picked up on Meridian's irritation before, now she (well, SILVERTONGUE) did.

"I don't know," said Meridian. "Don't you have, what, official privileges or something?"

Then Meridian had ended the call, leaving Kasey to ponder. Privileges. It was one way of looking at her court-ordered P2C service. The work was painless, granted, and the adults were nice enough, but even they were human, and as two chatted about their teething babies while packing up, Kasey yet again found herself on the fringe of a setting selected for her by someone else. She'd much rather look forward to college, a major in biochem or physics, a career at an innotech firm.

But regret, like guilt, was an unproductive emotion.

"See you tomorrow, Kasey," said Ekaterina. "Go home, Barry."

A grunt.

"See you," Kasey said to Ekaterina, and then, perhaps feeling ever so slightly guilty for not submitting their solution, complete or not: "Do you think we'll need a decision soon?"

Tremors had been detected off the coast of Territory 4, but pundits had also been predicting the "biggest megaquake yet" for three years running.

"Might happen in our lifetimes, might not," said Ekaterina. "Best to be prepared. Right, David?"

*Sir*s greeted Kasey's dad as he exited his private office. He nodded noncommittally in reply, refilling his mug at the water dispenser before shuffling back.

Kasey followed him, coming to stand under the polyglass doorway as David retook his seat at his desk.

When her mom was still alive, he used to sit in the same exact form, right shoulder hitched higher than the left, glasses fallen low, only it'd be at the foot of his bed, in pajamas instead of a suit, and he'd be hunched over blueprints instead of legislation that, if Kasey had to make an educated guess, concerned

HOME. As Genevie's last initiative, the Human Oasis and Mobility Equality act would have allowed cohorts of territory citizens to immigrate to the eco-cities even if they were unqualified by rank. Ironically, working on HOME often kept David *from* home, something Celia had resented their dad for. Kasey was more neutral. After Genevie's death, she accepted that loss changed people. It'd subtracted something from her dad, but was that bad? To be normal? It was worse to be unchanged. Unimpacted. To be fully aware, as Kasey was right now, that she *should* feel more strongly about her dad's absence but all she could muster was some half-baked annoyance at having to speak up to be noticed.

"How does one obtain a search warrant?"

David's stylus didn't stop moving across his desk. "You'll need to talk to Barry."

"We've talked." Technically. Her dad was the faster route, and fast, Kasey knew, was what she needed before her brain shut down this whole operation.

Seconds later, a search warrant app appeared in Kasey's Intraface. She selected it. A digital rendering of the P2C officer badge materialized before her chest.

Other dads went to their kids' swim meets and remembered their birthdays, but Kasey didn't value swim meets and birthdays and liked her dad as is, especially in this moment.

"I trust you to use it responsibly," said David. His stylus stilled and finally, he glanced up.

How they communicated: without words. One silent look

was their mutual acknowledgment of the incident that'd corrupted Kasey's life and nearly evicted her from the eco-city. She was only here due to David's intervention. He'd acted when it mattered most. Kasey respected that. Even related to her dad. David was no longer an architect. Kasey was no longer a scientist. Life went on, subpar for the course.

"I'll try," said Kasey, which was enough to satisfy David.

He looked back to his work. "Go in holo."

"I can't."

Another dad might have asked why. It wasn't like the weekly maximum, set by the Coles to preserve the "endangered spirit of humanity" in their tech-reliant worlds, was low.

"Then take the REM," said David, and Kasey commended her dad for being so solution-oriented.

Minutes later, she was on the duct to stratum-22, the REM immobilizer holstered at her side.

She'd been down-stratum before. Gone even lower than S-22 with Celia, who'd insisted lower stratums were more *real*, when technically, all stratums were equally real, built from the same raw materials, stacked to form one city lifted by antigravity and protected by one filtration shield. Any visible differences stemmed from how the stratums managed their residents. Upper stratum dwellers were encouraged to max out their holo quotas to lessen the burden on infrastructure, while lower stratums embraced . . . a different lifestyle, one that ingested Kasey the second she stepped out of the duct.

Heat. Stink. Clamor. Groaning pipes and rattling generators, trashbots and busbots working overtime to support the humans out and about, coughing, sneezing, and secreting other humanoid sounds as they traversed the corridors between unit complexes. Their ranks, displayed overhead in accordance with P2C's accountability laws, were the only virtual things to them. Everything else was in the flesh, like Kasey herself. Aside from her single-digit *2* floating overhead among a sea of 1000s, 10,000s, 50,000s, she fit right in. She'd rather not. Without Celia, this place was worse than she recalled. She breathed through her mouth to nullify the odor, and set her visuals to monochrome. A black-and-white world seemed less real and, consequently, less overwhelming.

The heat was the one thing she couldn't adjust, and sweat drenched Kasey by the time she arrived at her destination: GRAPHYC, a body shop that performed physical alterations deemed nonessential by medical hospels. Unable to imagine much demand when appearances could be modified in holo, Kasey relaxed as she went down the steps recessed between two ground-level stoops. Her rank blipped away as she pushed through the door and entered the private domain. Finally, a breather from her species.

This was her first mistake: assuming she understood other people.

Compared to the outside, GRAPHYC was positively arctic. Goose bumps sprouted on Kasey's skin. Her teeth chattered. Or maybe it was the machines, buzzing into her eardrums. The lights overhead were harsh. Industrial. The space—as windowless as a basement but large—was sectioned off into cubes. In one, an employee was plucking out teeth down an assembly line of unconscious clientele. Kasey stared, head ducking when Tooth Tweezer looked up. She hurried along, witnessing a number of other questionable things before she found what she was looking for:

An idle employee around her size.

You could never too be careful outside of holo, though, and Kasey's hand drifted to the REM as she closed in on the tattooist with spiky orange hair and golden temple studs. "P2C officer, here to conduct an authorized search of Unit Five."

"Be with you in a nano," said the tattooist, in the middle of cleaning his machine—machine slipping when Kasey flashed her e-badge. She flinched at the clatter—then at his shout. "*Jinx!*" he called.

"What?" Moments later, a person strode into the cubicle. She wore a fuchsia utility jumpsuit, sleeves of equally colorful tattoos, and black gloves that flecked red onto the cement ground as she snapped them off and tossed them into the trash bin. "Who died now?"

"*Jinx,*" moaned the employee.

"Joules, loosen up, will you?" Then she saw Kasey. Her eyes narrowed. The employee's stayed wide. Both looked at Kasey as if she was someone important.

She'd better start acting like it. She flashed her e-badge again, fresh sweat forming. "Authorized search warrant for Unit Five."

It came to mind, somewhat belatedly, that they couldn't

know what she was here for. Maybe they feared her because
GRAPHYC was in violation of regulations, or Unit 5 was
stashed full of contraband. Kasey didn't care—not today, not
with INTRAFACE LOCATED branded in her brain—but before
she could say so, Jinx turned to her employee.

"See?" She sounded more relaxed. "It's for Act."

"Who gives me the creeps."

"Don't worry. He's clean."

"How do *you* know?"

"I *know* because he's my tenant *and* my hire."

"Sure that's it—*ow!*" cried the employee as Jinx seized his ear.

"Up the back stairwell, first door to the right," she said,
presumably to Kasey, who would have followed the directions
anyway just to eject herself. She climbed the stairs to the
top landing; it was a jungle gym of obsolete gizmos. Cat
litter filled a boxlike apparatus that could have plausibly
been a washing machine, from pre-everfiber times, when
the fashion industry accounted for 20% of global waste-
water production and catchphrases such as *sustainable* and
recycled still fueled consumerism. *What a waste of space*,
Kasey thought, contorting herself around the obstacle and
stumbling—as if shoved—before the door. It loomed over
her. Unit 5.

The geolocation of Celia's Intraface.

With nothing left to troubleshoot, her mind dimmed. The
stairwell grew quiet. Had always been.

Her heartbeat was the loudest thing here.

What would a normal person feel, potentially moments from reuniting with their sister? Excited, most likely. Nervous would also be acceptable. Not scared, which was Kasey's physiological response of choice, epinephrine charting on her biomonitor. She wanted to run. Quelling the urge, she knocked and, when no one answered, bypassed the retinal scanner with her badge.

Possibility. Probability. The chances were next to none.

She pushed open the door.

And breathed out.

No Celia.

She ran a body heat scan. Negative. She walked in, looking for evidence of how this person by the name of "Act" might give anyone the creeps. Maybe she wasn't the best judge; she hardly put people at ease herself. But truly, this unit was the most mundane thing Kasey had encountered so far: boxlike, walls painted gray. Fuel-bar? Check. No bed; not unusual. The stasis pod, bolted upright to the back wall, could have doubled as one.

A more thorough inspection led Kasey to the fuel-bar. The cupboards yielded tins of protein blocks, vitamin cubes, and fiber powders. She studied the stasis pod. An older model, worse for wear and missing chunks of material on its right side.

A lot of chunks, actually, gouged out at fairly regular intervals.

Intervals like the rungs to a ladder.

It was a stretch of the mind—a biased mind, familiar with

ladders and primed to detect their patterns. Besides, what ladder went to the bare ceiling? Good question: Kasey looked up. The ceiling was painted the same gray as the walls. Nothing about it stood out.

Except for a speck. A paint bubble. A bead-like object, either attached by adhesive . . .

. . . or resting there, just like Kasey rested on the ground thanks to gravity.

To assume antigravity was at work in a down-stratum rental unit was an even further stretch of the mind than seeing ladders on the sides of stasis pods. The probability was absurdly low.

But Kasey was only here to rule out the near impossible.

She positioned herself under the speck, opened the search warrant app in her Intraface, and keyed CANCEL ALL ACTIVE FORCES into the unit override system.

For a second, nothing happened.

The bead fell.

She caught it in her cupped hands, like a raindrop from the skies. It was nothing so natural. The white kernel, no bigger than a tooth, possessed a smooth, machine-tumbled shape, and when Kasey nudged it onto its narrower side, she found a row of micro-lasered digits.

She could have magnified the numbers through her Intraface and matched them to the fourteen-digit sequence she'd memorized, given to authorities, and entered into her own geolocation tracker. She could have; she did not. She knew, intuitively, what this thing was. To whom it'd belonged.

Where it'd once resided: under the skin, at the base of the skull.

Might your sister not want to be found?

The kernel slipped through Kasey's fingers. She couldn't feel it fall.

Might this be deliberate?

Couldn't hear it bounce against the ground.

Beep-beep-beep. Sound, from inside her head. Text, flashing across her mind's eye:

BODY HEAT DETECTED

Behind her.

Like a cambot, she rotated and aimed.

He stood in the doorway. A boy. Face a blur to Kasey; she could only see in swatches. The white of his button-down shirt, sleeves rolled up. The gray of his waist apron, pockets swollen—

"Hands out." Voice too harsh, syntax too basic, but to Kasey's relief, the boy complied, slipping out one hand, then the other. He made no extraneous gestures. His movements were measured. Precise.

Slowly, she lowered the REM.

And fired when something furry brushed her ankle.

Whatever it was, it was gone when Kasey twisted around. Probably the cat, fled. The boy, in contrast, stood right where he was. Was he frozen in fear? Kasey couldn't tell, could tell that his eyes were black, as was his hair, parted sharply to the right, but couldn't read his gaze through the smoke rising from the scorch mark on the floor.

Say something. Apologize. "I mean no harm," SILVER-TONGUE suggested. Kasey hadn't realized the app was on. She closed it. She disliked stating the obvious, and as callous as it was, she didn't care about this boy's emotional state when hers couldn't be much better off. She nodded at the white kernel on the ground. "Tell me how you got this."

"Why should I?"

Quiet, but commanding. He wasn't cowed in the slightest. *Why should I?*—a challenge, cold and logical. Kasey found herself agreeing. Why, indeed, should he? What gave her the right?

"Because I'm a P2C officer." So much for not stating the obvious. Kasey drew a breath. "And that"—she nodded toward the ground—"belongs to a missing person."

Saying it made it real. That *thing* on the ground was Celia's Intraface, and Kasey's legs went weak. What was it doing here, with *him*? The REM rose yet again; she eyed the boy down its length.

"May I?" he asked, unfazed. He crouched when Kasey didn't object, scooped up the kernel, and straightened, graceful. He held out his closed fist, and Kasey reluctantly released one hand from the REM. The Intraface dropped into her palm. She brought it close, magnifying the lasered numbers.

1930-123193-2315. Her sister's. To cross-check, Kasey held the kernel in front of her right eye. A green ring appeared in her field of vision.

OBJECT IDENTIFICATION LOADING . . .

LOADING . . .

RESULTS: 18.2 / 23 grams Intraface, gen 4.5.

18.2 out of 23 grams. Kasey's gaze cut to the boy. "Where's the rest?"

Without asking for permission this time, the boy went to the fuel-bar and returned with a tin.

He handed it to Kasey. "She requested that I destroy it, after I extracted it."

Requested. Kasey focused on the word—*requested,* implying consent—to overcome her vertigo. *Extracted.* Blood and skin, sliced open. By him. What had Jinx said about him? *My tenant. My hire.* Kasey reexamined the boy. Sixteen like her, or older—the lean geometry of his face made his age difficult to pin. She was certain about two things, though: He was younger than most of the GRAPHYC employees she'd seen downstairs, and the exactitude of his person actually seemed befitting of his trade.

But who he was didn't change what he'd done, and with acid in her throat, Kasey glanced down at the tin in her hand. It contained a fingernail's worth of white powdery substance.

RESULTS: 4.8 / 23 grams Intraface.

"When?" she demanded, balling her toes as if she could grip the ground.

"A week before she left."

Overlapping with Celia's tech detox. Semiregularly, she would shut down her Intraface and give people no choice but to connect with her in person. Kasey hadn't thought much of it.

"And you carried out her request?" Her voice sounded too high-pitched and accusatory, as if the boy had killed her sister even though it was becoming clearer by the second that Celia had voluntarily come here, in her final days, and asked for this—and for him.

Second mistake: thinking her sister would rely on Kasey over a stranger.

If he was a stranger at all. "I did. She was a client," the boy explained, calm. "But to me, she was more than that." There was an intensity in his expression, emotions Kasey couldn't name but had seen before, somewhere. "So I saved it." He took the Intraface back from her; she let him, unable to stop him. "Even before I heard the news, I planned on reconstructing it. I wanted to understand what had happened to make her think she had no way out. After all, people who remove their Intrafaces tend to fall into one of two camps."

"Which are?" Kasey heard herself ask.

"Criminals, or victims."

Criminals. The word zapped Kasey out of her trance. "Which do you think she was?"

"Celia? Committing a crime?" The boy's gaze narrowed. "If she had any fault, it was for loving too much."

Definitely not a stranger, then. He'd obviously known Celia. Known her well. The look in his eyes—the intoxication, the all-consuming determination—matched what Kasey had seen in the eyes of people like Tristan/Dmitri. They loved Celia so much that they couldn't move on. They reacted with equal and opposite force to the force that loss exerted on them.

They were the normal humans.

And Kasey wasn't. Swallowing, she glanced again to the

powder in the tin. One misplaced grain, and the Intraface would never turn on again. It must have taken months to come as far as the boy had, and during this time, what had Kasey done? Dodged reporters. Accepted the tragedy. Thrown a party.

In the eyes of the world, she was more of a clown than a ghost.

She returned the REM to its holster and faced the boy, who'd answered everything he'd been asked. At a minimum, she owed him an explanation.

"I'm Kasey." As if that meant anything to him. "Mizu-hara." She couldn't remember the last time she'd introduced herself by her full name—wouldn't have been able to, outside, without tripping up a tapped bot and giving her location away to reporters. But here, in a private domain, she was safe. Physically.

Mentally, she felt more out of her element than at her party.

"Celia's younger sister," she added for good measure, at the same time the boy said, "I know who you are."

That threw Kasey for a loop. Then she recovered. The sound bite *had* gone viral.

If the boy judged her for dispassionately proclaiming her sister dead, he didn't reveal it. "Come back when it's ready."

Kasey's Intraface pinged with a new contact request.

ACTINIUM

Rank: 0

A normal person would've been grateful. He'd known her sister. He was someone who understood.

But that would have been Kasey's third mistake: assuming anyone would really understand her.

She left the room without a word, left the boy and her sister's Intraface with him, left the door open behind her, and took only the weight in her chest.

||||| ||

THE DOOR SWINGS SHUT BEHIND me, and I face the storm beyond the porch.

I've had plenty of terrible ideas, but this one takes the taro biscuit. With each step into the hailing rain, I wonder if I should wait. By tomorrow, the skies will be clear.

Then lightning flashes again, illuminating the body, and I remember this is a *person*. They might already be dead, but on the off chance they're not, I can't leave them to the mercy of the elements. So I keep on, toward the waterline and through the downpour, until after a light-year and then some, I reach them.

A boy—and not a bad-looking one, I decide at the next crack of lightning and thunder, if you ignore (or consider) the fact he's unapologetically naked.

Admire later. I'm trying to figure out how to transport him when the surf crashes into me and nearly knocks me over. Shit, that's cold. More waves are surging—I can hear them, roaring closer—and I was already drenched but now I'm inhaling rain-water.

Time to get out of here.

I heave my cargo up by the armpits and start hauling. The slick makes everything harder. The sand's become a swamp and twice, I almost slip.

Third time's the charm.

I land hard on my back while the naked boy lands on *me*, and maybe it'd be comical if he didn't weigh as much as Hubert. With a guttural cry, I push him half off. The effort leaves me winded, and I lie there, trying to catch my breath, while the sky waterboards me.

That's when his other half lifts.

He's awake.

I mean, he must be. Lightning—his hair's in his eyes and I can't see if they're open or not but—blackness—he's leaning over me and no longer crushing me and that's an improvement even if I'm still trapped. Beneath him.

A human.

The rain emits a faint sheen where it lands, creating the illusion it's evaporating off him. In reality, it's streaming down his hair, his face, and onto mine. I blink the water out of my eyes. My brain feels sodden. What do I do? What do I say?

"Hey." It registers, in the back of my brain, that this is my first time talking to another person in three years—a monu-mental moment, not that the storm cares. "Mind getting—"

The request dies in my throat.

My throat, twist-tied off in his chokehold.

What—*why?* My eyes burn. My skull balloons. *Just a bad dream. A bad dream.* But if there's one thing I've learned since arriving on this island, it's that nothing is a bad dream and thinking so is what gets you killed from starvation, dehydration, or—in this case—boys on the beach.

I scrabble at his hands. His grip is iron. I knee him in the balls. He doesn't flinch. Maybe he isn't a boy after all.

My tongue is meat in my mouth. My chest is lead. Lightning—a phantom ringing—blackness—a void.

The thunder goes quiet.

Then a blue light. A room, dimly lit, dream-hazy. A man in a white suit. A casket. My voice—*I won't let her follow me*—like a thought in my head, and I see myself, standing apart from myself, I reach to touch other-me but I can't feel her and am I . . . dead?

Find me, Cee.

No, not dead. Dead-me wouldn't be able to hear Kay's voice. The sound of it returns sensation to my limbs and skin—just in time for me to feel the boy's fingers loosen. His hands fall from my throat. His body thuds to the side. I hear U-me's voice, reliably monotone. "Strongly disagree." Then the rain drowns everything out like applause. It batters me, no-holds-barred now that the boy is gone. My gasps turn to gurgles and I choke again—on spit and *air.* I gulp it down, then finally roll. Onto my side. Onto my elbows. I lift my head, and through the rain, I see the gleam of U-me's metal body.

She's by the boy, who's now lying facedown on the sand. I don't know what she did—bot headbutt?—but it was effective. He's out, and I'm not strangled.

"Thanks, love," I croak, my voice a stranger's. "I owe you one."

"Agree."

Together, we consider the boy.

"Now, what are we going to do with him?"

8

"*SO HOW DID IT GO?*"

Where to even begin? Her sister's Intraface, or the boy who had extracted it?

"The party?" prompted Meridian, and Kasey cleared her mind. Right.

She shut the door to her gym locker. It stuck out even more now, as the only freshly painted one in the row, than it had with BITCH sprayed across it. Remarkable, Kasey had thought, that some people still had aerosols. Meridian hadn't been nearly as impressed. "Which one of you did this?" she'd demanded, causing a scene that Kasey found more irksome than the vandalism. She hadn't told Meridian, of course. She didn't tell Meridian a lot of things to avoid said-things becoming events (see Kasey's party, concocted by Meridian to flip off Kasey's detractors).

"Party was fine," Kasey said. "Crowded," she added as girls filled the locker room, clogging the air with chlorine and chatter and enveloping Kasey in déjà vu. If it weren't for swim class, the easiest way to fulfill the biomonitor's exercise requirement, she'd have holo-ed to school today. The trip to stratum-22 yesterday had drained her. She'd slept badly, checking her Intraface first thing this morning. Zero messages from Actinium. Cue relief. She wanted answers, but the idea of going through Celia's memories left her queasy.

And right now, the locker room humidity wasn't helping.

"That's it? That's all I get?" Meridian complained, following Kasey as she made for the exit—only to run into a familiar face.

Déjà vu round two.

"Oh, hey!" Yvone's hair was blond in person, not blue. Kasey, unfortunately, appeared exactly as she did in holo. Her name and rank were disclosed overhead per school rules, and as luck would have it, she was standing next to none other than the one true LAN, MERIDIAN, rank 18,154. The scene was just begging to be remarked on, and Kasey held her breath as Yvone smiled.

"You know, I can almost see the resemblance." Then she raised a hand—"See you around"—walked past, and Kasey relaxed, grateful Yvone had left it at that.

Meridian was understandably more baffled. "Uh, racist much?"

To be fair, Meridian and Kasey's geo-genetic profiles differed by a mere 7%. While cultural identities were preserved within families, the arctic melt had irrevocably reshaped society. Rising sea levels had caused continents to contract into territories, and people from different countries aggregated in whichever eco-city levitated above their general region.

But Kasey couldn't defend Yvone. She could only play along. "Look at her," Meridian muttered, and Kasey did, turning as they left the locker room to glance at Yvone's projected ID, having missed it before. "Strutting around when she just moved here."

YORKWELL, YVONE
Rank: 67,007

The rank, while low, wasn't what Kasey focused on. Rather it was the last name, familiar.

Where had she seen it before?

"I heard they applied to eco-city seven but got rejected," Meridian said as the fourth period bell rang, classroom doors opening and discharging students into the halls. They joined the tide of flesh students coursing to the cafeteria. "Makes you wonder how they got admitted to ours," Meridian muttered as they picked up their protein cubes. Then, while getting their nutritional IV poles: "Bet they're plants. What?" she asked as Kasey motioned for her to lower her voice.

"Synths." It was the proper term for people who'd undergone genetic modification to synthesize their own glucose from carbon and water, a process twice as efficient as intravenous nutrient delivery.

"You're missing my point," Meridian grumbled as nursebots inserted the IVs into their arms. "It's just not fair. My moms were up all last night trying to calm Auntie Ling down. Before you ask: application deferred again. Can you believe it?"

Kasey could. Meridian's relatives in Territory 4 had been trying to immigrate to the eco-cities for the better part of a year now, but they couldn't outrun one great-great-grandfather's legacy in the pesticide industry. No matter how cleanly they lived in the present, the damage to their rank was irreversible. Well, almost. Becoming photosynthetic was one way to boost rank by a factor of ten within a single generation. Kasey would have advised it—would have GMOed herself, in Meridian's position—except like most of Kasey's thoughts, it'd probably be taken as insensitive and offensive, so she kept it to herself.

"I'm sorry," she offered instead, the words useless.

"I mean, not like you can help, right?" said Meridian as they rolled their IV poles to the cafeteria courtyard, open-air—to the extent that it offered a view of the stratum directly overhead. Its underside, or undersky, drifted with clouds today, casting simulated gray light over the tables. As Kasey scanned for open seats, a shout rose.

"Lan! Over here!" A boy waved at them from a table of five.

"Seriously?" said Meridian, rolling over to the group. "Don't tell me you're skipping."

"Dr. Mirasol let us go if we finished early," said Sid, the one who'd shouted.

"Uh-uh," said Meridian, skeptical. "A whole *lunch block* early? Did you even check your work?"

One of the girls snorted. "What do you think?"

"Not my fault I'm a genius," said Sid.

Meridian rolled her eyes, then turned to Kasey. "Do you mind?"

Kasey quickly shook her head (the only socially acceptable response) and tried to come up with an excuse to remove herself, but Sid was already patting the space next to him, also leaving her no choice in that regard.

"Yo, Mizuhara," he said as she sat. "How are you these days? Up to anything shady? Kidding, kidding!" he said as Meridian glared at him.

"Fine, thanks," said Kasey, then nodded at the other faces around the table. Two familiar, two new, all from the science team Kasey was an ex-member of. Outside of the lab, they'd lost touch. Only Meridian had continued to sit at Kasey's lunch table after the science ban, placing down her tray loudly every day as if she were taking a stand on something controversial. She really didn't need to do that. Kasey was happy by herself. But word somehow reached Celia—*tell me about your new friend*—and Kasey reminded herself that having a lunch buddy was a pro, not a con. Social circle size was correlated with life span. She was the outlier, for being happier when the conversation at the table proceeded as if she wasn't there, topics bouncing from complaints about teachers to competition prep. Meridian shared news of her extended family's deferral and everyone booed. "Who do I have to kill?" asked Sid, earning himself a smack from Meridian, then a grudging smile.

People, Kasey noted, overreacted to signal their care. They cried and laughed and vowed revenge on the ones who hurt them. Finding completion in self-destruction, searching for the nonexistent, hoping and dreading in equal measure—

Ding.

Inbox: (1) new message

—comprised the miserable, helpless human experience Kasey didn't particularly want to take part in, but was sucked into anyway when she opened the message.

From Actinium. One word, no punctuation.

ready

No, Kasey wanted to say. *Not ready.* Except it wasn't a question.

Ready. Celia's Intraface was ready.

"—demonstration later. Oh shit," Sid said as Kasey looked up, bleary-eyed as if she'd just resurfaced from a 200 meter breaststroke. "I forgot we have a P2C officer here."

"Behave yourself," Meridian said to Sid, then to Kasey: "Linscott Horn is speaking on stratum-25 today."

"After school," added one of the girls. "We're picketing."

"What century are *you* from?" asked Sid, chomping into his protein cube. "*Hacking*," he mumbled through the mouthful. "Gonna disable everyone's rank. That will show Horn his bigotry isn't welcome here." He winked at Kasey. "Could use some help from a pro."

"Sid," said Meridian, a warning in her voice. "Cut it out."

"Just messing around."

"Well, it's not funny," Meridian snapped before Kasey could say it was fine.

An uncomfortable silence fell. No one spoke of it, but everyone had to be thinking about Kasey's science sanctions. Hacking was strictly forbidden. It was for everyone, but especially for Kasey. The presets on her Intraface monitored her compliance just like the presets on her biomonitor. One toe over the line, and P2C would know.

"Sorry, I can't," Kasey said, breaking the silence. She removed the IV from her arm and rolled her blazer sleeve back down. "I have plans."

"See?" said Sid, nudging Meridian. "She's in high demand."

The tension dissipated. The conversation resumed. Meridian caught Kasey's eye and mouthed, *Thank you.* As far as she knew, Kasey had lied to clear the air.

If only that were so.

● ● ●

This was Kasey's lie: She had no plans of going after school.

She left during study hall. Took the nearest duct down. Her classmates wouldn't notice her absence. Her teachers might, but it'd be her first strike. She'd survive detention, she thought as she pushed through the stratum-22 crowds, if she could survive this.

"Not again!" cried the tattooist when Kasey burst into GRAPHYC and cut straight to the back stairwell. The door at the top was cracked open. She entered without knocking.

Unit, empty. She looked up and found Actinium overhead, on the ceiling, sitting before a low tabletop laid with two
objects. One holograph projector, and a smaller device emitting a web of laser beams at the center of which, suspended
like a gnat, was the white kernel.

Celia's Intraface, exposed to the world. Kasey's scalp tingled. She became cognizant of her physical state: sweaty and
out of sorts, composure sorely lacking.

Unlike him. "You're early." His voice pervaded space like
a radioactive element. He rose; the table retracted. He strode
to the top of the stasis pod—or bottom, from his perspective,
and started to climb the makeshift rungs. The gravitational
force reversed halfway between the ceiling and the ground,
and by one arm he swung, released, and landed on his feet.

The move had clearly been perfected through practice. The
touch down, soundless. Still, the impact traveled through the
soles of Kasey's shoes. She took a step back. "You messaged."

"You have class," said Actinium, his tone flat.

Kasey crossed her arms. She may have seemed like the stu-
dious type, but she wasn't any more inclined to school than
she was to people, nor did she see how her school life was any
of his business. "How long?" she asked, piqued.

"Ten more minutes."

Ten minutes too long, then. The unit suddenly didn't feel
big enough for both of them. "I'll wait . . ." Kasey started,
and trailed off as Actinium went to the fuel-bar, opened a
cupboard, and took out a cannister labeled TEA and two
glass mugs.

. . . *outside.*

As he tapped boiling water into the mugs, Kasey analyzed him, looking for the traits Celia favored. Tall? Check. Dark haired and dark eyed? Check. Shoulder to waist ratio? There, Kasey paused. He'd seemed better built yesterday, at the end of her REM, but now she saw it was due to his posture. He was actually on the slighter side in terms of stature, Kasey concluded as Actinium turned around, handed her a mug, and leaned back against the fuel-bar with his own.

The silence grew into an unfinished breath. An unspoken name. Contradictory as it may have been, Kasey became convinced that the space, too small for the two of them, was made for three. It needed Celia. *She* needed Celia. Needed advice on what to say to the boy across from her, the common ground between them strong enough, in theory, to withstand any faux pas Kasey made and yet . . . she was scared. Scared of revealing that she grieved less. Understood less. Cared less, compared to Actinium.

She blew on her tea. It did not cool any faster. The law of thermodynamics didn't bend for her. The world, as usual, turned fine without her. Remembering that gave her the courage to finally speak.

"How long did you know her?" she asked at the same time Actinium asked, "Do you have any questions?"

Awkward. "That is my question."

Actinium didn't reply. Kasey was normally the one who discomfited people with her silences, but now she found herself in uncharted territory. "I looked you up," she said, and could have smacked herself.

"And?"

And she'd found nothing. Without hacking, she was as limited as anyone else. "You're a private person." She had to stop stating the obvious around him. "So I won't pry." Even though she already had. "I just wanted to know . . ."

How long I didn't know.

Actinium glanced down at his mug, concealing his gaze. "Years."

She'd had no idea. Kasey brought the mug's rim to her lips. The tea scalded like her shame. It was too nosy to ask how they'd met. Too nosy to ask anything about their relationship. *What else, what else?* She tugged at the collar of her school blazer—and it came to her.

"You're not in school." SILVERTONGUE chimed. "Either," Kasey added to appease it.

"Not anymore," said Actinium.

"When did you graduate?"

"I didn't." Wasn't this going well. "I dropped out seven years ago," Actinium added, saving Kasey from herself, "right before junior high."

Info: acquired. He was somewhere between her age, sixteen, and Celia's, eighteen. Kasey took a great gulp of tea— and choked when Actinium said, "You don't need to force yourself."

Then he nodded at her mug. "I was presumptuous," he

said, and for a moment, Kasey thought she heard a note of hesitancy.

"It's fine. Drinkable." She meant it as a compliment; it came out wrong, like everything else. She checked the time in the corner of her mind's eye. Two more minutes. Glanced to the ceiling, where the Intraface was still suspended among the projected laser web. "Can you bring it down?"

"Last time you didn't need my help," said Actinium rather pointedly.

"I didn't know who you were," Kasey retorted. Still didn't, apart from what she'd wrangled out. He worked at GRAPHYC, had a cat, and loved her sister, which frankly told her enough. At his core, he was someone she could trust. Someone a little reckless.

Someone ruled by his heart.

Actinium set his mug on the fuel-bar countertop. He walked to the stasis pod and climbed up the way he'd descended, flipping across the halfway point, landing on the ceiling, before looking down at her, gaze expectant.

Yup, definitely one of Celia's boys. Sighing, Kasey placed her mug beside Actinium's and wiped her hands on her blazer as she approached the stasis pod. The "rungs" were barely deep enough for her toes. She was so intent on not slipping that she didn't prepare for the reversal of force. Her stomach seemed to flip upside down, because she *was* upside down, hanging on to the side of the pod for a split second before she fell—

—and landed. Upright. Miraculously.

Less miraculously, when Kasey grew aware of Actinium standing before her, steadying her by the upper arms. Their gazes met; she was surprised to see his as guarded as hers felt. Then he let go, stepped back, and Kasey focused on the most important thing: She was on the ceiling. Feet planted firm, blood still flowing to her soles, the same 9.8 m/s^2 force that grounded all life on earth still grounding her . . . just elsewhere.

Awed, she sat on what was now the floor. Actinium joined her. The table automatically rose. The Intraface on it continued to reboot, its progress displayed on the screen. The space had felt too small before, but here, right now, Kasey was glad to have Actinium beside her so that she didn't have to watch the completion percent go up alone.

98%

99%

100%

The beams of light retracted. The Intraface floated down. Kasey didn't touch it. She waited for Actinium to insert it into the holograph projector.

Instead Actinium got to his feet. "I'll go."

Two words, quiet, but Kasey heard more.

I'll go to give you space.

"No," she blurted. Cleared her throat. "That won't be necessary." Looked away. "She would've wanted you here."

Actinium remained standing.

"Sit down," she ordered. He sat; she inserted the Intraface

into the projector before she could second-guess herself. A vertical beam rose from the top of the machine, fanning open to form a gray screen.

WELCOME, CELIA

The *wrongness* of being inside Celia's brain coiled like a snake around Kasey's own. Then Actinium opened a report of Celia's Intraface activity, and Kasey freed her mind.

Data. Facts. These were things she deserved to look at.

The data: Celia holo-ed 20.5 fewer hours per week than the average person. Her only apps were the standard downloads. The bulk of her Intraface storage was devoted to captured memories, tens of thousands of them, sorted by topic and date. A hundred thousand hours' worth of footage. They'd be here for years if they reviewed them all, so when Actinium suggested six months, Kasey nodded. Six months before Celia's disappearance it was.

She opened the appropriate folder, took a deep breath, and hit play.

It all came crashing in. Memory after memory after memory, the good the bad the damning. The first time they visited the sea together in person, and then—as Kasey learned reviewing the rest of the footage labeled SEA—all the other times Celia had returned by herself, at night, without Kasey knowing. Other secret nights spent at clubs. Sleepovers. Yoga and brunches with friends—so many friends; laughter and faces endless, people and places coming alive under the rays of Celia's attention.

Two weeks of memories reviewed, five and a half months more to go.

At four months to go, Actinium got up, went down, came back up. Kasey found a protein cube pressed into her hand. Later, she descended herself to use the ground floor restroom, and was startled to see that GRAPHYC had closed for the day. Time did not pass in Actinium's windowless unit— only Celia's life did—but outside day became night then day again. The morning news alert popped up on Kasey's Intraface. Tremors, detected off the coast of Territory 4. Pundit Linscott Horn's speech postponed. Meridian, messaging to ask Kasey where she was. No messages from David; safe to assume he'd spent the night at P2C headquarters.

Two months to go. Kasey looked up and met Actinium's gaze. His eyes were bloodshot; she imagined hers were too. But neither offered to take over for the other. An agreement existed between them, made at some point during the wordless night.

They were both in this to the end.

One month. One week. One day.

Then blackness. The final memory played. The tsunami of Celia's life pulled back, taking Kasey's with it. She felt like a corpse, deposited on the sand. Ears flooded, eyes brined. If senses were a nonrenewable resource, she'd just spent her entire allocation on a fraction of her sister's life. It was so much more saturated than hers. So much *more*. The world would have lost a lot less without Kasey, whose brain was already rebooting, compiling conclusions. They'd found no red flags. Nothing of surprise, secret nighttime sojourns aside (their absence would have been more surprising). Nothing, as Actinium had said before, that would have left Celia feeling cornered. The only victims were the ones she'd left behind.

Like Tristan/Dmitri.

I need to know if it was my fault.

Wait.

Where were the boy-specific memories?

Stored in a separate place, Kasey discovered. A folder labeled xxx. She opened a preview of it. A mistake. She closed it; this was where she drew the line. "You do it," she said to Actinium.

"There's another way." Actinium opened Celia's biomonitor data, and Kasey berated herself. Right. Emotions could be elucidated through numbers. She pulled up a monthly health report round-up. She knew what she was looking for: empirical evidence of heartbreak or trauma. Irregularities in neurotransmitter levels. Imbalances in mood. Data and charts, all of which she found.

None of which illustrated the picture she thought she was searching for.

Instead, for the first time in her life, Kasey had to read the numbers twice. She looked to Actinium, saw his eyes glazing over as he digested the data.

Not ready to do the same, Kasey stood, distancing herself.

Blood rushed to her brain, as if gravity had been restored and she might fall and break. She wanted to, for a frightening second. Break and join Celia in her senseless world. Because Celia was still dead. The sea had killed her.

It'd been killing her for a long time now.

++++ ||||

THE SEA'S ALWAYS PRETTIEST AFTER a storm. This morning, it shimmers beyond the sunken pier, sequined by the sun. The sky, I reckon, must be a cloudless blue. If only I could see it in color.

Then again, if only I didn't have boats to build and stranglers to neutralize.

I touch a hand to my neck. My windpipe's bruised, and swallowing kills. Turns out there are more ways to die on this island than I'd previously thought, like at the literal hands of a boy.

I could have left him on the shore. The storm might have drowned him. The ocean might have lapped him up and returned him to Joules-knows-where he came from. I could have disposed of him without lifting a finger, and it'd serve him right.

Instead, I kept him. Bound to M.M.'s bed, still naked—I refuse to dress my would-be murderer—but alive.

Because he's just like me. We both washed up ashore,

bare as babies. If he remembers anything, anything at all, about what's out there—other islands or the cities from my dreams—I don't care if he's the devil himself. He could be the answer to my past and my future. He could better my chances of finding Kay.

We'll see once he wakes.

Beneath my feet, the tide rises, slurping through the pier planks. The sea breeze tastes divine, especially after last night's events.

One last inhale, and I leave the pier. The nape of my neck prickles as I trek across the beach. It's strange, knowing there's another soul on this island. The house, when I return, looks different somehow. A floorboard creaks, and I jump, but it's just U-me.

The heebie-jeebies settle once I enter M.M.'s bedroom. It's bright at this hour, its eastward window aglow. The walls are papered with tiny flowers. The air is iridescent with dust, and sweet, too, the scent of yarn coming through the slatted doors of the closet, where M.M.'s sweaters hang in a row. I'd sleep here more often if doing so didn't make the rest of the house feel too empty. On the couch, I can convince myself I'm one of many guests, only passing through.

The boy, though, has made himself right at home under the blanket I spared to cover him. I sink into the sun-warmed rocking chair by the bed and watch him sleep—rather deeply, I think enviously, for someone restrained to the bedposts. I bet it's a dreamless slumber. I bet—I *know*—he didn't wake once last night. He was out like a light while I had to fight to keep my eyes open after my near-death experience just to avoid death-by-sleepwalking-into-storm.

If I'm awake, surely he can be too.

My patience drying up, I prod him. Poke him. I check that he's still breathing, and as I'm holding a finger under his nose, it hits me all over again.

A living. Breathing. Human.

The first in three years.

Will he be funny? Sarcastic? Charming? Or will he wake up still a murderer?

As if I might find the answers written on his face, I scoot closer and study him. He appears to be around my age, whatever that is. As for his looks, he's pretty, but plain. Nothing about him sticks out. Nothing is *striking*. His cheekbones, while high, could be more defined, and his jaw, refined, could be more chiseled. His hair is wishy-washy wavy and too short to be long, but long enough to fan out over the pillow, curling around his ears and neck, a dark gray mop over his brow, eyes interrupted only by the slope of his nose—a nice enough nose, but still boyish. *Boyish*—that's the word. Missing angles and gentle shadows, like the half-moon dwelling above his lip.

Which brings me to his lips.

Not too full, not too thin. Average, but here, it works. His lips are probably his nicest feature, and I run a finger over the bottom one before I can help myself, surprised by its softness. Do murderers have soft lips? I pick at my chapped ones, suddenly self-conscious. Then I chuckle. Me? Upped by a boy? Impossible.

Hold up.

Where did *that* thought come from?

I don't have memories of any boys. In fact, when I try to remember them, I end up with images of ice pops that melt too fast and sky-cities hovering over oceans. And Kay. Black coffee eyes. Bobbed hair. The rare slice of a smile.

But then, like some levee has broken, it all comes flooding back. Boys upon boys upon boys. Boys who talk more than they listen, who aren't as funny as they think they are but who need me like air, whose smiles are easily earned.

Only one boy is unsmiling. Black hair, swept to one side. Coal-dark eyes. When our gazes meet, it's like he sees me, not the version of myself I try to be to make others like me, but the parts I'm hiding, the secrets I keep from Kay, out of fear that they'll hurt her. I never want to hurt her or anyone or him.

A boy whose name I can't remember.

When I resurface, I'm out of breath. I glance back down at *the* boy to find my finger still on his lip and his eyes wide open, gray irises pinned on mine.

I withdraw my hand. "Finally," I say with feigned cool, folding my arms over my ribs. My heart pounds behind them. "You've wasted my entire morning."

Two seconds. That's all the prep time I get before the torrent.

"Where am I? How did I get here?" His gaze darts—left, right, left again, then finally up, to the bedposts. "What—" He tugs on his arms; the nylon rope holds. "*The hell?* Why am I tied up?"

So many questions. Do I even remember how to answer questions?

Where am I? "In my bed." *How did I get here?* "I carried you." *Why am I tied up?* "I like it kinky."

Maybe not.

"*I'm kidding,*" I say when the boy's face pales at least three shades of gray.

First impressions, take two: He doesn't look like a murderer, nor is he acting like one. But his voice is what sways me the most. Even panicked, it's . . . music. The sound of the sea as it sighs across the sand. It almost doesn't match his face, but as I'm thinking this, I find his face, paired with his voice, growing more beautiful before my eyes.

My takeaway? Voice-deprivation is real and could be the death of me if I'm not careful.

"Untie me," says the boy. The bed creaks as he tugs on his wrists. I resist the urge to jump to his aid. How I lived before is not how I live now. The shiny things in my dreams—the glass elevators and the boys with their white smiles—don't exist here. It's just me and my body's natural healing abilities. A beating heart trumps a soft one.

One wrong call is all it takes.

"Not until you prove your trustworthiness," I say, sitting back down in the rocking chair.

"*My* trustworthiness?" More thrashing and jerking.

"Stop fighting and listen." I wait for him. For several minutes, his breathing only ratchets up in speed. His distress rubs off on me, and I grip the arms of the rocking chair.

The wood is slick under my palms by the time he finally calms down.

"We'll begin with the question of why you're tied up." I start rocking at a grandmotherly pace, in hopes that it'll put him more at ease. "Last night, you tried to strangle me."

"I did not."

"You did."

"I did n—"

I yank down the turtleneck of M.M.'s sweater. That shuts the boy up. "You did, even if you don't remember. It was storming, too. You're lucky I bothered bringing you into the house." I tug the turtleneck back over the marks. "You're welcome."

I watch as the info sinks in. He's trying to reconcile it in his brain—what he's seeing versus what he believes. My truth versus his. I don't think he's *acting* forgetful, and I don't rule out the possibility that his behavior on the beach was a one-off thing, triggered by whatever he endured at sea. It's also worth noting that he seems scrawnier in the sunlight, and not nearly strong enough to choke me, and—no, I won't make excuses for him. He can explain himself.

"Where did this happen?" the boy finally asks.

"Out there." I nod toward the window. "This is an abandoned island. You're currently staying in M.M.'s humble abode. No, she's not around. No, I'm not sure where she is. It *has* been three years, though, so make of that what you will. For now, it's just us. You and me."

"Disagree," says U-me from the doorway of the bedroom.

"And U-me, the bot."

I wait for a reaction. Receive none. The boy says nothing for a long time. Then:

"*How*, exactly, did I get here?"

"I was going to ask you the same thing." I stop rocking and lean forward. "How *did* you get here?"

"I don't know."

"Think harder."

"I said, I don't know!" As quickly as his voice rises, it also ebbs. "Please—can I just be untied?"

My heart steels itself against his plea. *Remember your agenda.* "You really can't remember anything?" Naked *and* without memories—of last night and of his past. The boy and I may be more similar than I'd thought, which would be comforting— *I'm not the only one*—if I weren't relying on him for answers to help me find Kay.

"Try," I order. "Try to remember something. An image. A person. A place."

The boy's response is to tug on his wrists so hard that dark gray liquid wells at the rope.

Shit. I shoot up from the rocking chair as the liquid runs down to his elbows. "Stop that. *Stop.*"

I grab him by the forearms, only to be startled by the warmth of his bare skin. *A fellow human.* Who's now bleeding because of me. I thought washing ashore alone was bad, but how would I feel if I woke to some stranger interrogating me under duress?

I let go of him, my palms tingling where we touched. He tried to kill me. That still stands. But I'm alive. So is he. We're the only two people on this island. Coexisting in peace would be better than our current setup. Maybe this is a mistake, but—

"I'm going to untie you," I say, enunciating each syllable to buy time to think. *Lay down the ground rules.* "On the condition you don't try to kill me again."

Joules, save me—*that's* the best I can do? I have no way of enforcing this, and *certainly* no way of punishing him from the grave if he breaks his word.

Thankfully, the boy doesn't ridicule me. If anything, he's taking this too seriously. "'Again'?" he challenges. "How can it be 'again' if I don't remember the first time?"

I don't know. The semantics are beyond me. "Do you want to be untied or not?"

He nods. I wait. He catches on. "Fine. I promise."

"Sincerity, please."

"It's not sincere if I can't remember," he protests.

"Picture this: you, me, on the beach. Your hands on my neck."

The boy closes his eyes, a pleat between his brows. He's earnest, I'll give him that, and I take pity on him when he reopens his eyes and says, "I've never wanted to kill you, and I don't *think* I'll ever want to kill you, but I swear I won't act on those urges if they ever seize me." A pause. "Again."

"Swear on your life."

"On my life."

Future-me had better not regret this.

I untie him—then realize I probably should've warned him that he's got nothing on beneath the blanket.

"What . . . fuck!"

"Fuck," repeats U-me. "To engage in sexual intercourse, verb; to mess with, verb; to deal with unfairly or harshly, verb."

"Curse at your own risk," I say as the boy scrambles back into bed, drawing the blanket around him.

"What did you do to my clothes?"

Ripped them off you. The words come reflexively. Maybe I've said them to the boys in my past, but I know better than to repeat them to the boy in front of me right now, his eyes stretched to the whites. "You woke up like this, love," I say as gently as I can.

He shakes his head. "You did something to them!" He points a trembling finger at me, cheeks darkening—reddening, I assume. "You said so yourself! That y-you—you like it—"

"Joules, that was a *joke*."

"My name isn't Jules!" Emotions break over his face. I can't decipher them as easily as I used to, but I think I see fear. Disbelief. Anger.

"That wasn't what I was trying to say." My head's starting to swim. Just when I thought I'd pacified him, too. "Look, love. I'm sorry about your clothes. I know you don't trust me, and you don't have to, but you really did wake up like this. It's okay, though." I go to the closet, fling open the doors, and grab as many sweaters as I can carry. "We can dress you right now." I pile the sweaters over his lap, then sit at the edge of the bed. "Have at it."

The boy says nothing. Does nothing. Doesn't move.

His silence scares me. I reach out to him; he flinches away.

Been awhile since I've faced any sort of rejection. "Why don't you tell me your name?" I ask, hiding the sting of it. "Mine is Cee," I offer, to pave the way.

"I don't know my name." Horror fills his eyes. "I don't know . . ." His gaze drops to his hands, upturned in his lap. His voice hushes to a whisper. ". . . my name."

He stares at his empty palms as if he was holding on to his name a second ago. I, on the other hand, stare at his wrists. The crisscross of dark gray lines. The crusted zigzag down his arm. *I* did that to him. My own wrists ache. I rub at them, and hear myself say, "I couldn't remember mine, either."

Slowly, the boy looks up. "Really?"

"Mm-hmm." I don't like revisiting that time, but for the boy, I do. First week here, I had a roof over my head, and clothes, but I didn't know who I was or who I was living for. No one, it seemed, would miss me if I drowned, and so I almost did. In the tub. I fell asleep, and woke up with water in my nose and mouth but also a name like a heartbeat in my head.

"It took a while," I say, not wanting to give the boy a definitive timeline to compare his own progress to. "But it came back."

Cee. My name is Cee, and when the boy intones it—
"Cee . . . you said it was?"—something in me stirs. It's the first
time I've heard my name on another's lips since washing up on
the shore.

"Yeah," I breathe. "C-E-E, pronounced like the sea outside
that window."

I want him to say it again.

He doesn't. He looks at me, as if accepting this is reality, and
I look at him, too. He is real. I have to hold my own hands to
keep from touching him, because, apparently, as I'm learning,
that's how I connect to people. I want to feel their emotions. To
share them and to shield them. *I wish you were here*, I suddenly
think to Kay. I'd hold her and never let her go. But for now, as
incomplete as I may be, I'm not alone.

I'm not alone.

"—red on your face." The boy's voice draws me out of my
head. I've missed part of what he's said, but I'm already catching on quicker, and when he taps the corner of his lip, I swipe
at mine. A gray smear on my knuckles. I lick it, just to be sure.
Iron blooms over my tongue.

Blood.

His or mine, I don't know. Doesn't matter. *Red*, the boy
said.

He sees in color.

My stomach sinks. Still alone, in some ways. He has something I don't. Should I tell him? I decide against it. He has his
own missing pieces to worry about, evident when he asks me,
"What if I never remember my name?" His throat bobs as he

swallows. A lump grows in my own. I know what he's looking for—the reassurance that can only be found outside of yourself. The squeeze of a hand, or a promise.

"You will," I say, giving him both.

This time, he doesn't flinch from my touch.

10

THE MEMORY RUSHED BACK IN like the tide.

Saturday, six months ago. Temperatures set to an agreeable 26°C, when Kasey emerged from P2C headquarters on stratum-50 to find Celia waiting outside. She wore a baby-blue yoga set. Kasey was still in her school blazer. "My clothes—" she started as Celia took her hand.

"You won't need them."

A place where she didn't need clothes, albeit borrowed from Celia? "Where are we going?" Kasey asked, rightfully concerned as they made their way to the nearest duct. They hadn't always spent weekends together. For almost two years after Genevie's death, they'd barely spoken to each other. Then the incident had happened, tearing science out of Kasey's life. Celia had tried to fill the gap by reducing the time Kasey spent alone, in the company of her thoughts, as if they might be dangerous. Maybe they were. Kasey certainly wasn't breaking laws while watching soaps, shopping, or doing whatever it was Celia planned, which, by her sister's answer of "someplace special," could mean anything from a mud spa to rock climbing. Just last week Kasey had been roasted alive in something called a "sauna."

To make matters inconvenient on top of uncomfortable, the experiences, rarely ever virtual, predominantly took place in the lower stratums. But today, Celia didn't get off at stratum-50 or -40. Stratum-30 came and passed, then stratum-25. Six passengers remained as the duct continued downward, stratums blurring beyond the polyglass cylinder until Kasey deduced their destination.

"We shouldn't." Stratum-0 was off-limits; David Mizuhara had said so himself in one of his once-a-month messages.

"You've got to see it, love," said Celia as three more people got off at the next stop.

"I've seen the stratum." Kasey had holo-ed there on a class field trip.

"No, the ocean. Up close," Celia insisted before Kasey could argue they'd also seen the ocean from the Cole's unit while watching the sun set—another one of Celia's favorite pastimes. "It makes a world of difference."

"All right," Kasey conceded, as if they hadn't already arrived. "Just this once."

As the bottommost layer to the eco-city, stratum-0 functioned as part shipping dock, part observation deck. The lowest point of its bowl-like belly was formed completely out of polyglass, creating the illusion that the sea was beneath one's feet, and an unfortunate greenhouse effect. Perspiring, Kasey watched as Celia stared at the ocean. "Why do you like it so much?" she asked. Try as she might, she couldn't see what was so special about water, salt, and heavy metals.

"Because it's alive."

"We're alive."

"Are we?" Celia mused. Kasey pointed out they were breathing, to which Celia retorted, "Reprocessed air." Kasey would have said *clean*. "Our veins, shot full of chemicals." All nutrients were chemicals. "Minds, imprisoned." Freed from the material world.

"When I look at the sea," Celia continued, "I can almost hear it saying my name. It's comforting." *Unsettling* was the word that came to Kasey's mind, and Celia laughed at her expression. "You'll see what I mean."

"I don't think so," said Kasey slowly. "This will not be a repeated activity."

Celia only grinned.

The next day, to combat the heat, Celia bought ice pops from the observation deck concession stand. The ice pops made Kasey sticky *and* sweaty, the sucrose concentrate melting all over her hands and dyeing Celia's mouth a gratuitous Red 40. That didn't discourage her sister from eating three, or from coming back the next day and the next, until the inevitable happened:

Celia suggested they go to the sea itself.

The day was overcast, but clouds couldn't dissuade Celia. Via duct, she led them down to a boat rental set up in the waters beneath the eco-city. The existence of such an establishment amazed Kasey. Who'd bother coming here when around-the-world cruises could be enjoyed from the comfort of a stasis pod? Kasey's demographic, apparently. Puffy-faced teens high on organics, not one lash batting when Celia cut the line to rent a boat with HUBERT painted on its side.

Hubert came with the antiskins, goggle-masks, and P2C-approved toximeters required for all extra-city activities—gear they could have skipped if they'd holo-ed, Kasey thought as she zipped up her antiskin, trying not to think about the number of bodies that'd inhabited it before hers. She secured the goggle-mask over her face. It was huge, rivaling the goggles she'd worn back when she still had chem lab. Celia giggled, her own goggle-mask dangling around her neck.

The boat rental owner looked like she wanted to be here as much as Kasey. "Map's under the stern," she said when Celia asked for recommended attractions, before shouting, "Hey! Two to a boat!" to five teens trying to fit into one.

"All aboard," said Celia, hopping into *Hubert* while Kasey fished through a jumble of biodegradable floats in the compartment under the stern to retrieve the map. It was laminated in some contraband plasti-material, and unfolded to a whole lot of gridded blue, the only bit of land, labeled 660, a speck about twenty kilometers out northwest. "Where to?"

"Nowhere," said Kasey, holding open the map.

"Nowhere it is," said Celia. Kasey sighed. But later, she revised her opinion: sailing wasn't half bad. It was quiet. Peaceful. Celia cut the motor when they reached a calm patch of sea, and Kasey was just starting to relax when her sister began peeling off her antiskin.

"What are you doing?" Alarmed, Kasey watched as Celia stripped down to her clothes, then to the bathing suit underneath.

"Swimming, silly."

"We still need to get back." Leaving was easy; returning to the eco-cities was harder. They'd have to drop their antiskins into the appropriate hazard chutes and be decontaminated themselves, and if, for whatever reason, they didn't gain clearance . . .

"We could face eviction," Kasey finished, the word acrid in her mouth.

Celia's gaze deepened. "You're safe with me, Kay."

"*Both* of us," Kasey said. Misspoke. Celia never feared for herself and almost immediately, the seriousness evaporated from her sister's eyes. She leaned in and pinched Kasey's nose.

"With our ranks? We're invincible."

Kasey was silent. Meridian would've called Celia out for her entitlement. But wasn't that what rank was? A measure of what people were entitled to redeem after banking in good planetary stewardship? They were already being taxed for other people's mistakes, restricted to living in "e-cities," as Celia called them, because others had made the outside territories unsafe. What was wrong with reaping a perk or two?

Kasey wasn't sure. Right or wrong—contrary to what people wanted to believe—was often subjective. Self-interested.

Only numbers didn't lie, and numbers were what Kasey turned to as she stuck a P2C-issued toximeter into the seawater.

The contamination readings came in: safe for skin contact within a 1km radius.

"See?" said Celia, then jumped in before Kasey could get a word in edgewise. "The water's great! Come on."

Kasey, quite content where she was, tossed a float over the side for Celia. "Stay close." She didn't trust the waves to be as gentle as they appeared.

"Yes, Mom." Celia splashed Kasey. Kasey wiped the droplets off her goggles. "Join me. It'll be easier for you to save me from the sea monsters."

"Sea monsters don't exist." But neither did something called willpower around Celia, and eventually, Kasey followed Celia into the ocean. She could barely feel the water through her antiskin.

"This is how life should be," Celia said as the sun broke through the clouds.

The rays appeared gray through Kasey's goggles, the lens so scratched they'd gone cloudy. "Should be like what?"

"Like how it was before. No one living in a casket or in the shadow of the stratum above them. Just sun and sky." *Too much sun and sky is lethal*, Kasey wanted to say, but Celia went on. "It's like what Ester used to say to Mom. We need to remember what makes us *us*."

Emotions. Spontaneity. Self-awareness. Empathy. Kasey recited the Cole Humanness traits and Celia shook her head. "It's something more immeasurable." She floated onto her back, eyes squinting against the sun. "You know this thing called SPF? People used to cover themselves with it, for protection, and sure, it wasn't great if you forgot, but no one let it stop them from going outside. I wish we lived in that time. I hate knowing our home is trying to kill us."

Our home protects us. But Kasey knew Celia was referring to the world beyond the eco-cities, even if she struggled to grasp why. Celia was a star in their stratified society. She had no reason to look to the poisoned outside. It was Kasey who didn't belong—here or anywhere.

"It's just the way things are," she said to Celia.

"It doesn't have to be. You could change them for the better."

"I don't know about that."

"Confidence, Kay. You'll save the world someday."

"The world doesn't need saving." Not by Kasey, who barely understood the people inhabiting it.

"Trust me," said Celia. "It will."

• • •

They'd ended up checking out the island. Even gone back. Just never into the water—not when Kasey had been there to stop it. The sea was an unregulated territory, a fluctuating variable. The toximeter had cleared a portion of it as safe that day, but who knew if it would stay that way?

It hadn't. Each time Celia had swum in secret, she'd poisoned herself. It said so in her biomonitor report.

The blood charts: elevated levels of microcinogens most commonly found in deep-sea waste pipes.

The diagnosis: advanced organ failure and malignant cranial nerve sheath tumors.

The prognosis: one month to live without intervention.

And finally, a mandatory hospel summons, issued when ailments surpassed the biomonitor's capabilities. Celia had paid her in-person visit two weeks before disappearing at sea. The Mizuharas' designated family doctor had signed off on it.

Like everything else, Kasey hadn't known.

Her body cooled. Her blood pressure stabilized. Her mind overrode her heart. It'd never actually let her fall and break. Homeostasis had to be maintained. It was rational to let go of the irreversible. One month to live without intervention was the prognosis.

Celia had been at sea for three.

In one piece, Kasey descended from the ceiling. Actinium, too. He went to the fuel-bar and picked up a mug, the tea gone cold. Kasey faced him, the silence between them different now, devastated, vast, a wasteland of skulls.

The *crunch* sounding like the cracking of bones.

Kasey blinked, not trusting her sleep-deprived eyes. Actinium didn't blink; he simply watched as his blood dribbled onto the countertop, the flow quickening as he squeezed the mug—or what was left of it, glass shards driven deeper into his fist.

Have you lost it? Celia would shout; Kasey swore she heard her sister's voice. She'd seize Actinium's wrist and pry the broken glass from his grip. But Celia wasn't here. Celia was dead, and maybe that's why he'd broken it, Kasey thought, as if analyzing some case study around the P2C conference table, before the smell hit her. Iron.

Blood. More than she'd ever seen.

She started to approach Actinium like one might a wild beast. She couldn't fathom what he was thinking, could imagine his mind's eye—an eruption of biomonitor alerts—but not his mind. *Are you okay?* a better person would have asked, but instead, Kasey wanted to know *how?* How could glass yield to flesh? How could pain beget more pain? How could he be this calm?

How could *she?*

If they plotted their reactions, which one of them would be further from the mean?

As she struggled to compute, Actinium released the mug. The shards fell onto the countertop; the crimson puddle looked awfully like red ice pop melt. With his good hand, he opened the unit's door. "Come." His voice betrayed nothing. "It should be here."

Kasey, not sure what was happening anymore, came.

Down the stairs they went. GRAPHYC was busy this morning. Sedated clientele filled the operating rooms. None of them noticed the boy, bleeding, or the girl following him. They exited the body shop and ascended to street level. The alleyway bobbed into view—as did the copterbot parked in the middle of it, painted white and green.

Hospel colors.

Like lightning, it struck Kasey. Why Actinium had done what he'd done. Hospels, unlike GRAPHYC, admitted people based on need. Now they had a need—a biomonitor validated reason, a chance to confront the doctor who'd discharged Celia—and it was no thanks to Kasey.

A funny pressure mounted in her throat. Swallowing it, she climbed into a copterbot she should have summoned with her own blood. Actinium joined her, prompting the bot to chime INVALID: USER UNRANKED. A timely reminder. Out in the public domain, with both their IDs on auto-display overhead, it was impossible to ignore that [ACTINIUM, rank: 0] was a hacked account. Kasey was sitting thigh to thigh with a stranger.

But that was the thing about Celia. She brought people together despite their differences. And how different they were, Kasey thought, too shaken by Actinium's actions, calculated or not, to appreciate the way he reprogrammed the copterbot to register Kasey's ID even though it wasn't Kasey's emergency.

MIZUHARA, KASEY, intoned the copterbot as they lifted off the ground. HOME LOCATION, CONFIRMED. YOU WILL BE TAKEN TO THE HOSPEL ON STRATUM-10.

The unit complexes diminished beneath them, hedge-maze-like as they rose to the undersky of the overhead stratum. An aperture opened—in that stratum and every subsequent one. The copterbot shot through the eco-city like a bullet. Celia would've loved the thrill—*had* before the crash that claimed their mom and the Coles' lives. Kasey, less trauma-tized but also less accident prone, hadn't seen the appeal then and couldn't see it now. The ache in her throat spread, gripping her chest. She was out of the copterbot the second it landed, already walking toward the hospel before remembering Actinium.

"Go," he said when she turned back to him in painfully obvious afterthought.

"Your hand—"

"Needs to be seen in Emergency." He tilted his head to the side entrance labeled URGENT. "We can reconvene outside."

Fine by Kasey. Moral support didn't stitch wounds. He'd live without her. But was it too reptilian of her to accept his plan on the spot? She should at least pretend to care, to ask him—

"I'll be fine." Actinium cleared his throat, looking away as Kasey stared. "If that helps."

Yes, it did. She nodded at Actinium, and strode on. The automatic polyglass doors parted for her. The hospel lobby, with its parquet floors and hanging ferns, was styled much like the Coles' own unit. They *were* its founders, in case one couldn't tell from the wall banner commemorating the upcoming anniversary of their passing, or the sign-in bots stationed along the lobby perimeter. Designed in compliance with the Ester Act, the bots were clunky, their faces featureless and therefore impossible to confuse with any of the human nurses, who attracted incoming patients with their smiles. Not Kasey. She approached the bots first, only to learn that walk-in-appointment scheduling required personalized communication beyond the bots' authorization levels, forcing her to turn to the reception desk, where three human nurses sat. The air above their heads was unranked. Kasey's rank was gone too, when she checked. Puzzling—her Intraface labeled the lobby as public domain—until Kasey saw the brass plaque atop the reception desk.

PATIENT CONFIDENTIALITY IS A HUMAN RIGHT
YOUR PRIVACY MATTERS TO US

Patient confidentiality, for all intents and purposes, had killed Celia. Anger flared, hot in Kasey's throat. It must've scorched her voice when she requested to see Dr. Goldstein, because the smile dimmed from the middle nurse's face. "Reason for visiting?"

"My sister."

The nurse waited, then sighed when Kasey didn't elaborate. "Confirm your ID by looking at the red dot please," she said, swiping a holograph across the reception desk.

Kasey did as she was told, transmitting her rank, name, and residence via retina ID. The system approved her. Her Intraface downloaded Dr. Goldstein's soonest appointment slot and suite number. She was good to go.

"Wait," said the nurse, then reviewed Kasey's info as well. Seemed to defeat the purpose of a secure retina feed, but Kasey kept that thought to herself. Maybe this was the extra attention people craved, so she said nothing. Did nothing as the nurse paused, mid-review.

And tapped the nurse to her left.

It all happened in a matter of seconds. The microconversation (*It's her*—*Who?*—*Kasey Mizuhara*) conducted in a whisper, barely audible to the human ear, but human ears weren't what Kasey was worried about.

Like clockwork, the first reporter holo-ed in, alerted by the geolocation alert on Kasey's spoken full name. A dozen others followed, the public domain lobby a field day while Kasey, stuck in the flesh, couldn't log out. The elevator bank, labeled as private domain by her Intraface, was her only escape. She made for it, cutting through the semitransparent horde.

"Kasey! Kasey!" Thankfully they couldn't touch her—but then a question grabbed Kasey by the throat. "How are you feeling now that they've found the boat?"

She didn't stop moving—didn't change her outputted speed or expression.

The press excelled at extrapolating.

"KASEY MIZUHARA, LAST TO LEARN SISTER'S FATE," one enunciated as others blinked at her, snapping pictures with their Intrafaces, still snapping—just from a distance—when Kasey reached the elevator bank. She punched the UP button. The elevator arrived. In the privacy of its enclosure, she opened her Intraface. Fifty-five new messages, mostly from Meridian. None from David; didn't mean anything.

Kasey launched her daily news app. The headline glowed across multiple feeds.

BOAT WASHED ASHORE LANDMASS-660, BODY REMAINS MISSING

She waited to feel something, but felt nothing and realized this:

The boat did not matter.

The boat was inanimate.

The body did not matter. Found or missing, it'd be inanimate by now too, all because of the doctor in Suite 412.

"I'm sorry," Dr. Goldstein said after Kasey barged in, half an hour earlier than her appointment but he'd been seeing no one else. "A shame, what happened to your sister."

"Why didn't you treat her?" Kasey demanded.

"Ah." Dr. Goldstein seemed to visibly shift gears, confusing Kasey. She'd thought they were on the same page. "I'm afraid Celia didn't authorize disclosure to family members."

And Kasey was afraid she didn't care. "The Coles cured all cancers," she blurted, then stared at Dr. Goldstein, daring him to ask her how she knew.

"Not the new ones," Dr. Goldstein finally said. And then because Kasey must have appeared on the verge of hacking into the medical records herself, he went the extra kilometer. "Let me show you something."

They took the elevator all the way down to G3, the floor pitch-black before the motion-sensing lights flickered on, illuminating a room filled with stasis pods.

"All medical grade," Dr. Goldstein said as Kasey ventured in.

She knew without him saying so. She'd used them in her final science team competition, which was how she also knew what Dr. Goldstein would say next.

"What Celia had . . . it's rare. But what disease haven't we conquered? In fifty years, we might be able to transplant brains. In a century, we may reverse aging. All we need is time.

And this"—Dr. Goldstein patted a stasis pod—"gives us just that. Time."

Foreboding settled in Kasey's belly. "How many years did you tell her?"

"Now, you must understand, there's no exact—"

"How many?"

"A forecasted eighty, should the rate of innovation continue as is."

Eighty. The number passed through Kasey like a shock wave, immobilizing her.

Dr. Goldstein took it upon himself to fill her silence. "She came at a terminal stage." He assumed Kasey was in denial about the disease's severity. "Hid the decline well, I'll say." He assumed she felt guilt for failing to detect it herself.

Wrong. The only thing Kasey felt was her stomach sinking to the ground. "She agreed?"

"Why, yes, of course." He tapped the air with a finger and a holograph appeared.

The informed consent form.

The stasis pod sealing, scheduled mere days prior to Celia leaving for sea.

The bottom line, signed.

"Like I said, a shame." Kasey looked up from Celia's signature and found herself under Dr. Goldstein sympathetic gaze. "We were all set and ready for her before the accident," he said, and Kasey wanted to shake him, tell him it was no accident. Not the boat. Not the trip to sea. Celia had lied.

She hadn't signed her life away to a pod, no end date guaranteed. Dr. Goldstein could argue all he wanted that there was no life to sign away, no choice but death in their current day and age, and Kasey would agree with him. She'd have podded herself, if only to convince Celia to do the same, be there for her sister when she reemerged, eighty or a thousand years later.

But Celia's world was so much more than just Kasey. She lived in color. Lived for love and for friendships. She couldn't settle for anything less.

So she chose this.

"She chose to die," Kasey later recounted to Actinium. They were sitting on the rooftop of a unit complex in stratum-25, the copterbot parked beside them. It was programmed to deliver them home from the hospel, but Actinium had hacked it, coding it to take them wherever they wanted to go. That, for Kasey, turned out to be neither the Mizuhara unit nor Actinium's, both too steeped in Celia's memories. School had ended for the day, but she couldn't return there, either. There was the island, but what was the point of seeing the boat? She didn't know. Didn't know the point of anything anymore.

"She removed her Intraface so she couldn't be tracked," she continued. "She chose to die at sea."

Chose that instead of life, no matter what the chances of a cure might have been.

"She didn't choose anything," said Actinium, and Kasey shook her head. At first, after leaving the hospel, there'd been a vacuum in her chest. But now the ache was back, and it annoyed her almost as much as Actinium confusing the facts.

"She chose to swim in the sea."

"The sea doesn't come poisoned," Actinium said, voice tight, drawing Kasey's gaze to him. He hadn't sounded nearly as pained with glass in his hand, said hand now bandaged, when she glanced down at it. She'd assumed the hospel would erase the wound, but what, really, did she know about things like broken hearts, skin, and bones?

"Does it hurt?" she asked.

"No," said Actinium, and Kasey nodded, taking his word for it, blinking when he added, "I'm sorry."

"For what?"

"For scaring you."

"You didn't," Kasey said flatly.

To that, Actinium said nothing.

He didn't even nod.

Kasey looked away.

Her whole, uninjured hands fisted in her lap.

Down below, crowds moved through stratum-25's emporium, one of the few places to buy material products (like Actinium's current shirt, the other one too bloodstained to be worn in public). Vendor stalls encircled the piazza; a holograph of Linscott Horn glowed at its center.

"*Here's the problem, Pete,*" he was saying to the pundit in the armchair opposite him. "*When you're all living on the same planet, you're no cleaner than your dirtiest neighbor. And since the age of apes, mankind's dirt has always been Territories One, Two, and Four. When the rest of the world moved on to fission, they clung to coal. They dug deeper when they ran out, destabilizing the entire crust, causing the megaquakes that will plague us to the end of our days. Now, as other territories phase out of fission, guess what they do, Pete. Guess what they do. They start phasing in—"*

"Can we go?"

To Kasey's relief, Actinium stood, no questions asked. She wasn't sure *why* she'd asked, until the copterbot door closed, muzzling Linscott Horn, and she realized she wanted nothing to do with his words, or him, or with Meridian, Sid, and the other science team members, also here, perhaps in the square or set up on a rooftop like theirs, so preoccupied with exercising their freedom of speech when Celia couldn't even *breathe*, and neither could Kasey. The copterbot lifted, removing her from the same plane as her peers, but their actions still affected her. Her rank blipped away, suggesting that their hack was a success. Good for them. *Good for everyone in this world*, Kasey thought as Linscott Horn also disappeared, ostensibly as part of the hack.

Then the P2C emblem—two Earths linked into an infinity—superseded his holograph.

Simultaneously, a message appeared in Kasey's Intraface.

MEGAQUAKE WARNING

THE FOLLOWING IS A WORLDWIDE UNION—MANDATED BROADCAST

P2C WOULD LIKE TO REMIND ECO-CITIZENS TO REMAIN CALM

The reminder was unnecessary. As the Worldwide Union broadcast rolled—outside territory towers crumbling like blocks, bridges breaking over highways, residential condos disappearing under landslides, everything happening in real time, in real *life*—people continued shopping for underwear, protein cubes, and the few essentials still needed outside of holo. Nothing could reach the sky. Not the megaquake shock waves or the tsunamis they stirred up. Air was the only thing they shared with the greater world, and even that was filtered. The eco-cities had been built to protect the planet—and the people from it.

But the difference between *asylum* and *prison* was membrane-thin. It could be ruptured by the death of a sister, a treacherous lie.

Or a simple malfunction.

From above, Kasey watched it happen. It started with one person. They got onto the duct. The duct didn't move for them, for the same reason the copterbot hadn't responded to Actinium. Ranks were required to activate most of the eco-city's services, simple as that, but today, in a perfect storm with the news, people assumed the worst. What ensued was a spectacle so illogical and asinine Kasey couldn't watch it. Couldn't watch people stampeding for the ducts, so she watched the Worldwide Union broadcast instead. Saw reporters announcing radioaxons were already on the move, released by compromised fission plants. Stared at the graphs, concentric circles representing the radiated areas, blue swatches representing the trajectories of airborne radioaxons, numbers representing the already dead and soon-to-be-dead.

Kasey should have been one of them. Would have, if Celia had worn her antiskin in the water and Kasey hadn't.

Another P2C alert flashed on her Intraface—requesting P2C officer support on stratum-25 and help in restoring the ranks, something Kasey could have assisted with but she was unreachable, disconnected. Not even the screams of people below, overpowering the drone of the copterbot engine, could get through to her. Just moments ago, everyone had been so assured of their place in the world. Before *they* became *I*, no one cared when *they* died.

They don't deserve to be safe. I don't deserve to be safe.

"They've found the boat," she heard herself say.

"Where?" Actinium asked, as she knew he would. This boy who'd bleed for Celia, who didn't care about his well-being, just as Kasey no longer cared about hers.

"Landmass six-sixty," she said, and gave him the coordinates to the island.

#卌 卌 I

"AND THIS," I SAY, CONCLUDING the tour of the island, "is the ridge."

We stand under its elongating shadow. I make it a rule to never scale the ridge past sundown, and so finding new boat parts will have to wait. My accomplishment for today? Placating the boy beside me.

He's dressed now, in a sweater of his choice and cargo pants that reveal a little too much ankle. His hair spills back as he cranes his head. "You actually climb this thing?"

"Sometimes every other day."

"Why?"

He asks it like I'm out of my mind, and I get it. The wall of rock seems impossibly steep in the gathering dark. Just the sight of it causes my shoulders to spasm with phantom memories of pulled tendons and popped sockets. Once, I fell off about halfway up and saw my life flash through my eyes. I'm not exaggerating—before blacking out, I heard my skull crack and thought, *That's it. I'm dead.* I'm still not sure how I woke up sometime later with a killer migraine but no brains on the ground. My brain *does* die a bit now, at the idea of doing it all over again.

But the alternative—staying on this island, forever separated from Kay—is a fate worse than death.

I turn away from the ridge and its imposing height and start heading back shore side. "I'm looking for my sister," I say as a breeze snaps in, briny and cold. It sends a rustle through the skimpy shrubs clinging to the rock scape. Ripples flash across the rainwater ponds.

"I thought you said this island was abandoned," the boy calls after me.

"It is."

"Then where's your sister?"

He's falling behind, the snail. *Wait for him*—but I won't let him slow me down.

"Out there." I nod as I walk, tilting my chin toward the land before us, the shale that will eventually turn into gravel and gravel into sand. The island is small enough that if I concentrate, I can hear the waves, breaking upon the shore. "Somewhere across the sea."

"And you know this how?" asks the boy.

Turns out he isn't funny *or* sarcastic, and now that he's recovered from being scared out of his wits, he's starting to annoy me. "Where else can she be, if she's not here?" I say, splashing through a shallow pool of rainwater.

"She could be dead."

I stop in my tracks. The breeze stills. The island's gone

quiet, deathly so. I can't even hear the ocean anymore. "She's not dead."

"How do you know?" asks the boy, finally catching up. His voice is even more attractive breathless. His eyes, a limpid gray to me, gleam with some emotion. I think it's concern.

I'm both indignant and touched. He asks because he cares. His questions are legitimate and important.

I just can't afford to face them.

How do you know? I have neither the evidence nor the facts Kay would require. Only a conviction in my heart, a hope that thrives more on some days than others, a living thing I must protect at all costs.

I tear my gaze from the boy, point it forward, and walk. "I just do."

"So this ridge," he huffs, trying to keep pace. *Slow down*—but I go faster. Dusk creeps over the island, darkening the rock beneath our feet like rain. "What's on the other side?" he asks as we reach a shelf of shale, small enough to walk around, unlike the ridge.

I clamber over it. "Supplies for boats."

"You"—the boy struggles behind me—"build them?"

"No. I rent them from a shop on the beach."

"Have you ever reached land when you sail?" asks the boy, ignoring my sarcasm. Or not picking up on it. *Which?* I want to ask. *Joules, am I really that out of practice?*

"What if there's nothing out there?" the boy presses when I don't answer.

His question rushes through me like the wind.

"Why would you say that?" I demand, then inhale sharply. "Do you remember something?"

The rocks have diminished in size as we've covered more ground, but now they loom, shadows bleeding out from their bases, and the land, always so flat, appears pockmarked like the surface of some alien planet.

"No," admits the boy, sounding truthful.

"Look, love," I say as we finally reach gravel and I can see the back of M.M.'s house, silhouetted against the waterline by the dying light. "I don't know who you are or where you came from, but I've held up just fine these years on my own. I *am* going to get myself off this island, and I don't expect you to help. But you're not ruining my mojo. That's all I ask of you."

"Your mojo—"

"Uh-uh."

"—could kill you," finishes the boy.

"It wouldn't be the first thing to try," I say without breaking stride.

We don't speak for the rest of the walk.

• • •

For dinner, we have dandelions and eight-pointed-tree leaves. It's not exactly the best of introductory meals to island cuisine, and the boy pushes it around on his plate, appearing seasick. "You've survived on this?"

"No."

"Then what do you normally eat?" asks the boy.

"Taro."

"What happened?" asks the boy.

"I lost them to the sea."

"How?" asks the boy.

I lay down M.M.'s fork. Was talking always this tiring? "I packed all the taro I'd grown when I sailed to find my sister. But we ran into a storm."

"We," echoes the boy.

"Hubert and me."

"Hubert," echoes the boy.

"He's not around anymore."

Silence.

I lift the fork again, but don't eat. My stomach gurgles—no doubt with indigestion—as I wait. Wait for the boy to start spewing more questions, for his skepticism and incredulity.

"The taros," he says at last. "Are there any left?"

Finally. A question where the answer is literally in M.M.'s backyard.

I push my chair away from the table. "Let's find out."

We emerge onto the porch, into my favorite kind of night. Windless. Calm. The moon is just as white as the sun and the sky is a richer shade of gray than it would be during the day. I love the day too, but at night, when the beach is silver and the ocean obsidian, I feel like I'm missing out on less by not being able to see it in color.

Nights on the island are also cold, though, and I rub my arms as we head down the porch and around to the back of the house, where taros grow in a small plot of dirt. I squat by a row of them. Judging by the size of their leaves, none are ready to be harvested for their starchy tubers.

The boy squats as well. His body radiates heat, warming my right side even though we're a body-width apart. "The soil looks depleted," he says, and I glance to him. The moonlight contours his face, bringing out angles I didn't see before. "You should fertilize it."

I clear my head. *Focus on the plants.* "With what?" I don't exactly have bags of nitrogen compounds lying around.

"What do you think?" says the boy.

Oh.

"Ew." I shudder. Joules, no.

"Ew?"

"Yes, ew. That's gross."

He coughs. Suspiciously.

"What?" I ask.

"Nothing."

"What?"

"You just seemed so gung-ho about this survival thing," he says, absentmindedly rubbing at his wrists. "I figured you'd be okay with making your own fertilizer."

"Nope. Definitely not."

"No shit?"

"No shit."

Don't look at him. Don't make eye contact. Because it's over the moment we do.

U-me rolls out to see what's wrong. What's wrong is that

I've regressed to cracking up at potty jokes. But I can't control it. The laughter keeps on coming, wave after wave.

"Do you remember anything?" I finally gasp, cheeks cramping and chest burning, my body alive with the adrenaline I usually only get from climbing the ridge. "Something from your past?"

The boy falls silent. I immediately miss the sound of his laugh. "Should I?"

"Sometimes I find a memory when I rediscover things I know." I nod at the taros. "You seem to know gardening."

"I don't remember gardening."

"Where did that stuff about the soil come from, then?" To me, it all looks gray, and I tamp down on my jealousy when the boy acts like it's no big deal.

"I just do," he says with a shrug. But something about the gesture seems off, as if there's more weight on his shoulders than he's letting on. Seconds later, he rises and heads for the house.

Wait, I almost call after him, before checking myself. Boys come running to *me*. But it's chilly without him here. I rub my arms, the residual heat on my right side already cooling, then head back to the house as well.

• • •

I *have* to cross the ridge today, no excuses.

I'm up before the sun and head into kitchen for breakfast. The leaves somehow taste worse after watching the boy struggle to eat them. I chew on one as long as I possibly can, then spit the wad of fibers out the sink window.

The boy's asleep in the bed. I made the right call in insisting he take it. He looks dead, hair splayed over the pillow, eyes still beneath their lids. The only movement to him is the rise and fall of his chest. The rhythm hypnotizes me, and like a creep, I watch him sleep. Then I ease the bedroom door shut. Pad softly through the house, swiping a kitchen knife on my way to the porch, where U-me's waiting. She knows the routine. Grab M.M.'s fanny pack and go.

But today, I stop on the deck.

Do I trust the boy enough to leave him unsupervised?

He hasn't tried to kill me again—tall order, I know—but my throat's still tender. And though we shared a moment in the taro garden last night, this side of the island is my territory. Home. Out there, past the ridge, in the gray meadow with all the little shrines, even I feel like an intruder. I don't need an uninvited guest creeping around too.

"Stay here," I say to U-me. "Make sure he doesn't leave the house."

"Strongly disagree."

"Then what do you suggest I do? Tie him up again?"

U-me whirs.

I rephrase my question into a declarative statement. "I should tie him up again."

"Strongly agree."

"No, I can't do that," I mutter, half to myself. I can still see his panicked face, the whites of his eyes exposed with fear.

He's not an animal, but a person. A person like me. "I can't do that," I repeat, this time to U-me.

"Neutral."

"I've made the climb without you before."

"Agree."

"I'll be fine."

"Disagree."

"Paranoid."

"Paranoid: unreasonably anxious, suspicious, or mistrustful, adjective."

Yeah, that's not me. "Be a darling," I say to U-me, "and stay here."

Then I tuck the kitchen knife into the fanny pack and hop down the porch steps.

I'm not lying when I say I've climbed the ridge without U-me before. It just so happens that those were also the times I nearly fell to my death. But I have two years of practice under my belt, and I manage to make it up mostly intact, leaving behind only the skin on my palms. I tie the rope to the top; the descent is easier. I drop to the ground, stepping out of my makeshift harness and leaving the rope in place for when I return.

I weave through the meadow quickly, past the shrines, and reach the beginnings of the forest. The pines are too bushy, so I find a nice eight-pointed tree and start hacking at the base of the trunk with my kitchen knife.

Two hours and a dozen blisters later, the tree falls over. One down. I trim off the branches and start chopping the second. The sky darkens as I work. The air grows clammy.

Wiping sweat from my brow, I glance up to the trees ahead. They're dense, but it's almost as if they're not there. The Shipyard beyond looms up in my vision, calling my name.

Cee.

Cee.

Cee.

Right. Still on the island. Still losing my mind.

I lunch on some leaves, then fell one last tree. I tie the three trunks together with twine from my pack, strip down to M.M.'s holey camisole, and fill her sweater with rotting leaves and pine needles. That should do for fertilizer. The boy won't be expecting it. I smile a bit at the thought of surprising him.

The walk back through the meadow takes longer than usual, probably because I'm dragging three trunks topped off with a sweater-sack of mulch. By the time I transport everything to the top of the ridge and lower them down the other side, the clouds have thickened. It starts to drizzle as I lug everything across the rock scape, back to the house. I unload the trunks on the porch, prop the sack of mulch by the door, and head in.

I almost don't recognize the kitchen. The floors are polished, not a speck of sand in sight. The counters are clean. The old pitcher by the sink is filled with dandelions.

"Wow." U-me is either malfunctioning or self-actualizing.

"Wow," says U-me, rolling out from the living room. "Expressing astonishment or admiration, exclamation."

"Aw, U-me. You didn't have to—oh." I stop between the

kitchen and living room, the half door separating them swinging into the back of my calves. "It's you."

The boy sits back on his bare heels, a monogrammed towel in his hands and a pail of water beside him. His cheeks darken as he catches sight of me, and his gaze shoots down to my clogs. "You're tracking in mud."

Huh. I assume he's blushing, but I can't begin to imagine why. "How did you sleep?" I call as I go back to the porch to kick off my clogs. It's only his second day on the island. All in all, he's holding up rather well—better than me, on any given day, if he has the energy to clean.

"How do you feel?" I ask, returning to the living room.

"Fine," says the boy, terse.

"I brought back some mulch for the garden."

A grunt of acknowledgment. Glum today, I see.

Crouching beside him, I notice that his eyes are puffy and his nose is darker than the rest of his face, the shade of gray closer to that of his cheeks. Has he been crying? My heart twinges, and I squash the urge to ask if he's remembered something. The question killed the mood last night and created unnecessary friction. It's a sore spot for him, not having memories, like not being able to see in color is for me.

"You don't have to do this," I say instead as he tackles a stain in the wood that looks like it's been there since the beginning of time.

"It's filthy."

"It's fine."

He keeps scrubbing.

Sighing, I grab a towel from the bathroom and join him on the floor. Our elbows bump; he jerks away. Then he stills.

"Your hands."

I wince as I dunk the towel into the pail of what turns out to be salt water. "It's nothing."

His fingers close around my wrist.

At first, I let him inspect my pulpy palms. Then the warmth of his touch spreads under my skin, making me more aware of it—and of the holey camisole barely covering it, turned sheer by the rain and revealing bits of me that would mean nothing to U-me, but the boy is not U-me. The boy can see—has seen, judging by his cheeks—and now I'm blushing too, which is ridiculous. I'm perfectly comfortable showing off my body, at least in my memories. What's different?

For one, past-Cee was much better groomed. I tell myself that my embarrassment has nothing to do with the boy, who gives me his solemn diagnosis. "Infection could set in," he says as I tug my hand out of his.

"I'll heal." I grab the towel and attack the stain, stopping only to insist "really" when he doesn't join me. He's unsatisfied by my reply; I can tell from his expression, the same as yesterday's when I explained my plan to find Kay. I have proof of healing, though, and from injuries much worse than this. I'd just rather not get graphic. Cleaning seems to be more the boy's speed, and eventually he returns to it. We work in silence, the rain on the roof quieting as we finish. He goes to the garden, and I head outside, taking advantage of what cloudy daylight remains to cut the trunks into rough log shapes for Hubert 2.0. I'll have to name him. Or them.

Or her. *Leona.* The name pops into my head. It sounds fierce. I'm going to need fierce if I want to get off this island on a raft. Because frankly, that's what Leona's going to be. A raft. I have neither the skill to craft a proper boat, nor three more years to spare.

Too soon, the last of the light fades, forcing me back into the house. I soak off the day's grime in the tub. As I'm drying off, a mouthwatering aroma wafts into the bathroom. I follow the scent to the kitchen, where, on the table, rests a bowl. The steam rising from it smells like mashed potatoes . . .

. . . *swirled with butter and sprinkled with chives. The flavors melt across my tongue, as if they're real. I know they're not, but what* is *real is the smile Kay gives me from across the table* . . .

. . . the edge of the table pressing into my stomach as I lean in, drooling, until I see the bowl's contents.

Taro, not potato.

The door behind me opens. I whip around as the boy walks in. "You harvested them?"

"Just two," he says, washing his hands at the sink.

"Just?" Joules, there are only twelve plants in all.

The boy turns off the tap. *Plip-plop-plip.* The last droplet falls. "I'm not going to let us starve."

Even before he faces me, I can imagine his expression. I draw it from his voice—from the preemptive edge to it, as if he senses my hackles are raised.

He's not wrong. "It's not about *us*." I eat only what I need and stockpile the rest. I bake unappetizing biscuits because they will keep. Mashed taros? That's a luxury I can't afford. "I need to ration for the journey," I say, and catch the look on the boy's face, a flash so quick I would've missed it yesterday but already, I can read between his lines. The thinning of his lips? That's his skepticism.

What if there's nothing out there?

The softness in his eyes? That's pity I mistook for concern.

She could be dead.

He thinks I'm delusional, and that angers me. Scares me— *what if he's right?*—and when we're trapped in a tiny kitchen together and he's a meter away, I'm breathing in his doubt and I need to push it out and so the words leave my mouth before I can think any better of them. "Unlike you, I have someone waiting for me."

And then I can't see his face, or what my words do to it, because all I can see is Kay's, blurred through my tear-chafed eyes. Hers are dry. She's whole; I'm broken, I shouldn't be— Mom was barely in our lives—and I wonder what's wrong with me but that's not what I say.

What's wrong with you? I ask Kay, and the memory shatters. The boy is gone and I'm alone now, back in M.M.'s kitchen. My hands grip the table. Droplets dot the wooden surface. I wipe them off. Wipe my face. Sniff. In the memory, we were young, but was the last thing I said to Kay just as regrettable? Did I get to tell her I love her, and if not, will I ever be able to?

I will. I have to. I lift the bowl of mashed taro, appetite gone, but food is food and can't be wasted so I taste it. It's good. Sea-salted. A feast for my guilt.

I stomach what I can and leave behind more than half for the boy. For when he returns.

If he returns.

I keep watch by the kitchen window until night falls, then curl up on the couch, feeling dejected and pathetic for it.

"I hurt him," I lament as U-me rolls over, stationing herself before my knees.

"Agree."

"He's never coming back." Melodramatic, I know, but I can't help it.

"Disagree."

"You sound confident," I mutter, laying my head down on the couch arm beneath the windowsill, my eyes fixating on the ceiling above. I guess we *are* on an abandoned island with limited real estate. He'll have to return eventually. No guarantee we'll be on speaking terms, though. *I'll miss his voice*, I think, and groan, covering my eyes with an arm. I wish I could share my emotions with U-me and have her tell me I'm being irrational. Kay would. I've known the boy for, what? Two days? Three years without a human fix and two days later I'm addicted. Past-me would laugh at current-me, unable to sleep and heart leaping when finally, sometime around midnight, a sound comes from the porch. Whine of the front door, then creak of the half door separating the kitchen from the living room. Footsteps, soft.

And him. His outline fuzzes through my lashes as I pretend to be asleep, stirring only when I hear him stop by the couch.

"Cee?" His voice is a murmur of moonlight. I am the sea, pulled toward it. I don't fight my reaction or act on it. Just let it swell, welcoming the physical yearning after so lengthy a drought.

"Mm-hmm?"

"I didn't want to wake you," says the boy, still whispering. I open my eyes fully. He stands at the other end of the couch, in a slant of moonlight coming from the window behind my head. His face is pale. Tired, but not upset.

I'm tired too, and too relieved for pretenses. "I wasn't actually asleep," I admit, sitting up. "I was waiting for you."

A beat of silence, slightly awkward. Too honest? Maybe. Well, better say what I've been waiting all night to say. "I'm—"

"Sorry." The boy steals the apology from my mouth. "For making you wait. And for earlier. I may not understand your way of life, but I can respect it. As for the taros . . ." He begins to explain how the tubers multiply as they grow.

I cut him off. "I trust you."

The words feel right, even if they surprise me. They seem to surprise the boy more. His lips stay parted for a second. Then they close. He looks away. "You know nothing about me."

His silence says the rest. I *know nothing about me.*

If only I could take back my words from before or give him some of my memories. But all I can offer is, "I know you're good at cooking and cleaning and gardening, and probably a whole lot else. And I'm sorry too." My throat grows thorny and I look to the window, the glass reflecting my face. "I say things I don't mean sometimes, when I'm scared."

"Do I scare you?"

"No." His questions only watered the uncertainties already seeded within me.

"Even though I tried to kill you?" asks the boy. "Supposedly," he adds, grudgingly as ever.

That makes me smile. "What can I say?" I turn away from the window. "I enjoy living on the edge." I lay myself back down, stretched out like how I was before except I feel more vulnerable now, less like part of the couch and more like a flesh-and-blood body as our gazes meet.

"I'm glad you're here," I murmur. Not that I'd wish this island life upon my worst enemy, but I think he knows what I mean.

I wonder if he's glad I'm here, too.

If he is, he doesn't say so. Only, "You should take the bed."

"I like it better here."

Silence.

Stay with me, I think as the boy takes a breath.

And says, "Good night, Cee."

"Night." I watch as he goes, something yawning open in my chest. It hurts like a wound, even though I'm used to being alone.

Except I'm not alone. Alone is an island. It's an uncrossable sea, being too far from another soul, whereas lonely is being too close, in the same house yet separated by walls because we choose to be, and when I fall asleep, the pain of loneliness follows me as I dream of more walls—this time between me and Kay. I can feel her in my mind, but I can't feel *her*, and so I break the wall, tear it apart with my bare hands, to find nothing on the other side but whiteness, blindingly bright, and the cry of gulls.

12

THE COPTERBOT LANDED ON THE gray sands of the shore.

This was it. The island. There was the house up on the rocks, looking no different than it had since the sisters' last visit four months ago. It just felt like a lifetime, and Kasey a changed person.

Or so she thought. Her vision of how this would go—starting with having the grief-stricken courage to expose herself—vanished like the fantasy it was when the copterbot door opened on Actinium's side and her brain defaulted to logic mode. She caught his arm. "The radioaxons—"

"It's safe."

Safe. *You're safe with me*, Celia had said, her expression harrowingly similar to Actinium's as he went on to say, "I wouldn't put you in danger," before his gaze fell to Kasey's hand, still on his arm.

She knew what he had to be thinking: She hadn't reached for him when he'd cut himself. Hadn't seemed nearly as concerned. But that damage was visible. Repairable. Radio-axon poisoning was neither and all the more dangerous for it.

Still, she forced herself to release him. Watched, helpless, as Actinium stepped into the open air in nothing more than the black button-down and jeans they'd purchased on stratum-25. He turned back to her, offering a hand. She didn't take it. She told herself it was because of his bandages but in reality, she was afraid he'd feel her fingers shaking in fear for her own life despite losing one so much more vibrant than hers.

By herself, she climbed down, disoriented, as always, to enter a new world. That's what Landmass-660 felt like to her. It didn't technically belong to any outside territory, but it was as far "outside" as Kasey had ever gone, and nothing like the eco-city. The ground here was alive, sand shifting under her feet. The sky above was mold-gray and far deeper than the ninety meters allotted per stratum, and wind existed, explod-ing in erratic, sneeze-like bursts. Was it spreading radioaxons? Suppressing the thought and the panic it sprung, Kasey looked to the house on the beach as a figure emerged on its porch, waving at them. Actinium waved back, leaving Kasey no choice but to lift an arm too, trying to wave but not quite able to because this wasn't right. She should have been here with Celia.

Waving at the woman in the iron-on pug sweater with Celia.

They'd met Leona upon docking *Hubert* at the pier. She'd shown them around the island, from the cove to the levee, a holdover from pre–arctic melt times, even though she'd been under no obligation to do so, or to treat the girls like her own. Yet she had, and as she jogged toward them, the sand beneath Kasey's feet liquified and her mind sank. If it hadn't been for Leona, Celia might not have returned to the island. Might not have snuck out, poisoned herself again and again—not that Leona could have known, which only angered Kasey more, to see the grief on the woman's features when ignorance still protected her. She started to back away, but then Leona's arms were around her, her voice by her ear—"Oh, Kasey"—and Kasey's vision darkened, a memory dragging her under. Midnight. A knock on her door. A whisper—*Still up?* Her sister's heartbeat against her brow. *You belong here.*

"The boat," Kasey managed to choke out.

A nod against her shoulder. Leona released her, and Kasey noticed something troubling about the scene other than Celia's absence from it.

"Where's your mask?" Not just that, but antiskin. Goggles. Leona was wearing no protective gear.

"Didn't Act tell you?" asked Leona. "The island's safe."

Act. The familiarity of the nickname did not slip by Kasey unnoticed, nor did the ease with which Leona took them both by the arms. As they walked down-shore, Kasey thought back to all the times Leona and Celia would chat on the couch while Kasey fiddled with Leona's teachbot—a gift, Leona explained, from her sister. Had Kasey missed news of Celia and Actinium's relationship then? Or had Celia deliberately kept it from Kasey because she knew Kasey's shameful secret—that she had trouble remembering Celia's boys?

Which was it? she wanted to ask Leona, followed by *How is the island safe?* But whatever questions she had were blasted away when they reached the cove and Kasey saw it.

On the rocks before they curved into the cove. Tugged out of the tide's reach.

The boat hadn't made a lasting impression before. Now the sight of it speared Kasey. She stopped in her tracks, her inner world grinding to a halt as the world outside continued to roar with the wind and the sea. A squeeze of her arm—"Take as long as you need; I'll be in the house"—and Kasey found herself left by Leona. Alone with Actinium.

"I can wait at the house too."

Kasey shook her head. Last time, she'd said Celia would have wanted him here, but the truth was, Kasey did too, needed Actinium here to remind her that love was pain, and pain was approaching the boat when all she really wanted to do was retreat from it. With every step over the brine-slick rocks, she realized she was no better than the people at her party. She half expected Celia to spring up from the hull and say "Surprise!" until the very end, when Kasey was practically upon the boat, the unequivocally, indisputably empty boat.

She crouched beside it. She refused to think of it by its painted name. To her, this was a *thing*, the hearse that'd delivered Celia to her watery grave. If it were sentient, she'd want to hurt it, but it wasn't, and it was already damaged, bow dented and gunwale half gone, evidence of the abuse it'd suffered at sea. Had Celia suffered? Had she known hunger? Thirst? Or had it been quick? Kasey hoped it was. Hoped it was the death

Celia had wanted, as foreign as the concept seemed. As the waves shattered on the rocks around her, she felt Actinium's presence at her back. He remained standing. Kasey appreciated that. If he knelt too, and contributed his grief to the space, she'd actually drown.

Rising, she wiped the sea spray off her otherwise dry face.

As promised, Leona was waiting back in the house. "We'll have it transported to the eco-city," she said as Actinium and Kasey came through the door and into the fuel-bar, where two kettles were going on the stove.

"Keep the boat here," said Kasey. The island was classified as private domain, prohibiting non-residents from holoing in. That, along with Leona's lack of an Intraface, would offer her ample protection from the press.

"Then we'll send it over to Francis," said Leona. "He'll patch it up, make it good as new."

He could destroy it, for all Kasey cared, but she nodded for Leona's sake—then stiffened.

Voices. Inside the house.

Peeking into the living room, she was taken aback to see the Wangs, Reddys, Zielińskis, and O'Sheas with their twins. It was literally the island's entire population, minus the temporary vacationers and old Francis John Jr., the handyman who lived in the woods. The couch was crammed, the overflow sitting on the floor, spread with grandmother Maisie Moore's monogrammed towels, everyone huddled around Leona's small holograph projector and none, to Kasey's growing dismay, wearing masks.

The air above her head shifted; she glanced up to see Actinium, leaned in beside her. He took one look at the living room and sighed. An odd sound, coming from him. Even odder was his mutter, something about "going outside."

Before Kasey could ask what was wrong with inside, a scream bounded toward them.

"Act!" Roma, one of the nine-year-old twins, burst into the kitchen and ran for Actinium, skidding to a stop upon seeing Kasey. "Who's that?"

They'd met before, but Kasey didn't blame Roma for forgetting. Celia was the one who'd spent hours making mud-patty cakes with the twins, while Kasey stood off to the side, not very good with children. She was worse at introductions, so she left the honors to Actinium.

"A friend," he said. Not quite true, but Kasey supposed *friend* was easier for kids to understand. Simple, clear-cut—

"A *girl* friend?"

"No," Kasey said as Mrs. O'Shea's voice floated in from the living room.

"Actinium? Is that you?"

The next thing Kasey knew, islanders were piling into the fuel-bar. She edged out of the way as they beelined for Actinium, shaking his hand, hugging him. Actinium reciprocated far more woodenly than Kasey would have expected from him. "You told them," he said to Leona, sounding aggrieved, and Kasey sent him her sympathies as the mob swept him into the living room.

"They were all rushing to evacuate!" Leona called after them. "I had to explain!"

"Explain what?" Kasey asked Leona as the kitchen emptied. "Why doesn't anyone have to evacuate?"

Leona lifted the kettle from the stove. "Because the air is filtered. Act built a shield around the island."

Kasey blinked.

She knew perfectly well what Leona meant by *shield*, as an eco-city denizen protected by one. A filtration and force-field system, invisible yet impenetrable, sieving out toxins and shielding city infrastructure from the effects of elemental erosion. Before the science ban, Kasey had spent an entire summer deciphering shield mechanics and equations. She could recreate a miniature model if she tried. But around the whole of this island?

"That's . . ." Kasey trailed off as the pieces fell into place. Leona not wearing a mask. The people's warm reception. And Actinium. Come to think of it, he'd reprogrammed the hospel copterbot like it was nothing, with all the cool-headedness Kasey had witnessed during their first meeting, but those impressions had been erased, like recessive genes, by the episode with the mug. Even now, Kasey could smell the blood, but maybe she'd been too quick to judge.

". . . a big project," she finished, the words feeling inadequate.

"It's my fault," said Leona, smiling sheepishly as she filled the mugs on the table. Kasey set more out. "Thank you, dear.

It's like what I told you girls: I just can't bear to abandon Maisie's home." Yes, Kasey remembered Leona saying so one time after Kasey pronounced the house structurally unsound. "But with all the talk of worsening storms, Act wouldn't put up with me staying on the wrong side of the levee."

"So he built a shield for you."

"For everyone," said Leona, and Kasey nodded. It wasn't the first over-the-top thing a boy had done to woo her sister. The son of an illusion-tech CEO had inscribed every undersky in the eco-city with love poems dedicated to her. In Kasey's unsolicited opinion, Actinium's grand gesture was superior. Impressive, actually. *Amazing*—the word that'd eluded Kasey.

"He only got around to checking the shield on my side of the levee this month, though," Leona continued. "So I invited them over for my peace of mind." She gestured at the living room and Kasey looked to it for a second time, gaze pinpointing Actinium. He was facing away from her, talking to Mr. Reddy.

The back of his shirt was soaked through.

How—when—where? It took Kasey a second to figure it out. On the rocks. He'd been standing behind her. The sea must have sprayed him then. Strange, that he hadn't moved away.

Then her attention was drawn to the center of everyone else's, to the holographs of tsunamis and landslides befalling ten out of the twelve outside territories, the rest left to contend with microcinogen and radioaxon fallout far more pernicious than the initial megaquake.

It was the moment people had failed to prepare for, as if

preparing too well made an event inevitable. A logical fallacy. So was human exceptionalism; 99.9% of species went extinct. The end of their road was not an *if*, but a *when*. The world would end.

Was ending before their eyes.

As it should, Kasey couldn't help but think, and startled as one of the twins began to cry. The sound was louder than she expected; she'd unwittingly drifted into the living room to better see the broadcast and as Mrs. O'Shea changed the channel, Kasey found herself staring at her dad. "The Planetary Protection Committee is set to convene at 17:00 Worldwide Time today," came the broadcaster's voice-over as David Mizuhara took the P2C podium. "Together, with Worldwide Union officers and delegates from the twelve territories, they will determine humanity's next step during its most critical hour."

The audio cut to her dad's press briefing. His monotone voice filled Leona's living room. "Here at the eco-cities, we thought to delay the crisis via lifestyle change, but despite the best efforts of P2C and those under its jurisdiction, the crisis has come to pass. Nevertheless, we remain committed to the health of this planet and its people. As such, we've been recruiting solutions for the better part of eighteen months now. And I can assure you . . ." A pause that would be misinterpreted as losing his place in the Intraface-fed lines but Kasey knew, from the way her dad pushed up his glasses, it was because he had seen a factual error. "I can assure you we have the best options, going forward, under our consideration."

There it was. The factual error. The blatant lie, unless Barry had found a promising submission in the last—Kasey checked her Intraface time—eighty-four hours.

David Mizuhara went on to talk about Environmental Control and Alteration Technologies. But even if every outside territory followed ECAT cleanup protocols, the balancing agents being pumped into the atmosphere wouldn't be able to neutralize the deadly compounds before their chemical bonds broke and re-formed into deadlier ones, the entire process expedited by increased global temperatures. It was as Linscott Horn had said, Kasey thought darkly. The dominos had been set centuries ago. One quake, and they all fell.

The people had brought this upon themselves.

"Live updates can be accessed through the Worldwide Union forum-feeds," said the broadcaster, voice returning. "The world will be watching, and we will be unpacking developments as they occur."

"See?" said Mrs. O'Shea to the twins. "Experts are going to make things better."

She said more. The broadcaster said more. Both their voices faded as Kasey retreated back against the wall—the wall giving way to a door. It closed behind her, sealing her into the bathroom, Celia's favorite space in the whole house. Eco-city showers relied on UV and pressurized air, and everfibers, like the sweaters Celia had gifted Leona, were self-cleaning. Using water for anything other than hydration was wasteful. But here, there was a tub and a non-fuel-bar sink. Kasey ran the tap to drown out the news, and as the water gushed, her rank flashed in her mind's eye.

Rank: 2.19431621

Rank: 2.19431622

Rank: 2.19431623

Her heartbeat rose with her rank: 105 bpm. 110 bpm. 115 bpm. She looked up at the mirror over the sink. She imagined breaking it with her bare hands, like Actinium had.

Couldn't do it, in the end.

• • •

The world will be watching.

Everyone will know you didn't help.

No one saw Kasey leave the house, or run to the pier. She stopped when her toes met the edge.

Couldn't jump, either.

The ache in her chest returned, metastasizing to her lungs. She took a deep breath.

And let the pain out.

|||| |||| |||

THE SCREAM SPLITS THE DAWN when I'm halfway to the house. It propels me into a sprint, over the porch steps and into the kitchen, my eyes darting around to see who's hurt, who's died, but it's just the kettle, come to a boil on the stovetop.

Right. People can do more things than die.

Like prepare breakfast in my absence. "Morning," says the boy, bustling about the kitchen with a towel tied around his hips like an apron. "Where'd you . . ."

He trails off when he sees my sorry state.

To paint a picture: I'm soaked up to the waist and dripping all over the floor. My feet are caked in sand and some stray kelp's plastered around my ankle. I have no idea what I can say to dodge the boy's inquiries so I don't try, offering up "beach yoga" as my explanation before I climb onto the kitchen counter and toss the house key onto the highest shelf.

There. Now, I might fall and break an arm in the middle of

the night, but at least I won't wake up like I did this morning, standing waist-deep in the sea as the surf hurtled toward me.

Clambering down, I brush past the boy. I'll field his questions later. But once I'm in front of M.M.'s closet, hunting for dry clothes, his words from the other day resound in my skull.

Your mojo could kill you.

I grip the edge of the closet door. Normally, I can trick myself into seeing the hilarity of sleepwalking to the shore. But today, my mind refuses to reframe the shit I can't control. Thanks to the boy, it's stuck on the possibility that I *could* really die the next time. It's bad enough for me to assume there *will* be a next time.

"Hey."

I take a deep breath, let it settle my nerves, then release the closet. "Yeah?"

The boy stands in the bedroom doorway. He's removed the apron, unveiling his outfit of the day: an M.M. pom-pom sweater and hair, freshly washed, that drips onto his shoulders. It's a good look. Would be better if his lips weren't parting to release a flood of questions in three, two, one—

"I'd like to join."

I blink. "Join?"

"Beach yoga," says the boy, and oh, love. He believes me. Why wouldn't he? The truth—that I sleepwalked to the beach—is just too out there for him to arrive at on his own.

Let him believe it, then. My problems aren't his, and what he doesn't know can't hurt him. "It's an advanced class," I say, untying my wet cargos and nearly dropping them before remembering such a thing called propriety. I glance at the boy; he's already turned around. "Not sure you can handle it." I step into a dry pair, cinch the waist, and tell him I'm good.

"I'm a quick learner."

I turn toward his voice—and back up into the closet.

He's stands in front of me, long-lashed eyes slightly hooded. I don't think we've ever been this close before—conscious, that is. Can't forget about the time he almost crushed the life out of me.

"Some other day," I say, flustered at being caught off guard. "Gotta run."

I wait for him to move and let me pass.

Instead he leans in. His head tips down beside mine, hair dripping onto my shoulder.

"Don't go."

His voice holds a command, a plea, and an invitation all in one and my stomach answers with a clench of hunger. My veins throb with blood and I know what I want to do—press him up against the closet and devour him, as I would any other boy who speaks to me like that.

Except this isn't like him. This isn't the boy I've been getting to know. Nor is it the unhearing, unseeing boy who tried to strangle me on the beach, but—*Careful, Cee*, says a voice in my head as I cup his cheek and turn my head a fraction, my lips brushing his ear. "Unless you want to be kneed in the balls again," I whisper, "you're going to step aside."

For a long moment, nothing happens.

Then he stumbles back. He clutches his face like I slapped

him. He shakes his head, mouth opening, closing, eyes looking to *me*, as if *I* can explain his strange behavior, before frowning. "Again? You've . . . done it before?"

His voice is back to normal. My heart rate sure isn't; my brain's confused and whiplashed and it takes a lot of effort to think of a comeback. "Clearly, I didn't do it hard enough to leave an impression," I say, deliberately eyeing his crotch.

Then I get the hell out.

"Stay," I order at U-me as I hurry down the porch, swiping my fanny pack on the way.

I trust you, I said to the boy.

You know nothing about me, the boy said to me.

The score chart as of this morning:

Boy: 1

Cee: 0

• • •

Don't go.

I can't unhear his voice no matter how I try, and believe me, I try. I chop trees so single-mindedly that the hours run together. The sun's setting when I finally drag all five trunks to the ridge; I curse when I realize my maximum load of two trunks per climb means three separate climbs.

Better start now.

The sun is already lower by the time I complete my first ascent. I quickly unload the two trunks at the ridge top. As I prepare to head back down for two more, a sound comes from the shore side of the ridge. I freeze. Again—same sound.

A voice.

"Cee!"

I peer over the edge.

Oh my Joules.

The boy is *climbing. Without. A. Rope.*

I throw him mine—and not a second too soon. He grabs it just as he loses a foothold. My stomach plummets as he plummets, and my heart snaps taut when the rope halts his fall.

"You're going to get yourself killed!" I shout. Something glints at the base of the ridge. U-me, loafing around. Failed at her supervision job and can't even be bothered to be useful now. "*Help him*, U-me, for fuck's sake."

Slowly, she rolls beside the boy as he relocates his footholds. "Strongly disagree. Disagree. Neutral. Agree."

Eons pass before the boy reaches the top. I grab his hand and tug.

"*Explain*"—he lurches into me—"*yourself*," I puff out.

"Let me—help."

"No. Absolutely not." Forget about his weird behavior this morning; I'm not about to let my first guest fall to his death before my very eyes.

The boy finishes catching his breath. "The sun's setting."

"So?"

"So we should get going." He grabs a log and moves toward the edge, as if the descent is as easy as stepping off.

I seize him by the back of his sweater. "Okay, first, you don't *descend* with the logs. It's hard enough carrying them to the top. Let the rope do the rest of the work."

"Any other pointers?"

No. No pointers. You shouldn't be here. But the sun isn't slowing for us as we argue, and at some point, the boy's going to have to climb down on his own anyway since I can't strap him across my back like a log.

I blow a long breath past my lips. "Listen closely."

I show him how to tie the rope around himself like a harness, then send him on a test climb down the ridge side.

He didn't lie—he *is* a fast learner. And with him here, I don't even have to climb the logs to the ridge top. He can stay at the base to fasten them to the end of the rope, and I can stay at the top to pull them up. The sun sinks past the horizon as we lower all five logs down the shore side of the ridge. We complete our own descent in the after light.

"Thanks," I say later as we're dragging the logs across the shale. "But never again."

"I won't bog you down."

"Don't care."

"There's nothing else to do."

"Remind me to dirty up the house for you," I say, and he snorts. The sound suits him, fits nicely into the repertoire I've collected for the boy-I-think-I-know, a boy whose mysteriousness begins and ends at his lack of memories and who, for the most part, is the opposite of dangerous. The opposite of suave. It's somewhat of a shame, I think, glancing sidelong at the boy as he wipes the sweat from his brow, because I guess there *are* a number of human debaucheries I miss and the boy, while a decent helper, is far from an (in)decent partner in crime.

At night we still go our separate ways—bedroom for him, couch for me—but he's up in the morning, ready when I am, and after some verbal sparring, I let him come that day.

And the next.

We build a routine. I chop down trees. He drags them to the base of the ridge. Transporting them over to the other side takes half as long with our human pulley system, and time goes by quicker when split with someone. Before I know it, I'm only three logs short from finishing Leona, and the boy and I have even wandered through several conversations.

"How do you think of me?" he asks when we're dragging logs through the meadow on our fourth and likely penultimate outing. For a second I'm not sure what I would say. *You're fine/helpful* sounds lukewarm while *You're pretty great* would be coming on strong. Luckily the boy clarifies by adding, "Do you have a placeholder name in your head?"

Ah. Nope, just *the boy*. "Would you *like* a placeholder name?" I ask, arching a brow.

"Depends."

"Oh, come now." I nudge him with an elbow. "I'd pick a good one."

"It'll be weird if it's random."

"It won't be random," I promise.

"Dmitri?" I pop seconds later.

"Sounds pretty random to me," says the boy.

The grass ripples around us as we slip through it. The blades tickle, and I scratch my ear. "What's wrong with it?"

"I don't know."

"Then there's nothing wrong with it."

"It's too . . ." The boy trails off. I wait, and sigh when he remains tight-lipped.

"Fine." I have other contenders. "What about Tristan?"

"Same issue as Dmitri," says the boy as the last of the grass parts, the meadow behind us and the ridge towering over us. "They're both . . ." His forehead wrinkles as he thinks.

"What?" I prompt. I refuse to let him off the hook this time.

"Promise not to laugh."

"Promise."

The boy offloads his logs at the ridge base. "Hunky."

I howl.

"You promised!"

"I know. I'm horrible. I'm sorry." *I think you're plenty hunky*—but the boy looks mortified enough. "Just—*hunky*."

The boy is not amused. "What term would *you* use?"

"'Smoldering,' maybe. 'Dark.'"

"Do I *look* dark to you?" demands the boy.

"No tragic backstory?"

"Nope. Tragic, right?"

My abs ache as my laughter finally releases me. We're standing in the shadow of the ridge. Not working. Not moving. Just talking. And I don't want it to end. "Heath?"

"No."

"Stop rejecting my names."

"Stop pulling them all from the same hat." Then the boy frowns and looks at me closely. "Are these coming off the top of your head?"

"Yes?"

"Maybe names are like faces in dreams," says the boy. "Maybe you only know the ones of people you've met before."

"You'll have to write that theory down. Publish it in some peer-reviewed journal when we get off the island." *Be scouted by an innotech firm.*

Now where did that come from?

"Am I?" asks the boy, distracting me.

"Am I . . . ?"

"Getting off the island." He speaks without bitterness or blame, his words as soft as the rain that begins to fall. He faces the ridge. "You don't have to answer that," he says, and starts climbing as I stand, speechless at the bottom.

Great. Just great. He's not allowed to *say* something like that and leave me agonizing over what he really means, because there's no way he's *that* neutral to the idea of being left behind—

Or is he?

I stare at him over dinner. As we wash the dishes. He gives me nothing to work with. We part for the night, and I'm left tossing and turning on the couch, his question gnawing at me.

Am I getting off the island?

The raft *could* be big enough for both of us, if I keep building it. Food is the real issue. We haven't stockpiled enough for two people on a journey of indeterminate length. I could set sail first, I decide, and spare the boy a watery death if I fail. And if I succeed, and find Kay, then I'm sure she'd help me rescue the boy as well. But why do I assume he needs rescuing at all? What if *he* also has someone he needs to find, someone he doesn't remember? And even if he doesn't—if he's truly alone—does that discredit his desire to go home? Is his life worth less than mine just because he isn't missed or loved?

"Still up?"

The whirlpool in my head stops at his whisper. I nod, say "Yes" in case it's too dark for him to see. He comes around to the front of the couch. I sit up and pull my legs in to make room. The cushion beneath my feet flutters as he sits, and something in me flutters too, adjusting to his presence across from me.

I wait for him to address what he said back at the ridge.

I don't expect him to ask, "Do you ever dream about things you can't make sense of?"

"Sometimes." Sometimes, scenes from my dreams seem too good to be true. Like the blueness of the sea, the crystalline sky, and the white ladder running between the two. "But mostly, I dream about my sister." Or swimming in the ocean, which usually ends with me waking *in* the ocean. "What about you?"

For a minute, it's just the sound of my even breathing and the rain, gentle outside.

"White." The boy speaks in a whisper. "In my dreams, all I can see is white."

"What kind of white?"

"Just . . . white." A measured breath. "A white worse than nothingness. The kind that makes you go blind."

His voice is hushed, his fear barely audible, but there.

It hurts me to hear it.

I inch over to him as he says, "I don't know how you did it, living so long here on your—what . . . are you doing?"

"Combing out the dreams," I say, one hand on his shoulder, the other running through his hair.

The boy is stiff, but doesn't move away. Doesn't move at all when I replace the hand on his shoulder with my head. "And this?" he asks, voice airless as if he's stopped breathing.

"Listening to your fears. Rest your head on mine."

After a second, he does—very, very carefully, as if our skulls might break. As the weight of his head settles, so does the breath in his chest. He resumes breathing; I'm close enough to feel it, now that we're sitting arm to arm, in darkness and silence still as water.

Eventually, I break it to whisper, "Can you hear my fears?"

"No," admits the boy, and just as I'm wondering if he thinks this is too weird and dorky, he says, "I hear the sea."

I smile. Might still be smiling when I drift off, into a dream where me and Kay are walking along the beach and Kay bends down, picks up a shell. *A Fibonacci spiral,* she says to me, holding out her palm. Normally, such a dream would have me sleepwalking to the shore but in the morning, I wake to light from M.M.'s good old window and something thumping under my cheek.

A heartbeat.

My own heart, sleep-sluggish, wakes up once I see gravity's work. Overnight, my head appears to have fallen onto the boy's chest and we *both* appear to have fallen flat onto the couch. His one arm dangles to the ground while the other rests over my waist. His head's angled back, the pale column of his throat exposed.

I touch my own throat. The bruises have finally stopped hurting. That night of thunder and rain feels like a week-old dream. The boy beside me (under me?) is warmer than any carpet-blanket, and I'm tempted to lie back down, but rafts don't build themselves and at last, I lift his arm, lift myself, and carefully reposition the limb over his stomach.

I grab a taro patty left over from last night's dinner and eat it on the porch. The tide rises with the sun. The boy doesn't wake. *Let him rest.* I don't need his help today when I'm only three logs short of completing Leona.

Three logs short of setting sail.

I feel none of the joy I did when I finished Hubert. Instead, the taro patty sits like a boulder in my stomach, and I do everything slowly—checking my pack, climbing the ridge, even going through the grayscale meadow and its creepy shrines. I cut my trees with precision, trying to make each stroke count. All the while, the forest keeps on calling my name. Beckoning.

Cee.

Cee.

Cee.

Fuck it. I toss down the kitchen knife and rise. It's just the foggy trees and the Shipyard, deeper in. What do I have to be afraid of?

I follow the call of my name, venturing into the trees. My steps, loud at first, quiet down as the pine cones underfoot decay. No beetles today. The island isn't exactly a menagerie, crossing *predators* off my list of things to worry about. But as the fog thickens, strung between the trees like cobwebs, I'm also reminded of how alone I was before the boy washed up— and how alone he'll be when I leave.

I shake off the thought. We've only known each other for one week. Kay and I have shared—and lost—years together. Nothing can compare, and when I reach the clearing in the forest and see the Shipyard, surrounded by the piles of junk I scavenged through to exhume Hubert, it rushes back. Every ridge crossing. The broken arms and ribs. The pain and joy and hopelessness, to have come so close and lost it all to a storm. But despite my worst fears, it didn't take three more years to find another way off this island. This really is a best-case scenario. Leaving will hurt, but I'll survive. Nothing can kill me. Kay is waiting. I hear her. Her voice—it's coming from the pool.

Cee. An ash-gray leaf lands in the middle of it, quivering the surface. My ribs uncurl in reach, and I stumble to the pool rim, my face perfectly reflected in water still as glass.

It shatters as I step in.

The water closes over me. My thoughts dilute. My eyes open. The pool's shockingly deep. I part the water before me like a curtain, revealing the bottom. It's plush with moss and speckled with toadstools, some as small as pebbles, other as big as dinner plates, glazed with light from above. Shadows gather, cloudlike, as I dive deeper. The water goes on forever and ever, and at some point, I begin to see.

In color—just like my memories and dreams—I see Kay. We're in a shoebox of a room, lying on the same bed and curled like kidneys, knee to knee. My fingers comb through her hair as I talk to her and my words appear on my hands, wrists, arms. They darken into bruises. The walls around us move away. Now I'm alone and speaking to a man in a white suit. Eighty years, he says, but I can't wait that long, so I walk to the doorway and step out, into the ocean waiting beyond. Water licks my skin; the sun bakes it dry as I'm washed ashore. A woman runs out to greet me; she wears a baby-blue sweater with iron-on pugs. I gave her that sweater, and she gives me a mug of tea and together we go to see a wall of concrete, soaring into the sky.

The images come faster and faster.

And freeze.

I choke as something cuts into my midsection, digging in as it draws me up and up and up.

Turns out it's the boy's arm, a vise around my waist when we break the surface, and though it doesn't *feel* like he's trying to kill me, I still panic. "The fuck do you—"

I break off. My eyes widen, absorbing the turquoise water around us and the gem-green trees, hemming in the Shipyard.

Turquoise.

Green.

My vision blurs, unable to process. To focus. When it finally refocuses, it's on the boy, his face mere centimeters from mine, his breaths ragged on my lips. His are pink. His hair is a dark, dark brown, strands matting his forehead. His eyes are the color of the sky.

Color.

Joules, I can see in color.

A voice worms through my sensory overload. It's the boy's, ordering to me swim.

Hard to obey when he's holding on to me like a floatation device. "What are you doing?" I snap, pushing him before he can answer.

We separate with a splash. The boy sloshes backward, floundering, then regains control of his limbs. "What does it look like?" he snaps right back, treading the water.

"Like you're trying to drown me."

"I was *saving* you." He spits out a leaf. "You weren't moving!" he cries when I glare at him in disbelief. "And you were under for at least three minutes."

Yeah, right. Three minutes, and I'd be blue in the face. I only choked on *one* mouthful of water, and guess who made me do that?

"I counted," says the boy, swimming after me as I paddle to the rim. "I waited as long as I reasonably could and only jumped in when I had to." *Blah blah blah.* I hoist myself out of the pool, flopping onto the green dandelions. "Because believe it or not—" The boy flops beside me, panting. "—this is not my idea of fun." He glances to me. "Say something."

"Sorry to break it to you, love, but I don't need saving."

"Got it," says the boy, adopting my annoyed tone. "Will keep that in mind if you're ever hanging off the edge of a cliff." Then he sits upright and wrings out M.M.'s sweater. It's blue. Brings out the color of his eyes.

"What?" he asks when he catches me staring.

I'm still peeved at his meddling, but also curious. "What color is my hair?"

"Black . . . ?"

"And my eyes?"

". . . Dark brown." He looks me over, brow furrowing. "Are you okay?"

I don't answer.

Black hair.

Dark eyes.

Just like Kay.

Relief trickles through me. I don't know what I expected. We're sisters, after all. But I feel closer to her than ever, especially with the new memories.

The memories. They were cut short. There are more, I'm sure of it. My eyes snap to the pool, the source of everything, before I was interrupted—

The boy grabs my hand and pulls me to my feet. "We're heading back now."

"Says who?"

"Says whoever didn't just try to drown themselves."

Grumbling, I follow him through the forest, too wet and too tired to pick this bone with him. My whole being buzzes. First memories, now color. It's overwhelming—and probably the reason why I screw up an hour later, after we've gathered the trees, lowered them down the ridge, and it's time to descend ourselves. I go first, barely a meter down when I lose my foothold. My hands shoot out, grappling for a dip in the rock. I miss, and my other foot swings free.

Above me, the boy shouts. My eyes shut on instinct, and I brace myself for the hard bite of the harness up my ass.

It doesn't come.

The rope goes slack. Untied.

I keep on falling.

14

SHE WOULD NEVER SEE THE body.

Never know the moment Celia died.

Another sister might not have been able to make peace with that.

Kasey could.

She just couldn't make peace with her peace.

Beyond the pier, the sea that'd spoken to Celia spoke to Kasey, too. The wind whispered in her ear. *Unfeeling. Defective. Deficient.* The world had been saying those things to her from the start, from the vandalized locker to the public outcry, when she stomached what others could not. She'd gone numb as Actinium bled, and accepted the fatality of Celia's prognosis, no questions asked, while he thought to call the copterbot. Even now, the ache lodged in her chest felt like a foreign body that did not belong, and the soreness of her throat, chafed from the scream, was pain she had to resist swallowing. It was human to inflict hurt on yourself and unto others, to let down the levee in the face of the storm, like the literal one currently brewing, dark clouds gathering where the ocean met the sky. Waves churned past her toes, two meters below, and over the churn, his voice reached her.

"Don't jump."

In the past, she would have found the warning insulting. Why would she do something so reckless as exposing herself?

Now Kasey was glad she seemed more emotional than she really was. "I'm not."

"Good." Actinium reached her side. Together they stood at the end of the pier, looking out at the sea as the air thickened, heavy between them. "Because the shield doesn't extend that far."

"The shield you built."

She emphasized the *you*. Actinium didn't reply. When Kasey glanced to him, he was looking on ahead resolutely, as if he knew she held her preconceptions of him like a deck of cards, and she was reshuffling with his every word.

I won't pry. That's what she'd said before. But Kasey couldn't stop her curiosity from burgeoning. Usually it annoyed her when people were inconsistent, but the mystery around Actinium felt curated, his contradictions too precise. Was he logical? Emotional? Authoritative, or uncomfortable around people? For someone who modified bodies, his own person was very unadorned, down to his mannerisms and speech, prompting Kasey to ask, "Do you actually work at GRAPHYC?"

The question seemed to catch Actinium off guard. "Yes," he said, and paused, then added, "part-time, Jinx would say."

Kasey was with Jinx on this one. Piecing together her sister's

Intraface, valiant as it was, seemed like a misuse of work hours. "What do you do?"

"I design the implants and digi-tattoos."

"Do you have any yourself?" SILVERTONGUE claimed the question was intrusive, but it was unrelated to her sister. Actinium shook his head, and she pressed, "Then how do you know if you're any good?"

"I never said I was."

To anyone else it'd sound like modesty, but Kasey heard the words he'd left out.

I never said I was. I'm better at other things.

Like coding. Engineering. He was obviously smart. Talented. Had he stayed in school, an innotech firm would've scouted him. With a team and resources, he'd be developing projects with even greater impact than an island-wide shield. But then, maybe he wouldn't have met Celia. Maybe Kasey was just bitter that he'd turned away from a future she would have wanted for herself.

"What are you thinking?" Actinium asked after a minute, and it surprised her that he should care, and for a heartbeat, she entertained a silly notion, that maybe he'd taken the brunt of the sea's spray *for* her. The physics of projectile motion checked out. The motives didn't. Actinium loved Celia.

Loved the things she loved.

Unlike Kasey, who still didn't see anything magical about the sea when she gazed at it. "That this was Celia's favorite place on the island. The pier."

"A place in between land and water, where there is power in a single step."

"You disagree." She made it a statement; she didn't pretend at uncertainty when she was certain. "Why?" she asked, less certain about *how* she could infer so much from his tone alone.

"I think most choices are made before you reach the edge."

Kasey agreed with him. She'd tried to jump. To expose herself. To bleed. But she was only fooling herself; she'd never choose self-destruction. Her brain was too solution-driven.

Or should have been. Because at this very moment, her Intraface pinged with a reminder from P2C headquarters that the emergency meeting was about to start and she was faced with the other choice she'd made: the choice not to help. Kasey swiped the message away; others took its place, namely unread ones from Meridian.

Where are you? Have you seen the news? Are you home?

Home. The nature of it—bubble-wrapped and safe—felt as alien to Kasey as it had to Celia.

"Actinium." His name burned her lips. She looked to him just as he looked to her, and for a heartbeat, she saw something in his gaze. A wavering. His lips parted.

But Kasey spoke first. "I have something to confess."

Celia had loved the sea. Loved the whitecaps that foamed like milk, the waltz of sunlight atop the peaks. Kasey did not. The sea was a trillion strands of hair, infinitely tangled on the surface and infinitely dense beneath. It distorted time: Minutes passed like hours and hours passed like minutes out there. It distorted space, made the horizon seem within reach.

And it was the perfect place for hiding secrets.

I killed Celia. I knew visiting the sea in person was a bad idea. I didn't stop her. But as much as guilt would have substantiated her humanity, she couldn't summon it. Anger was the easier emotion to access. Celia had been foolish to swim in the ocean, but she shouldn't have had to die for it. Someone—a person, a company, or multiples of each—had polluted the sea. In secret. It'd gone unreported. Unremedied. Kasey had been punished when she'd broken international law; had they? If not, why should she help them? Why better a world when *better* for Celia had meant choosing where and when to die?

A barrier in Kasey fell. The solution spilled out of her. All of it, including the final piece she'd told no one of. She waited for Actinium's disgust, his horror. Receiving neither, she barreled on.

"I can help," she finished, breathless. "But I don't want to."

Her confession. Science was impartial to everything and everyone. It either worked or didn't. It didn't say who deserved to benefit. The solution existed; therefore, it had to be shared.

"I don't want to help," she repeated, more quietly, as lightning flashed in the distance. The storm rumbled in. The rain thundered down.

Actinium was right; the shield ended where they stood. Kasey could almost see the arc of it before her eyes, where the rain passed through less forcefully, misting over them. Nervous, she looked to him, this boy who'd used science for the people's good. What would he think of her now?

As she waited for a response, a gale swooped in from the sea. Filtered by the shield or not, it felt real. It tugged at Kasey's clothes, dampened her face. It swept Actinium's carefully parted hair into his eyes, obscuring his expression. But his voice rang as clear as it had since day one.

"Who said anything about helping?"

||||| ||||| |||||

MY FIRST THOUGHT IS THAT I'm not dead.

My second is that I'm hanging without a rope halfway down the ridge, clinging to it by a rock, and I've almost certainly dislocated my right shoulder and I'm still dead because there's a long way left to fall and my fingers are slipping and *oh Joules, what a shit way to go.*

"Strongly disagree." Pressure—under my left foot, alleviating some of the strain in my arm.

U-me. Her fans whir as she supports me with her head. Whatever she was designed for, it wasn't this. We're both going to end up as rubble below if I don't do something fast.

Think, Cee. My eyes roll from side to side, then down.

The rope.

Part of it is a neon-orange puddle on the ground, but the other part still dangles down the ridge face, no longer tied but caught in the hands of the boy, his figure backlit at the top.

"Tie it!" I'll take the two of us over if I grab it now. Surely

he knows that. "Snap out of it!" I scream when he doesn't move. "Come on! Be a—"

Acid shoots up my throat.

"—*hero!*" I choke out.

"Hero," intones U-me dutifully as rocks tumble out from beneath us, free-falling to the ground with a telltale *pock-pock-pock*. "A person who is admired or idealized . . ."

I can't hear the rest. My vision is spotting and it's impossible to see the boy's features, let alone figure out what the hell is going through his mind as he just stands there, rope in hand. Meanwhile, the pressure is back on my fingertips. Pain sizzles white-hot down my arm. *This is it.* The cords in my neck tense. My lips part for one final shout—

—and close when the rope brushes my cheek.

It moves as the boy moves. He's a blob to me at this point, but I think he's making tying motions with his hands, and if he's not, I'm dead anyway, so I seize the rope, pincer my knees, and worm down its length as much as I can before my arms give out.

Sky. Air. Ground.

The impact jettisons the breath out of my lungs.

I don't know how long I lie there, on my back, before a face eclipses the yellow sun.

The boy's.

"Cee, can you hear me?" He sounds distant. "What hurts?"

"My shoulder." *And everything else.*

The skin on my arm burns as the boy slides up my sweater

sleeve. He slips one hand through mine and holds my elbow with the other.

"Okay," he breathes, almost to himself. "This will hurt before it gets better."

"What—"

The boy tugs on my arm. Someone screams. I think it's me. I claw at him—*Make the pain stop make it stop*—while my muscles flex against the pressure, the tension in my shoulder mounting until it feels maxed out—

The ball slides back into the socket.

The boy helps me sit up. When I'm ready to stand, he drapes my good arm over his shoulder and uses his body to support me. Either I'm shaking, or he's shaking, or we're both shaking. Our first few steps almost send me sprawling back on the ground.

The rest of the walk is a slow, silent hobble.

Halfway through, U-me suddenly speaks without prompting.

"Hero: a person who is admired or idealized for courage, noun."

I feel the boy stiffen under my arm.

"Hero: a person who is admired or idealized for courage, noun."

The sun descends from its midday summit.

"Hero: a person who is admired or idealized for courage, noun."

Hours later, we finally reach the house. The boy guides me to the couch, then takes off without a word. I have don't have the mental or physical capacity to wonder where he's going. My head lolls back, and I stare at the ceiling, tie-dyed violet from the sunset.

Joules.

What a day.

Yes, I gained a shit ton of memories. Yes, I'm also seeing in color. That may explain why I was careless in my climb, but it doesn't explain the untied rope. I haven't had such a close call since I perfected my knot technique two years ago.

I try to think back to the scene right before the fall. U-me was at the bottom of the ridge. The boy was at the top.

I didn't *see* him untie the rope.

I wasn't looking at him either.

What am I thinking? If killing me was his goal, he could have done it while I was flat on the ground. A rock to the temple. It would have been over in a second. Instead, he hovered over me, his face shining with sweat and worry, and maybe he could have faked the emotion, but he couldn't have faked the pounding of his heart. He fixed my shoulder, half carried me back, and now nothing adds up. Not the untied rope, or the way he froze at the top while I hung on for dear life.

Unless it was just that: He froze up. It's not every day you have to be a hero.

I know one thing for sure: I don't *want* to believe the boy had anything to do with my fall. He's become more to me than a visitor or a guest. He's a friend. And as his friend, I drag my ass off the couch when he doesn't return by night.

He's not on the shore, or at the sunken pier, awash in the midnight tide.

The same tide rushes into the cove, a secret place tucked past the rocks west of M.M.'s house. The sand glows with all the colors of mother-of-pearl in the moonlight. The boy, a mere blip against the waterline, is indigo.

He doesn't turn as I approach. I sit beside him. For several minutes, the only sound comes from the surf, shushing the night as it tumbles in.

"It's my fault." His voice is low and dark with shame. "Back on the ridge, when I saw you fall . . . My whole body . . ." His pain is palpable and I find myself rubbing circles onto his back. His muscles bunch under my hand. "Locked." He lets out a frustrated breath. "Except that's not the right word."

I might be battered and bruised, but he sounds scarred. And who wouldn't be? He's not like me, hardened by the brutality of island living.

"Hey," I say gently. "No hard feelings. You managed in the end."

"But what if I didn't?"

"You did. That's all that matters."

He shakes his head. "I don't have any memories. I don't have a name. All I have are my current thoughts, the things I feel and think and want. If I can't even act on those, then . . ."

He doesn't finish. Doesn't need to. His unspoken words live in my heart. They're the same ones that keep me up at night, when I worry Kay's face is fading. I worry who I would be without her. Just some girl on an abandoned island, with no past to draw on, no future to live for.

Who am I? he wants to ask. I can't answer that.

But I can offer *something*. "Hero."

"What?"

"You do have a name. Hero."

The boy breathes in. "That's—"

"U-me's pick. And mine, too."

Some names are found. Others are earned.

This one is both.

The boy, Hero, frowns. "It's cheesy."

"Well, it's either that or Dmitri. Cheesy or hunky. Take your pick."

He sighs. Not calmed. Not comforted. I'm all for exploring emotions, but his are a swamp right now. They'll only suck him down. I need to distract him. Pivot his mind.

I have an idea as to how.

"Let's try something," I say.

"What?" asks the boy.

"Turn toward me."

He does.

"Close your eyes."

He does—eyes flying open when I kiss him. Briefly. It's more of a peck, for his sake. I know what I like. The boy, though? I giggle at the look on his face. He scowls; I make my expression serious. Not everyone is as touchy-feely as me, and I ask if he didn't like it.

To which he responds, reluctantly, "I wasn't expecting it."

Not the same as not liking it, then. Grinning, I lean in and kiss him again. His lips are soft—softer, even, than when I traced them with my finger. A stir goes through me, not necessarily because I feel *for* him but because I simply feel. Him. I reach him. I say to him *It's okay* and *You're not alone* and *We don't have to overthink—we can simply live.* Kissing is just another means of conversation.

And conversations can't be sustained by one side, so when he doesn't respond, I pull back. "Right, then. What were—"

Oh.

My eyes widen as he replies.

Recovering, I slide a hand up his chest. He questions by leaning in. I answer by drawing him closer by the collar of his sweater.

He bears us down into the sand.

We break apart only when we run out of breath. I keep on running out of breath as his mouth drifts to my neck. My hands knot in his hair, holding on as my insides melt, brim, spill. I am vast as an ocean, the only sea I don't have to cross, and for the first time in a long time, I remember what it feels like to drown in myself.

• • •

We kiss until our lips swell. We speak in the language of tongues and teeth.

And then we speak more. I tell him about Kay, about my color-blindness, about my sleepwalking. He shares his cold, sterile dreams. I ask if he remembers being a doctor because he didn't do a half-bad job on my shoulder. He thinks I could have been a boat builder after I tell him about Hubert. He asks me more about Kay and I tell him what I can remember, and when I run out, he asks me about me, and I tell him, too, though the words are less sure and more shy, tentative. We talk about nothing and everything, and it's . . . *nice*, so nice that even when it gets colder, it's warm enough with him here.

We fall asleep on the cove, in each other's arms.

But my dreams take me far out, to the sister still waiting for me across the sea.

16

KILOMETERS OF SEA FLASHED BY as they neared the eco-city.

The ocean does not come poisoned.

Within the confines of the copterbot, Kasey glanced to Actinium.

People poison it.

Their eyes connected, black on black.

Not just the sea, but the land and the air. There are many in this world who live at the expense of others, and they need to pay.

Pay, Kasey had echoed on the pier, not sure if she'd heard right over the storm.

Yes. Actinium had met her gaze head-on, and in his, she saw herself—and the fire she was missing. *For what they did to Celia and others like her.*

She hadn't known how to reply. Not at first. Then the ache in her chest had pulsed like a second heart. The heart said *yes.* Between them, they shared an ocean of loss. It was under their chins, threatening to drown them the moment they sank. And

Kasey chose to sink. The world was ending. People were dying. But how many others were consuming more than their fair share when Celia could taste no more? Emitting carbon, when Celia, who'd never polluted in the first place, could exhale no more? The planet wasn't a single-occupancy home. Those who trashed it and got away? Who profited off other people's pain?

Save the deserving. Make the murderers pay.

She might not have been brave enough to poison herself, or sad enough to cry. But she was angry enough, and that made her feel alive.

As their copterbot waited in line to clear decontamination, Kasey linked into the video and audio feed of the P2C meeting taking place at the HQ conference room. She stayed on mute and listened as an eco-city 6 delegate spoke.

"All predictions remain in flux. But with ECAT, I reckon we can neutralize up to eighty percent of airborne microcinogens."

"And how long will that take?" asked Ekaterina, standing at the front, David beside her like a potted plant. For once, it frustrated Kasey to see him so passive.

"Like I said, it really depends—"

"The question, Officer Ng," Ekaterina cut in.

"Eleven months to two years. A lot can change—"

"And where, may I ask, are impacted peoples going to stay for a year?" A snap of Ekaterina's fingers and holographs appeared, destroyed territory cities fountaining up in the center of the conference room. "Already, we have twenty million dead and ten million missing. More will succumb to the complications of prolonged exposure. A projected hundred million casualties are expected by the half-year mark. Territory hospels are failing. Their governments will follow." Mutters, quieting when Ekaterina said, "We eco-cities are vulnerable too."

Not to toxins, Kasey knew, but to hysteria. During the first wave of natural disasters, people had tried to claw their way into the eco-cities, forcing the adoption of a rank-based admission system. Who's to say it wouldn't happen again?

"Now," said Ekaterina. "Does anyone have a better proposal?"

Silence.

Kasey pressed UNMUTE. "I do."

||||| ||||| ||||| ||

I STEP OFF THE PIER and stroke into the sea. I don't tire. Don't falter. I go as far as the horizon, and beyond. The sun rises, transmuting the water around me to gold. I could swim for days.

But I stop when I see the empty sky.

There used to be a city suspended in the air, made of disks of varying diameters but all stacked together, forming a 3D teardrop.

Now it's in flaming pieces, bobbing in the ocean, and there isn't a soul in sight.

"*Kay!*" Her name bursts from my lips before the thought shudders through my brain—that this is our home. *Was* our home, before I somehow ended up on the island. "*Kay!*"

A hunk of metal floats past me, sending up a wave. I swim faster, into the wreckage, but I'm too late. I spent too long on the island, too long building my boat, too long with Hero, the boy who washed ashore.

I stop swimming and sink.

Too late . . .

Too late . . .

I wake with a start.

Choke on salt water.

It's under my chin. Under my toes. All around me. Sea, and nothing else.

So this is how it is. A nightmare within a nightmare. A wave claps over me. Salt water rips up my sinuses. I breathe it in to wake up faster.

But I don't wake. The sea spits me back out, swallows me again, and again, and in between the rounds it sinks in: It's finally happened.

I've woken up in the ocean.

My senses return. I've lost the clogs on my feet, but I've still got on M.M.'s cargo pants and sweater, and they're weighing me down. Come the next wave, I duck under, shucking both. Breaking the surface, I try to orient myself. The steel-blue waters are never-ending, but my eyes latch on to a smear of beige in the distance.

The shore.

I throw everything I have into the swim. Sand scrapes my knees—in the shallows finally. I part crawl, part paddle, the surf growing feeble but I am too. For a moment, I don't think I'm going to make it. The sea tugs at me, refusing to let go.

Then I'm being lifted out of the water. Arms wrap around my shoulders and brace under my knees. The cold assault of air is agony. I see his face, his lips, forming a name that looks like mine. I try to say his—*Hero*—but my mouth won't move.

My scalp is too tight. Any moment now, my skull's going to burst through, and—

And—

And—

And—

• • •

For a while after I come to, I lie, alone, in the dim of M.M.'s bedroom, remembering everything that happened. Waking up in the ocean. Swimming to the shore. Blacking out from the pain—the worst I've ever felt.

There's no pain now. No feeling at all. My limbs feel like newly set gelatin. My arms won't support me when I try to sit up, and my head bangs into the headboard on my way back down. A curse rips from my lips, and the door whips back on its hinges. Hero rushes to the bedside. He helps me up. He hands me water I didn't realize I desperately needed until it's trembling in my hands. I drain it. He sets the emptied glass on the rocking chair, then sits beside me, the mattress dimpling.

I look at him. He looks at me.

I know what we're both thinking: I woke up in the ocean today. I warned him last night this could happen, but now that it's actually happened, it's scary. Ten times scarier than falling off the ridge. I should address it.

"About today . . ." I look down at the blanket in my lap, suddenly at a loss for words. I feel stripped bare of my usual defenses and when Hero's arms go around me, I let myself be enfolded. I bury my face into the scratchy knit of his sweater and let myself be cradled. *I don't need saving*—but honestly? I wouldn't mind it, every now and then. Certainly didn't mind it today. I'm tired. Tired of chopping down trees and wearing ugly sweaters and eating the same three things. I miss Kay. I miss my life of sequined dresses and fancy mashed potatoes and boys—

Scratch that. The boy I have here does just fine.

"So," I start when I begin to feel more like myself. I push back from Hero's chest to make myself audible. "Still up for beach yoga?"

He peers at me through his lashes. "Was that what today was?"

"Advanced-advanced. What, scared?"

"Very," he admits. "But sign me up."

"Done. We meet at eight a.m."

Speaking of time . . . I glance toward the window.

"You were out for a day," supplies Hero.

A day. My gut knots. Even if it was a dream, the fear of finding Kay too late is very real, and now my sleepwalking habit has sent me an ultimatum: Find Kay or drown.

Good thing Leona's almost built. I just need to tie all the logs together and fashion the oar.

When I'm feeling up to it, and with Hero's help, I make it onto the porch, down the steps, and to the house side, where—

The sand beside the rocks is empty.

No Leona.

No logs.

No pieces on the beach, when we scour. And we do, for hours, until at last, I go back to the house and stand by the hollow in the sand where Leona should be but she's not. Not coming back. I have to accept it.

Leona is gone.

• • •

This time around, I don't even have the heart to despair. I tell Hero I need a moment alone, then head straight for the sunken pier and stare hard at the horizon, mind churning.

Honestly? Leona was just a raft. Losing her doesn't hurt nearly as much as losing Hubert. But I could explain Hubert; I saw his remains with my own two eyes.

I can't explain this. Rafts don't walk.

Unless they do here, where sleep-swimming is also a thing. I'll blame the island. I have to. Because if I don't . . .

Again, rafts don't walk.

But people can.

Me or him. Me. It had to be me; I've done some strange shit while unconscious. But when I look down at my hands, I find no marks. No sign that I dragged a raft to the sea before I nearly died in it. I press my palms over my eyes, press harder when I see his face. It fades, but then I remember the heat of his mouth on mine, the sand damp beneath my shoulders, the stars light-years above us, the moment everything went wrong because I was happy. Happy without Kay. Hell, give me a few more nights like that one, I might not even be *upset* over losing Leona.

Which means I'm done. Done thinking about boys, done with delays. I need to find Kay *now*. I need to build a boat *now*.

I *can* build a boat now.

The solution's been staring at me this whole time. I just hadn't been desperate enough to see it.

I dash into the house, tripping around U-me and knocking my bad shoulder into the bedroom door on my way in. Barely wincing, I beeline for the bed, flinging off the comforter and sheets, chucking pillows to the ground until I've stripped the mattress down to its hunter-green polyurethane casing.

I step away and dust off my hands.

Meet Genevie the mattress boat, my ticket off this island.

Genevie *thwack*s onto the floor after I heave her off the bed frame, then thumps sideways as I push her upright to fit her through the narrow doorway.

"Strongly disagree," says U-me as I'm dragging the mattress through the living room.

"Don't judge a book by its cover," I grunt, aiming a kick at the couch. The pathway widens, and Genevie unsticks herself as I tug.

Getting Genevie out onto the porch is the hardest part. The rest is a breeze. Using the kitchen blowtorch, I melt the bottoms of several storage bins and attach them to the head and foot of the mattress, constructing what looks like a backless armchair. I then wrap rope over the tops of the storage bins, forming a makeshift rail that runs lengthwise down either side of the mattress. It'll be something to grab on to in case it storms, which I dearly hope it won't.

I fill the bins with my supplies—an extra sweater, mason jars of water, as many taro biscuits as I can afford to take without letting Hero starve—and then drag Genevie out on a test float. The sun is setting by the time I'm done. Hero still hasn't returned. I sit on the porch in wait while keeping watch over Genevie. When he finally appears, I jump to my feet. "Where have you . . ."

I catch sight of what's in his hands.

He offers me the oar. I inspect it. The handle's cut smooth. The paddle is flat and thin. "You *made* this?"

"No, I rented it from the shop on the beach."

It's an echo of what I said to him before, when he asked if I'd built Hubert and I tried testing my sarcasm on him, with no idea if it landed. It did, apparently, and he remembered, and suddenly the oar weighs a ton in my hands.

"You . . ." *didn't have to.* But I leave it at *you.* Hero. The boy who is trying so hard to be someone, someone I don't want to suspect for Leona's disappearance, especially when I notice the dirt on his sweater and the scratch running up his forearm and disappearing under his rolled-up sleeve. He must have crossed the ridge for wood.

Slowly, I tie the oar to Genevie. So much for my contrived dilemma. Just nights ago, I was debating the ethics of leaving Hero to set sail first. Now I see my true, self-centered colors. Hero, meanwhile, has seen them all along. Joules, he's made me an *oar* to send me off.

"Look," I start. "If I make it—"

"You will."

He speaks with a quiet, steadfast conviction I would have craved before. Now it makes me feel like a bad person. My gaze drops to the sand between our feet. "You weren't nearly as confident two weeks ago," I mutter. "What happened to doubting my mojo?"

"You happened," he says simply, and I glance back to him, see our too-short time together in his eyes. We've made do, come to know each other the best we can. Imperfectly, incompletely, our conversations like crumbs and yet these are flavors I'll never forget. I'll never forget the night we listened to each other's fears, and the more recent one. As if recalling too, Hero's cheeks pinken. "Your heart is set." He shrugs, and like that night in the garden, the gesture reveals the very tension he tries to hide. "I don't see how you could fail."

Waves crash on the shore nearby. My voice is small in comparison. "I'll come back for you."

For a moment, Hero doesn't reply. "I don't think you will."

There it is. That maddening honesty of his. "You don't know that." It hurts to hear him say it. A lot. Hurts more when he doesn't refute me. When he offers me a hand, I don't take it.

"Walk with me?"

I don't respond.

"Please, Cee," and I hear what he leaves unsaid. This might be it. Our last night.

I bite my lip and glance at Genevie. I don't want to let her out of my sight.

Hero notices. "We can walk it, too."

I take a breath. "Her."

And so that's how we end up strolling the moonlit shore, a mattress in tow between us.

Genevie is not as into the walk as we are, and Hero runs out of breath before I do.

"She's heavy," he says when I smirk.

"Not as heavy as a real boat."

"You've carried a boat?"

Carried, pushed, climbed a ridge with a hull tied to my back. "Yeah. *And* Hubert was made out of metal."

I say it to sound impressive but Hero actually looks concerned. "Wouldn't that weigh . . ." A pause. "One-point-five tons?"

I laugh at the specificity of the number. "Want to know what I think?" I take the rope from his hand. "I don't think I'm strong. I think *you're* weak."

"Am not."

"Prove it," I say, and yelp as he sweeps me into the air, only to lose his footing in the sand. We both go down.

"Thanks, love." I roll myself onto my back beside him, arms spread wide. "Really needed to have my point demonstrated to me."

"It's the sand," he insists, but there's an undercurrent of laughter to his words and—sure enough—a smile to match on his face when I turn to look at him. The moonlight glosses his brown hair to black, an ink spill on the sand. His upturned right palm is mere millimeters away from mine. I could take it. I could roll over and take from him more than just his hand. But tomorrow, I will travel light, without him or his emotions. I may not know what the standard protocol is for leaving someone behind on an abandoned island, but this, this distance, feels right. This night feels right—clear and crisp, the polar opposite of the night that heralded his arrival.

Perfect departure weather.

"First impressions of me," I say before my throat can close. "Go."

"When I found myself tied to your bed?" Hero pauses. "That you were going to eat me."

"Very funny."

"Maybe I come from a scary land. A place where people eat people. Maybe I come from there."

"The stars?" I ask, both our eyes on the night sky overhead.

"Mm-hmm."

"Which one?" I ask, and look in the direction of the finger he points.

"The thing about stars," says Hero, voice soft, "is most of them appear close together, but not many actually are. None are meant to pass each other in orbit."

"That's not true," I surprise myself by blurting. "Binary stars." Then: "My sister." Hero will know what I mean. I've told him about our differences, from our hobbies to our personalities. Kay's the one who would use terms like *binary stars.* I, in contrast, hear Hero talk about the stars and can't help but wonder if he's making some metaphor about us.

"We're not stars," I declare. We're already in each other's orbit. Hero's business is mine, whether he likes it or not. "We get to choose the places we go and the people we find."

"Do we?" Hero wonders. "I don't think either of us came here by choice." Fair enough. "And I think we have even less choice over the ones we're meant to find." He lowers his arm and folds it beneath his head. "That first day, I kept trying to put myself in your shoes. Couldn't. It frustrated me, seeing the way you lived your life. Then I realized it was because I could never do it. I might have survived, but you . . . you kept your-self alive. Kept her alive, too. In here." He taps two fingers to his chest. "So I know you'll find your sister. Even if it takes you far away from here."

I miss Hubert, I decide. I miss the simple emotions he inspired in me, nothing like this hopelessly tangled mess I feel now. "You could sound more sad."

Hero doesn't say anything. I peek over at him and see his half-lidded eyes on the moon.

I look to the moon too.

Minutes later, he reaches for my hand.

His fingers say what his voice does not.

More minutes later, his voice drifts through the night. He asks if I plan on staying out.

"Yeah," I murmur. "I think so."

I don't want you to see me go.

My hand goes cold as he releases it. He sits up, gets to his feet, and says, "Be right back."

I sit up too, twisting around to watch as he jogs across the shore. He disappears inside the house and remerges moments later, stuff piled in his arms. A pillow and blanket, I see once he nears. He props the pillow against Genevie's side and spreads the blanket on the ground. Then he stands there, for a silent beat, and it takes everything in me to stay sitting, to not run after him when he finally turns and walks back to the house, a solitary figure in the dark.

Swallowing, I lean against the pillow, pull the blanket over my shoulders, and face the sea. Hours pass. The surf recedes. The sky peels back, the horizon gum-pink. I stare at the colors changing, and remember doing something similar from a glass cone of a room, way up high. Watching sunrise. With Kay.

It's time to go home.

• • •

U-me rolls down to the shore as I'm pushing Genevie into the surf.

"Take care of him, U-me." *Just in case.*

U-me's not programmed to vocalize a response to a direct command, but I know she hears me. She was the first one who did on this island. Before Hubert, and before Hero, she was all I had.

"I'll be back for you, too," I say, and to my relief, U-me, unlike Hero, believes in me.

"Strongly agree."

Overcome, I drop a kiss on her bulky head. Then I seize the oar Hero made for me and row into the sea, toward the rising sun.

18

THROUGHOUT THE COURSE OF CIVILIZATION, humans had looked to the heavens for answers. In stars, they found maps. In suns, they found gods.

In the sky beyond the sky, they thought they'd find a second home.

But when faced with the question of where to house displaced coastal and island communities, the founding Mizuharas hadn't looked up, but down.

Ocean deep.

Science backed the decision to build the first eco-city prototypes on the seafloor. Hydraulic-pressure turbines were more efficient than their air counterparts, and the sea was also a natural buffer against erosion. As long as you didn't (1) build over a tectonic region, or (2) use materials that would react with saltwater electrolytes, the cities could theoretically last a millennium.

But not everyone was married to the idea of a plankton-like existence, and as the beta-testing population grew, so did demands for better conditions. The people, Kasey imagined, likely made the same arguments as Celia. Why should they have to sacrifice access to basics such as sunlight and air while the rest of the world went on with their day-to-day, unaffected lives?

And so the seafloor eco-cites were abandoned. Forgotten. Beta-testers had signed non-disclosure agreements that allowed their memories to be cognicized post-experiment, and knowledge of the first-gen eco-cities died out of the populace, living on only among the world's governing bodies and the Mizuharas.

As a member of both, Kasey had immediately thought of the underwater cities when presented with the annual science competition challenge: Save the world from an asteroid on course for Earth.

The rest of the team had had their doubts. "Dinner's on me if this works," Sid had said.

They'd won.

By proving the first-gen eco-cities could contain the entire human population if everyone were stored in a medical-grade stasis pod, their team modeled a scenario where mankind skipped the worst centuries of hellfire and sooty-darkness by waiting it out in stasis under the sea. It wasn't glamorous, but it was more realistic than manipulating space time or diverting the asteroid, and less of an upheaval than an extraterrestrial exodus.

"Hibernation," Meridian had dubbed the solution, which Kasey now posited to the P2C and Worldwide Union officers through the conference room speakers. Asteroid fallout, carbon emissions, and radioaxon releases all had something in common: Time was the best medicine. Climate might change. Oceans might rise. Species might mutate, or vanish. But given enough time, nature would do what nature did best: break down the elements that didn't belong.

"An advanced barometer will measure outside conditions," Kasey explained. "When habitable thresholds are reached and verified, stasis-pods will open."

She finished to a deathly silent room.

"It's decided," said Ekaterina, setting off a chorus of protests, Barry's among them.

"No offense to Kasey—"

"None taken."

"—but let's be realistic."

"Do you have a better idea?" asked Ekaterina. To the room at large: "Well? Do any of you have a solution that can be implemented with available resources, on a universal scale?"

"Universal *if* all parties can agree," said Barry. "We can't speak for the territories or their governments."

"But we can convince them," said Ekaterina. "I want PR teams on this, stat. We'll host conferences in all of the territories. Kasey will lead a portion of the presentations."

"A student?" said one of the Worldwide Union officers incredulously.

"Her name is rather well known," another muttered.

"For a scandal!"

"I suppose she'll be seen as a neutral party, above the geopolity establishments."

"She's a P2C officer!"

"Enough," Ekaterina said, clapping her hands. "Kasey, what do you have to say?"

No reply.

"Kasey?"

"You may use the solution." Heads turned toward the conference room door as Kasey stepped through, in person and alone. Actinium was waiting outside headquarters. *She told me if there was anyone who can change the world, it's you*, he'd told her before she exited the copterbot, and Kasey had wanted to scoff. Then it came back to her, what she'd said to Celia that day in the water. *It's just the way things are.* Both of them had been wrong: Celia, in thinking Kasey wanted to save the world, and Kasey, in accepting the status quo.

"I'll do whatever you need me to do," she now said to the policymakers in the room. "On two conditions."

|||| |||| |||| ||||

TWO DAYS.

That's how much time passes before I wonder if sea monsters exist.

I know, I know. Not exactly the best thought to have when you're traversing the great blue in nothing but a mattress boat. But I can't help it. There's not much else to do out here besides think, row, and rest.

Right now I'm resting, the oar laid across my lap, and all around me, the water's glass-still, mirroring the clouds in the sky.

Maybe it's that—the clouds are making me pensive. Or maybe the clarity of the surface is drawing me to the mysteries still beneath it. That's what we do as humans, right? We unwrap the secrets of one thing and move on to the next, like kids tearing into presents, leaving a trail of ripped paper in our wakes.

It's kind of sad, honestly.

The thought rings through me. I double over, hands splayed on the mattress encasement, *remembering*.

"It's kind of sad." I'm in a boat and Kay is sitting across from me, the sea glittering around us. The sun beats down, warming my skin as I say, "Everyone's so focused on outer space, but we haven't even finished exploring Earth."

Kay considers my words. "Like the sea."

"Exactly! Like the sea."

"Maybe it's not sad," she says. "We would have drained it long ago if we could, just to find the secrets at the bottom. And then it'd be like everything else. Discovered."

I blink. Then smile. We don't have many shared hobbies or talking points, and I'd almost dismissed the idea of visiting the sea when it came to me in the middle of hot yoga. I'm glad I didn't. It's brought us to the island, and Leona, and to moments like these, when Kay reveals that she understands me more than she lets on. I reach for her—

—My fingers grasp the air.

My surroundings haven't changed. The sea is still glassy, the sky still cloudy. But everything is different. I *feel* different, my head swimming with names.

Leona.

Who else is there? Did I know a Hubert? A Genevie? Why have I forgotten them? And Kay and me. On a boat. In the sea. Is that how we were separated?

I take deep, calming breaths, like I did in yoga. That's right. I actually did yoga. I remember now. But I've either gotten rusty or I was never any good because my body won't calm. I plunge the oar into the water and start rowing to distract myself from my building panic. I wish Hero were here. But then I'd have to tell him: Even now, years later, I don't remember everything.

What if I never do?

Not even after finding Kay?

I ease Genevie into choppier waters. The sight of normal waves relaxes me, and I'm about to set the oar back across my lap when my grip tightens around the handle. I raise the oar, paddle poised in the air as something cuts through the water in the distance, swimming toward me.

Not something.

Someone.

20

SHE'D COME A LONG WAY. From the girl she'd been two weeks ago, hiding behind her own kitchen island, to this: standing center stage, in the flesh, before a full auditorium. Five hundred holographic people in attendance, yet the questions were always the same. *How long before a consensus is reached?* Not up to Kasey. *How long will rollout take?* Too long, if it went like these questions. And most popularly:

"How long before it's safe to repopulate Earth again?" asked a person in the front.

Longer than people would like, and in the past Kasey would've hesitated before giving the distasteful answer. But the beat of her second heart made her fearless. "One thousand years."

The audience reacted violently. Kasey expected no less. At every presentation (and this was the eleventh) someone argued that radioaxons decayed in less than a century, so why, then, the millennium? *Why* not? was Kasey's question. Allow the sea to reuptake a millennium's worth of carbon emissions while they underwent stasis. Wipe the slate clean. Save future generations.

But she kept her mouth shut. People wanted the quickest, easiest solutions. To solve their most immediate problems, they could steal from any future other than their own. And to think they acted like Kasey was the villain, shortchanging them, when she was offering them a deal to better the world.

Well, offering it to some of them.

"You expect us to spend a thousand years holoing through our lives?" one audience member asked, as if holoing were a prison sentence.

"No," answered Actinium, more diplomatically than Kasey might have. She was glad to have him on the stage at her side.

Condition one: I get to present with a partner of my choice.

"Unlike commercial ones," Actinium explained, "medical-grade pods administer a version of general anesthesia." This was key: Only in pure stasis could they shave extraneous habitat mass down to zero and lower per-capita storage volume. "The passage of time won't be experienced."

The voices dropped to unsettled mutters.

A hand rose in the back. Actinium nodded, and the person asked, "How can we possibly expect to return to the same standard of living if we abandon the planet for one thousand years?"

Standard of living? Kasey's teeth clenched. "Standard of living" was the reason why so many had refused to move to the eco-cities in the first place, only to decry the imposition of ranks later, when outside conditions deteriorated enough to impact their day-to-day lives.

"How do our homes and streets stay clean?" said Actinium, turning the question back to the asker. "Bots already perform ninety percent of infrastructure maintenance in territories and eco-cities alike. A degree of rebuilding is inevitable upon re-habitation, but automated reconstruction measures will be put in place in advance to lighten the load."

A lull, as people absorbed this information. Then came the surge.

"Is *everyone* in a pod?"

"How will we ascertain outside conditions?"

"You say Operation Reset will erect habitability barometers around the world," someone said—the only one, apparently, who'd bothered reading their press release. "And that once certain conditions are met, the pods will transport everyone to the surface. But how can you be sure of those conditions? One thousand years is a long time."

Finally. A worthwhile question. Because the person had a point: Barometers only measured what they were programmed to measure. Even if correct levels of sunlight, water, and minerals were recorded, humans were finicky. One oversight—a new species or disease—could mean the difference between survival and extinction.

There was only one way of knowing *habitable* for sure, and it called on Kasey to break the law a second time.

||||| ||||| ||||| ||||| |

IN THREE COUNTS, HE REACHES the mattress boat. It's faster than I can react.

Too fast.

That's what gets to me. Not the fact he *swam* the whole way, or his ability to find me at all, but his unnatural *speed*. His hands clamp onto the mattress's edge, his fingers white against the hunter green, and I can't move. I'm paralyzed as he claws onto Genevie. She lurches, and my legs crumble. I collapse as he stands, water pouring off his person and pooling around his feet.

"H-Hero?"

He steps forward. I scuttle back, hand colliding with an object—the oar. I seize it by the paddle and stand as he takes another step forward. I shove the handle between us, gaze finally rising to his face—

His blue eyes are unblinking.

This isn't the boy who cleans the house and grows the taros, who walked Genevie the mattress boat with me and showed me the stars. He's wearing an M.M. sweater, sure, and he has the hair and lips and eyes. But this isn't *my* Hero.

This is the boy who tried to kill me on the shore.

"Don't move!" The wind steals my voice, but it doesn't matter; he can't hear me. Can't see me. Just takes another step forward, crossing the midpoint of the mattress. Genevie sinks lower into the water. *"Don't come any closer!"*

One more step, and the paddle knocks into his chest.

He stops.

Everything stops. My breath. My heart. The sea itself, even though I know that's impossible. The sea is unending.

So is this moment, right before he lunges.

22

IT BEGAN WITH A SEED. Celia had planted it, and for two years after Genevie's death, it grew inside Kasey before germinating on a day like any other: lunchtime, eighth grade, Kasey eating alone in the alcove where the cleaningbots were stored while her peers navigated cafeteria waters she didn't care to swim, and the question flitted through her mind— why? Why didn't she feel drawn to the same things as her peers? Why was she different?

What's wrong with you?

She set to find out.

She'd been eleven years old. Top of her class, and the youngest, but not exactly well versed in international law. She saw nothing scandalous about her project. Humans already came in more forms than flesh, such as holographs, and DNA could be recoded to enable processes like photosynthesis. What did it matter if other functions were coded too? If the Intraface didn't just supplement the brain, but supplanted it?

A lot, according to the Ester Act, passed precisely to draw

a line between humans and machines, a boundary arbitrary to Kasey but intuitive to her fellow peers. They must have stumbled across her project because one day, the cafeteria went quiet when Kasey entered. She got in the protein cube line; someone moved away. "Deviant," muttered the person behind her. Kasey ignored it. She advanced through her day as usual—until Celia appeared.

"Show me," her sister ordered before Kasey could ask why Celia, a freshman in the adjacent secondary school, was waiting for Kasey outside the science team lab during fifth period.

"What?"

"The . . . *thing* you've been working on," said Celia. "Or say it's a rumor. That it's not true."

Saying so would have been untrue, so Kasey showed her sister, leading the way to the cleaningbot closet in the basement of the school.

Celia had taken one look at revamped model-891 and spun on her. "*Why?*"

Celia had rejected Kasey's solution to her pain before but that was because Kasey hadn't addressed its origin. "We could bring Mom back, if we had her memories." As holoing and GMO procedures demonstrated, people remained people so long as they retained their brains.

"And why *this*?" Celia cried, pointing at revamped model-892.

"It's me." An upgraded version, with behaviors and thoughts more closely aligned to the average person's. The only thing left was figuring out how to code reactions to novel situations. As a part of her research, Kasey had been studying facial expressions for weeks. Now it came in handy, enabling her to identify the emotion on Celia's face as horror.

The magnitude of her error finally dawned on Kasey, if not its nature. That would be announced to her minutes later, when word finally reached P2C authorities and school security came to remove Kasey from the premises.

Suspended at home, she awaited her fate. Eviction seemed likely. She envisioned it to prepare for it, eliminated her fears one by one. Then David Mizuhara struck a deal with P2C: Kasey could stay.

Just not all of her.

After submitting herself to the science sanctions, her biomonitor tweaked and her Intraface modified with trackers, she'd returned home to find Celia waiting for her. The relief on her sister's face convinced Kasey she'd made the right choice. Without science, her heart was hollow, but Celia's could beat for the two of them.

How naive she'd been.

Condition two: Lift the sanctions on me.

Her request for a partner had been granted easily. This one, not so much.

"She's extorting us!" Barry had cried, one raised voice among many in the P2C conference room. "I knew it! Why else would you withhold the solution until now?"

"Because it violates international law," Kasey had deadpanned. And explained how. And after some debate for the sake of debate, laws, people seemed to realize, would have to

208 • JOAN HE

be bent. Red tape snipped, regulations loosened. Drastic times called for drastic measures. Kasey didn't know how to feel about it—that it took the world ending for five years of her life to be returned to her. But what was done was done.

She had much left to accomplish in the days ahead.

It'd start on this stage, with Actinium.

"One moment," she said to her audience. She wouldn't explain how they'd accounted for any loopholes in the barometers. She'd show them, just as she had shown Celia.

She stepped behind the stage.

||||| ||||| ||||| ||||| |||

HE SIDESTEPS MY THRUST AND grabs the oar. The paddle pops out of my hands and into my chin. My head snaps back, light exploding behind my eyes. A splash. It's me, I think. I've fallen overboard.

But I'm still on Genevie when his hands close around my throat. He lifts me right off my toes and squeezes until his lifeless blue eyes are all I can see.

"H-H-H—" *Hero.* If I could just cover his mouth with my own and breathe his name into him, if I could just—bring—him—back—

My vision flickers. Goes. *Kay.* Her face—every detail of it startlingly bright, as if there's a projector behind my retina, beaming her straight onto my brain.

Cee.

Find me.

My eyes fly open. My legs are already drawn up. I kick out, feet slamming into Hero's abdomen. He rocks back but doesn't let go, taking me with him.

Into the sea we fall.

24

THE DARKNESS DEEPENED AS THE duct whisked Kasey to the storage unit beneath the stage. Recessed lights in the high ceiling flickered on as Kasey walked past several stasis-pod prototypes and tanks of solution. She came to a pod in the very back and stood still for the retina scanner.

USER CLEARED.

The doors hissed open.

‖‖‖ ‖‖‖ ‖‖‖ ‖‖‖ ‖‖‖

THE SEA RUSHES BETWEEN US as we plunge, ripping us apart. But the moment we resurface, he's swimming for me again. My back bumps into Genevie. I try to hoist myself up by the elbows, but he's too fast and yanks me under. Bubbles bulge from my mouth like jellyfish, swimming up to freedom as we go down, into darker and darker blue.

Cee. Find me.

Strength returns to my limbs. I fight him off and swim for the light above, head whacking into something as I break the surface.

The oar—the first thing that went overboard. I grab it before it bobs by and whip around, swinging it with everything I've got.

Smack. The ugly sound of wood against wet skin. And bone. Skin and bone, splitting. Scarlet, spilling down half his face.

The impact is still vibrating in my arm when his whole body goes slack. He sinks, water closing over the top of his head, and he's gone.

Just like that.

I stare at that spot of sea, expecting him to resurface. I wait and wait, treading water until my legs burn.

"Hero?"

My voice is broken, my vocal cords crushed. I'm still seeing Kay's face, clearer than ever, and it's compelling me to get back onto Genevie, to find her, to sail away from the boy who just tried to kill me but *Joules dammit*, fuck me, fuck reason, fuck *everything*—

I dive.

I don't know how long it is before I see him, suspended like a specimen in the middle of the deep. I pull him to me and swim us both back up, gasping for breath as I grab one of the ropes I tied along Genevie's side. I push him on first, then clamber on after, trembling.

"Hero?" His skin's almost sheer, his eyelids purpling like his lips. The sea water has washed away the blood, but the gash in his temple unzips to the bone.

"Hero." I clutch his face. "*Hero.* Wake up, love."

He doesn't wake up.

And after an eternity of begging, I finally check—

He's not breathing.

His heart's not beating.

Rain falls, silver needles melting into the sea, washing the salt out of my hair, bringing it down my temples and cheeks as I stare at the boy in my lap.

The boy I killed.

The rain stops. The sun rises. Sets. It's night when I finally wrap my hand around the oar.

I row.

Back to the island. I try to carry him to the house. Buckle.

We fall into the sand, just like we did that night beneath the stars.

I drag myself over to him and lay my head on his chest. We lie there. How long, I don't know. Maybe hours. Maybe days. I lose track of time.

I do know that the whirring begins at dawn. The vibration starts somewhere beneath his sternum and spreads outward, humming into my cheek. My mind's too numb for thoughts, but my body reacts. I lift myself and stare down as color returns to his face and the gash to his temple fills itself in with silvery skin that turns a shade of flesh.

And then Hero, the boy I killed, takes his first breath.

26

"*ACTIVATE.*"

From the depths of the pod, a pair of lights turned on.

"Hello, C," Kasey intoned.

The lights blinked.

‖‖‖ ‖‖‖ ‖‖‖ ‖‖‖ ‖‖‖ ‖‖

CEE. FIND ME.

The voice takes over my body and mind. Emotionless, I move, not understanding what I'm doing until it's already done.

I've carried Hero back into the house and placed him on the mattress-less bed frame. I've tied him—everywhere. Arms. Legs. Body. All trussed to the bedposts. He'll be in for a nasty surprise when he wakes, but I don't care. Can't care. Can't feel relief over the fact he's still alive. Can't feel apprehension over the ramifications of the only human I know being . . . not so human after all.

I don't know what he is.

I don't know if I'm like him.

There's only one way to find out.

I step out of the house and onto the sand. Grains push through my toes, dry and cold, then cold and damp. As I walk, I imagine the stars above me to be a million blinking eyes. What do they see? A girl in a baggy sweater, drawing a not-quite-straight trail of footprints down the beach?

Stars or eyes, they can't know my intentions, and when I reach the waterline, I realize neither do I. I'm just following the pull of my gut, the same one that draws me to the pool beyond the meadow. Now it leads me to sea. I bet it always has, even when I'm asleep. There's a fishing hook caught inside me. The silver thread of moonlight spooling over the waves is the line. It disappears into the waters of the deep.

Without thinking, I step in. The surf immediately washes over the backs of my feet. *Welcome*, it seems to be saying, clasping my ankles like the hands of long-lost friends. The water's cold, but I don't mind it, don't feel it as I take another step in, and another, each one easier than the last. It could be even easier—and faster—if I lay myself down and close my eyes, let the waves carry me out like a raft. But I can't do that, can't surrender the little control I have over what I believe. And what I believe is simple:

I could still turn back, if I wanted to.

The waves reach my chest. The water buoys me off my toes. I stop walking, and swim. My strokes are flawless. My strength is endless. I swim until the eyes of the universe blink their final blinks and the moon submits to the sun. Mist blankets the waves, silver. I enjoy the light of the waking day for all but a moment before I take a deep breath, and plunge.

I dive.

And dive.

The distance between me and the surface widens. I've gone too deep. The weight of the world above could pulverize me. But I can't bring myself to panic, not even when the pressure in my chest builds and the primal need for air wins out over the need to survive.

I breathe in the ocean. It scorches my nasal passage and blazes down my throat, burning every centimeter of the way. Pain without panic. Without panic, my body keeps on breathing and breathing, drowning and drowning.

Then the pain stops.

Everything's quiet as I dive, deep and deeper.

Deep, past schools of speckled fish, slim like darts. Past fat brown fish with noodle-like whiskers. Past fish with fins sharp as knives . . .

Deeper, to a place where there are no fish . . .

The puffer fish tattoo on the bodyworker's arm flexes as she wheels in a pushcart filled with scalpels. I know I should be scrutinizing these archaic-looking instruments before they go into my brain, but I can't look away from the fish, especially when it changes color, from blue to violet, then hot pink as she hands me a flask.

"Drink up."

She snaps on a pair of gloves as I down the stuff. It's thicker and sweeter than I expected. I cough on the dregs. "Nice tat," I croak as she takes the empty flask.

"Eli can throw one in for an extra fifty while you're under. Right, Eli?"

A grunt comes from the next-door operating room, followed by the squeal of a drill.

This is what I want, *I remind myself. A place where they don't check ID. Someone will take my place in this chair the moment I'm out.*

No one will remember I came through.

"Maybe in the future," I say to the bodyworker as she puts on a surgical mask, then goggles. They remind me of Kasey. I swallow.

"In a sec, the neuron-damper will kick in. The operation itself will last fifteen minutes. You're free to pick up two doses of pain-killers on your way out. Post-surg complications are on you. Got any burning questions, ask them now."

"I'm fine, thanks."

The bodyworker pauses and finally seems to see me. For a second, I think she's going to ask if I'm sure I want to do this. It's not every day someone requests an Intraface extraction. I also don't look like the typical clientele.

"It might leave a scar," she says in the end.

A scar. *I almost laugh and say,* Have you seen my face? *But of course she hasn't. I'm hiding beneath a millimeter of concealer. My brain is high on psychdels. Without the pills, I wouldn't even have been able to walk myself down here. A glance at my vitals would reveal everything wrong with me.*

But here they don't check. And if they do check, then they're under no obligation to care. This body shop is the opposite of every-thing Ester stood for, but I don't think it undermines the human experience. If anything, it celebrates the fact that our bodies are ours and we're allowed to treat them to nonessential procedures. Nonessential experiences. That's all I wanted—to live and laugh without consequence, to feel the sea like people did in the past.

And look how that turned out.

"Hey." *Fingers snap in front of my eyes.* "You okay there?"

"Yeah." My breathing has quickened. *Thinking about your upcoming death is no fun.* "Yeah. Just feeling the drug."

The bodyworker frowns. She's about to say something else, when another voice interrupts.

"Jinx. I'll take this one."

The memory fades as I reach the bottom of the sea.

It's flat, without the ridges, grass, and trees of the land above. Just pebbly sand that stretches on and on, and I don't know why I swim in the direction I do—it's all more of the same—until something sparkles in the distance.

A house-sized dome, emerging from the sand.

It's silver, like the lid to a fancy dish. It lifts like a lid too, when I reach it. I swim in without a second thought and it sucks me down, dumps me—seawater and all—onto some slick, cold surface.

Coughing, I push onto my hands. The ground beneath my fingers emanates blue light—dim, too dim to illuminate anything beyond the curved walls to my immediate right and left. My eyes burn when I squint to see more. Weird. They didn't sting before, even though I had them wide open in seawater. I also wasn't freezing before. Now I shake from head to toe.

I slosh to my feet—and almost faint. Static sands the backs of my eyes. My nerves feel singed. My spine crimps, and I double over, water geysering from my mouth and nose. My esophagus burns like my eyes by the time I'm done.

Then the dam breaks. *Emotion* and *thought* chainsaw through me, and I scream as the numbness is drained from my veins, all the pain gone for a split second before it's back, tenfold, because I remember.

I remember.

Hero . . . trying to kill me . . . but I killed him . . . he was dead . . . but then he was—is—*alive* . . . and I—I walked right into the ocean, swam and dove down and I *drowned* but kept on swimming, kept on diving until I reached the bottom and here I am, here I fucking am, inside some strange dome on the seafloor, alive, but have I ever been? Alive?

Have I ever been alive?

I reach for the wall for support—and flinch away when my touch triggers a row of lights to blink on. I'm in a tunnel that winds downward, built of some smooth, matte material.

Slowly, careful not to touch any more walls, I walk down the tunnel. Lights pop on anyway. They're the only sentient things in this cold, inanimate place, and the deeper I go, the more I lose my senses. I stop smelling the seawater. I stop hearing. The air is too odorless. Too quiet. Misgivings mushroom in my gut, but my gut nevertheless tugs me forward, brain telling me to turn around, but then what? Swim back to the surface? Confront the fact I literally *dove* to the bottom of the ocean? How long did it take? How much time has passed since I tied Hero to the bed? I don't know. I don't know what I'm more scared of: the questions ahead of me, or the answers I left on the island.

My feet pad on without a care, then stop on a patch of blue-lit floor that looks no different from the other patches of floor—until a disk of it sinks. I'm taken like a pill, swallowed into the ground. The disk deposits me somewhere at least 500 meters beneath the surface of the seafloor. I step off the disk before I can stop myself, into the darkness.

Without fail, the lights come on.

28

"*HELLO, C*" *WAS SIMPLY A* placeholder command, chosen by Kasey on the fly. After P2C agreed to endorse Operation Reset (and renamed it as such), she and Actinium had worked late into the night to build the model she now rolled onto the stage. It was harmless and mindless, at a glance, like all bots under the Ester Act, prompting confusion from her audience when she said, "This is the secondary barometer, meant to serve in conjunction with the primary system."

"Looks more like a cleaningbot than a barometer to me," someone predictably argued, and Kasey could have sighed. People. Always so quick to judge by appearances. When would they learn that all the important things were on the inside?

"There are two classes of re-habitation determinants," she said, and projected a slide on the screen behind her.

RE-HABITATION can be defined as:
- fulfillment of **survival motivations**, or the ability to attain and maintain physiological health

- fulfillment of **happiness motivations**, or the ability to attain and maintain psychological health

"Once the primary barometers indicate that the toxicity of the land, air, and seas have fallen within acceptable levels, the secondary barometers will be released from their own pods and sent to locations all over the world. They will be outfitted with biomonitors to track caloric intake, sleep cycles, and other measurements of survival motivations. When those are sufficiently met . . ." Kasey highlighted the happiness motivations. ". . . the biomonitor will measure stress levels and emotional well-being."

Actinium started the time-lapsed simulation. The SURVIVAL MOTIVATIONS bar filled in; a second bar appeared underneath, labeled HAPPINESS MOTIVATIONS.

"The bot starts off focused solely on survival." A shell of a human, like Kasey herself. "But when conditions grow more favorable to re-habitation, the bot will seek fulfillment through other avenues. Goal-setting is one example. Goals give the bot a sense of purpose. Any progress toward a goal will be positively reinforced by the release of identity-reaffirming memories. Identity building will enable the bot to develop more abstract goals, such as those pertaining to the environment outside of itself, increasing fulfillment *and* the scope of what it can measure.

"This feedback loop will continue until happiness reaches a certain threshold and activates the final goal, in the form of a command. This command . . ."

The HAPPINESS MOTIVATIONS bar crept to completion, and the bot turned toward Kasey.

卌 卌 卌 卌 卌 ||||

IN A CAVERNOUS ROOM, SUFFUSED in blue light, I stand before a maze of walls. Each wall is an arm-span wide and spaced by narrow corridors. I have to angle sideways to fit.

As for why I'm trying to fit, I'm not sure. Not sure why I turn right, right, left, then right again, and come before the dead end that I do. I walk in closer. Faint lines run through the wall's expanse, dividing it into uniform rectangles, imprinting upon it a pattern of man-sized bricks. My right hand, developing a mind of its own, shoots out and splays itself in the center of one of these bricks. Its outline glows blue. Then, slowly, the brick slides out like a drawer. It floats down, lowered by some invisible mechanism, comes to a rest on the ground, and I realize it's no brick, but a casket, like the one I saw in my fragmented memories, when Hero choked me and I was lapsing in and out of consciousness. My gaze rises, to all the bricks in the wall before me, and around me. So many caskets. Are they filled with bodies? I don't want an answer. *Get out*, screams every fiber of my being, but my feet remain planted on the ground, even when the casket that slid out hisses, releasing a cloud of chemical smelling steam. The topmost surface retracts like a lid and—

And—

But there is no "and."

"And" means incomplete. "And" means still searching.

Before, I was both. Incomplete and still searching.

But now—

Tears, hot in my eyes. They blur my vision. Still, I see her. I see her as clearly as I do in my dreams. *Clearer.* Because this isn't a dream.

I choke back a sob and whisper her name.

30

KASEY STARED AT THE BOT, and the bot stared back at Kasey as best it could without real eyes. Outwardly, it was even more clumsily designed than a cleaningbot, but its core system was kilometers above.

It had a goal.

It could develop a plan for attaining that goal.

And in time, it'd have the memories to color the goal as congruent with its self-concept. That self-concept was key. The bot would see itself as a protector. Above its survival, it would value a person, someone they would try to locate, the moment Earth became re-habitable, because the thought of life without this individual would be unbearable.

Unlike Kasey, the bot would be the perfectly calibrated human. She'd make sure of it.

"This command," she repeated as the bot rolled toward her, "is 'Find me.'"

ⷭ ⷭ ⷭ ⷭ ⷭ ⷭ ⷭ

TURQUOISE GOO SLUICES OFF HER body as she sits up in the casket. Her eyes stay closed. Is she okay? Is she hurt? I can't tell; a skintight gray suit covers her from the neck down. It looks thin. She must be cold.

"Kay . . ." I reach for her, then stop. Now that I've fought back my tears, I notice she's different from how I remember her. Older. Closer to twentysomething than sixteen. Her hair is short—*shorter*, I should say, than the bob I'm used to.

But what do looks matter? She's Kay. *My* Kay. My mind floods—not with memories this time, but emotions. The pain of not being able to share her world, and the love in spite of it, when I realize we will always be there for each other when it matters most.

"Kay." My voice wobbles. "Open your eyes, love."

She does, and every fear I've had these last three years—about forgetting her or perishing before I find her—melts as our gazes meet and lock and she smiles.

"You've finally found me."

32

AT THIS POINT IN EVERY presentation, all hell broke loose.

"A bot that can pursue *happiness*?"

"With emotions?"

"That's a violation of the Ester Act!"

Trust people to always state the obvious.

"Would you rather it be a human?" The auditorium quieted at Actinium's question. "Think of this as a clinical trial; the bot will test the treatment before it's released to the masses. Does someone want to volunteer in its stead? Be the guinea pig?" Silence. "I assumed not."

"The bot's happiness is just a means to an end," said Kasey, who had less patience for the audience than Actinium. The bot continued to roll toward her from across the stage. "Once it completes the 'Find me' command . . ."

The bot reached her.

IN MY DREAMS, WE HUG. We cry. We hold each other so tightly our limbs become one.

But there are no hugs. No tears. Not from Kay's end, anyway. She hasn't moved since opening her eyes, and though I know she needs time and space, my worry builds until I can't stay silent any longer.

"Are you okay?"

She draws a breath, reminding me to do the same. "Yes." She lifts a hand, her nails trimmed practically short as always, and slowly curls her fingers shut. "Just the side effects of . . ." She trails off.

"Of . . . ?"

"Take a seat, Cee."

"Okay . . ." I look around at the seatless space. "Um—"

Four faucet heads rise from the ground before the casket, shooting out beams of red light that crisscross to form a cradle.

"Sit," Kay repeats, and though I trust her, I still prepare to butt-plant on the ground as I lower myself onto the light-cradle.

It holds.

A nervous laugh escapes me. I just dove to the bottom of the sea, and now I'm sitting on some chair made out of light while Kay's in a casket. Also, Kay is *older* than me, which—unless my memories are screwed up *and* spotty—isn't right. I should be two and a half years older.

But I feel small under her gaze.

Guess I'll start with the whole bottom-of-the-sea thing. "I thought we lived in some city in the sky," I begin. "Which, I know—ridiculous." *So is this*, says a voice in my head. "I've been having trouble remembering things, but I thought—"

"Tell me about your life on the island, Cee."

"Oh." Something in me sinks. I'm not sure what, or why. "It's been all right," I say with a shrug. "Not exactly comfy, but not bad, either."

She's nodding along, but she's not really listening. Instead she's looking at a . . . projection of some sort (*holograph!* I remember triumphantly) that's rising up from the foot of the casket, filling the air between us with translucent images of graphs and numbers. She frowns as she considers them. "Calorie readings are a bit on the low side . . ."

"Oh yeah. There was a bit of an issue with the taros—"

"But happiness levels . . ." The frown deepens. "Cee. Has something happened?"

"I don't think so?" I try to mimic Kay, squinting at the graphs, but all the numbers are backward to me. "What's wrong, love?"

"Well there's this spike right here . . ." She's talking to herself again, but I look to what she's referring to: a graph with a line, mostly stable, before the line randomly jumps up.

"It's been nine hundred eighty-nine years," mumbles Kay, "so it's close to the estimated date, but if not for this spike . . . perhaps a couple years later . . . Cee." Her gaze cuts to mine and I sit straighter. "Are you sure nothing unusual has occurred during your time on the island?"

"Unusual . . . like suddenly being able to see in color?"

She shakes her head. "Anything else?"

"Sleepwalking?"

"No, that would be . . ." More muttering. From what I recall, Kay never thinks out loud. She's rubbing her right wrist too, like it pains her. She's never done that before, either.

Concerned, I look to the graph again. I see the words HAPPINESS MOTIVATIONS running beneath the X axis. "I mean, like I was saying, living on the island hasn't exactly been a blast, love. Maybe things got a little better with Hero around, but—"

"Who is this 'Hero'?"

The sharpness of her voice startles me. "A—a boy."

"A boy." Kay's gaze darkens. "Has he tried to hurt you, by any chance?"

The question prods at a memory of Kay telling me to be careful. She did that each time I went out. I smile. "Aw, love, I can take care of—"

"Cee. Tell me. Has this Hero ever tried to kill you?"

Kill.

I suddenly remember that we're at the bottom of the sea, that I *swam* here after . . . after . . . he tried . . . and I *did*. Kill. I killed him.

I didn't mean to. And: "He didn't mean to." It sounds absurd, once I say it, but it's true. The boy who tried to kill me didn't recognize me, didn't know me. He wasn't Hero.

Kay sighs. "Well, you're safe now."

"So are you. You have no idea—" My voice breaks. *No idea how hard I tried to find you.* But words can't convey that, so I violate my promise to give her space and lean in, through the holograph, and hug her.

She's motionless under my arms. Then slowly, she pats my back.

"Cee," she says when I pull back but keep my hands on her shoulders, marveling that she's *real* and *touchable* and *right in front of me*. "Please. Have a seat."

I plop back in the light-chair less warily this time. "Are we leaving now?" The room is cold and I'm not even the one sitting in goo.

"We are," says Kay, then grips the sides of the casket. She pushes to her feet unsteadily. I reach out to help her, but my limbs won't move. She steps one foot out of the pod, blue goo running down her leg and pooling on the ground, and my body stiffens. Her other foot joins the first, and my vision dims.

"Kay?" My voice sounds weak, weaker than it did after Hero choked me. Dread swirls in my stomach, gathering speed like it's going through a drain. "What's . . . happening . . ."

34

"... *IT TERMINATES.*"

The bot had found her. Once they refined the design, it'd do more than that. It'd take her out of stasis. Then it'd be up to Kasey, or whoever was designated as "re-habitator zero," to wake everyone else up after confirming the habitability of outside conditions.

The bot's job was done.

And so with a whir, it powered down.

‖‖ ‖‖ ‖‖ ‖‖ ‖‖ ‖‖ ‖‖

"*CEE.*" *ALL MY OTHER SENSES* are fading, but I can still hear her crystal clear. "You should understand by now."

She takes a shaky step closer. My fingers and toes go numb, as if in response. I can't move anything but the muscles in my face as she stops half a meter away and says, "You're not really human."

My mouth opens. Closes. Opens again—

"I know something happened to me." Something that explains how I washed back ashore, alive, after rowing Hubert out for seven days, and how my eyeballs didn't burst from the pressure of diving to the bottom of the sea. How Hero could have come back to life.

But none of that changes what Kay means to me.

"And I know I might not be . . ." *human, not human* ". . . like you," I gasp, unable to choke out the words. *I'm not like you. Not as smart as you. Not as strong as you.* "But I'm still your sister, Kay."

"My sister is Celia." She doesn't say it cruelly, just as a matter of fact. "And Celia died a long time ago."

Died.

I swallow the obscene amount of saliva pooling in my mouth and almost gag as it slithers down my throat. "Then who am I?"

She glances over me, quiet. "You're artificial intelligence prototype-C." When I don't react, she sighs, as if she was trying to spare me. "A bot."

The words glance off me, missing the mark. I shake my head. I know what a bot is. A bot is U-me. I'm not U-me.

"When you couldn't see in color," says Kay, "that was because you hadn't yet unlocked your next level of self-actualization. And once you saw in color, you felt a stronger pull to the sea, yes?"

No, I try to say, but find that I can't. Can't seem to lie, because yes, the day after my world filled with color, I did wake up in the sea.

"It's a part of your programming. As a built-in safety, you're drawn to all bodies of water, not just the ocean."

Which would explain my jumping into the pool—*no, stop.*

"We designed you to be mechanically hardier than a real human for sustainability reasons, but you experience the same pain and psychological trauma. And while your intelligence is set to the fiftieth percentile, you possess an internal search engine that allows you to learn new skills in the absence of external models."

Say something to make her stop. "But my memories . . . all my memories. Of you. Of *us* . . ."

"Seventy percent were Celia's, retrieved from her own brain."

"Seventy?" The number feels wrong in my mouth, too precise and too incomplete.

"Five percent had decayed with time," says Kay, as if memories are made of wood. "Ten percent, we enhanced."

"We?"

"My team and I."

A team. Multiple people, privy to things inside of my head. I want to crawl out of my skin. "So you . . . built my memories." Like a boat? A raft?

"Coded them," corrects Kay, and then before I can even ask, "all but for fifteen percent. Overall well-being improves when your brain is allowed to fill in the gaps, in whichever way is best suited for your circumstances."

It sounds smart and logical and like gibberish. "But *why*? Why give me these . . ." *memories.* No, they can't be memories if they're manufactured. "Why give me this at all?" *If I'm not her?* Denial chills my spine. My need to find Kay is real. Our kinship, our bond. My memories are real, and this . . . this whole situation is fake. A dream. I'm not here. I'm still on the island, still Cee—

"Deep breaths, Cee."

Fuck it, I don't want to—

I start taking deep breaths.

As I sit, locked in my own skin, Kay looks over me. Her face goes mask-still, but her eyes give her away. I see the calculations being conducted in them. She's weighing the costs and benefits. Choosing between what makes sense—

She sighs.

—and what will make me happy.

"Cortisol, negative one point five."

The fear bubbling in my stomach calms to a simmer.

Kay sits at the foot of the casket, covering the holograph projector. The translucent numbers and graphs between us vanish. We're eye level now, and Kay makes sure to look at me as she speaks.

"I know these three years haven't been easy for you, Cee. So allow me to explain. You were designed to find me."

She goes on. She talks about a time when Earth was failing, its air, water, and land poisoned by humankind. Scientists came up with all sorts of ways to clean things up, but every innovation had an unforeseen side effect. Some of what she says rings true within me, and I know I must have a buried memory to match. But when she gets to the megaquakes and the casualties, numbering in the hundreds of millions, the ringing stops. I guess that's where my—Celia's memories end.

"But why me?" I ask after she explains the solution she proposed to the world. It's brilliant, of course. All of Kay's ideas are. "Why not send out a . . ." *No, no, no.* ". . . a *real human*?"

"You're better than a real human, C. Real humans, well, they die. Or they lie," she says, voice roughening, "to further whatever self-interests they may have. You can't die, and your data logs true. Besides, consider the ethics. You're the final bot, released only because your predecessors successfully reached progressively higher happiness thresholds. Bots A and B faced far harsher environments, suffering immensely in their struggle to 'survive.' To ask humans to do the equivalent? That plan would never pass." She frowns as tears fill my eyes. "Cortisol, negative two point zero."

"I have loved ones, too," I whisper as my emotions dampen yet again.

"The boy, Hero? Oh, Cee." Kay speaks as if I'm the younger sister, green and naive. "Some people bear a grudge against humanity and can't be stopped, no matter what you do."

"That's not Hero," I blurt. "He doesn't have a grudge against anyone."

"I know," Kay says quietly, rubbing her wrist again. "I'm not talking about Hero."

And neither was I. Hero wasn't the loved one I was referring to. Not entirely. He's not the one I see in my dreams, not the face right before me.

My hands begin to shake at my sides. "So what now?" I ask, before Kay can notice and dial down my emotions. "What are you going to do, now that I've found you?"

What's going to happen to me?

"Set the pods on course for the surface, where everyone will be released from stasis," answers Kay.

Stasis. Pods. Stasis pods. The vocabulary returns to me like it's always been part of my world. *I am Celia*, I think. *I am Celia.* But I am also Cee, and I can't help but acknowledge that when I say, "What if I lied? What if my data is messed up and Earth isn't re-habitable?"

"Possible," says Kay. "But not probable."

"What if?"

My hands are balled so tightly that a little bit of feeling prickles through them. Kay notices, but lets me have my pain as she decides whether or not to entertain my "not possible" scenario. She rubs her wrist, and this time, the gray material covering it slides up enough for me to see a green-black line encircling her skin.

"If I had reason to believe your systems were malfunctioning," she finally says, "I'd check the surface for myself."

I can't look away from the line on her wrist. "And if things weren't right, you'd go back to sleep?"

"No."

"Why not?"

"The pods run on a closed, infinite energy loop. Opening them breaks the loop and weakens the electrical balance of the solution. In time, the body's cells will resume aging."

It takes me a moment to understand the implication. "Then you . . ."

"Yes. If, hypothetically, I were to be woken prematurely, there would be no way of returning to complete stasis." Her gaze narrows. "But I'd release the next C-model to run its trial, and it'd been in charge of waking the second re-habitator zero come time."

I imagine this playing out. Kay, alone in this facility forever. Or Kay, living out the rest of her years on the island, as lonely as I was. It feels like a kick to the kidneys. "Why did you volunteer for this?" I croak.

"I'm the creator of the idea."

She says it like it's the most logical conclusion. But it's not—at least not from the sister I knew. Kay accounts for the risks, however slight. She had to have been okay with a chance of dying alone, without being joined by the rest of the world.

I confirm my hunch by looking into her eyes. In the depths of her pupils, I see cold fire, the same kind that consumed her years ago, when she was lost in the world of her mind and I was too distant to notice. But then we repaired our relationship and slowly, that fire abated.

What has happened since I—Celia died?

I look back to the line on her wrist. It shouldn't be there. Never was, in all my dreams and memories. Who did this to her? Who hurt her while I was gone?

"Kay." I don't care if I'm in danger. I want to touch her, to cup her cheek and prove I never left her. "You have me. You've always had me."

The facility quiets.

I can hear a thousand things I didn't hear before. The lights, drawing energy from generators embedded in the walls. The sea, pulsing around us. The beat of our hearts, mine and hers, in perfect sync.

Kay clears her throat.

"I'm sorry, Cee. I had to program you with a terminate function. There was no other way Operation Reset would've passed the international board of ethics."

"Kay—"

My body goes rigid as she stands. Or tries to. Even if the blue goo was supposed to preserve her body cell for cell, her muscles are clearly still weak after a thousand years of disuse, and she sits back down on the compartment's edge, bracing her hands on her knees to try again.

The moment stretches out before me, forking in two paths. In one, I let her stand. I let her be the person I always knew she could be, someone who's going to save billions of lives. The other path . . . I won't let myself envision it. It's selfish and it's wrong and it's . . . it's *right*, to want to live. *A* right. *I deserve to live*, I think as the word *terminate* boomerangs through me, shattering me where it hits, breaking bone and bonds and beliefs I thought I needed but all I need—all I *want*—is to see the rest of the stars in the sky with Hero and taste every unmade taro recipe and hear the words left for U-me to define and *feel* all the life I—Celia, Cee—have yet to live.

Kay would want that for me.

Which means the person before me isn't Kay. If Kay were actually here, with me, she'd be thinking of a way to get us out of this situation.

But she's not here.

In this room at the bottom of the sea, surrounded by billions of people depending on me to die for them, I am on my own.

Not-Kay starts to rise, and my mind scrambles.

"You—" A string tightens from my belly to my throat, straining to fish up a feeling, a memory, a something, anything to stop her— *"You never saw her die!"*

Silence.

Stillness.

Then it starts. In her eyes. Emotion, spreading slow. She's thinking that I shouldn't know this. There's no way I *can*, but apparently I do and it's the truth: Kay never saw Celia die. This must be one of those learned memories she was talking about, something of my brain's making, best suited to my circumstances, and it works, because after a moment, Kay sits back down, as if the strength has been stolen from her legs, and like a scale, strength tips back into mine. The bonds around my limbs weaken. Feeling prickles back into my skin, then freedom—a glorious rush—and before I can give my body permission, it rebels against its oppressor. My mutinous hands shove into Kay's chest before either of us realizes what's happening. She falls backward into the pod. I see her shell-shocked eyes there, then gone. I've heaved the lid shut.

But there's blue goo on the ground, evidence of what I've done.

And the pod door is glowing with words:

POD-BREECH DETECTED.

POD-BREECH DETECTED.

SOLVENT WILL SUSTAIN ELECTRICAL BALANCE FOR

192 HR.

191 HR 59 MIN 59 S

191 HR 59 MIN 58 S

191 HR 59 MIN 57 S

And my heart is hammering. I could reverse this. I could open the pod. My heart is not my body my heart is not my body my heart—

Is broken. By the one I thought I loved.

So it joins my body on the goo-splattered ground and on my knees, I sob.

36

"GOOD WORK," EKATERINA SAID AFTER the presentation. The message arrived in Kasey's Intraface with a *ding* that must have reverberated in Actinium's, too. Ever since the day on the pier, and more so after building the demo-bot together, their minds had felt connected, and as they parted at their respective ducts, his going down and hers up, she knew they were thinking the same thing.

Oh, what P2C didn't know.

Yes, the solution was universal. Everyone could and would be put into stasis. Earth would clean itself, and be repopulated—by the ones who could be trusted not to ruin it again. As for everyone else? They could sleep on. Kasey and Actinium would ensure it. It was a simple bit of programming: a perma-lock command on the pod, activated by rank, or whatever empirical measure of planetary stewardship they decided upon. It wouldn't kill those people—not in the same way they'd almost killed the rest of them, and might yet still if they were allowed to return.

But one thing at a time. First, Operation Reset needed to pass. Seven out of eight eco-cities currently supported it; eco-city 6 was still on the fence. Kasey didn't blame them. It was one thing to ask your citizens to spend at least 33% of their waking moments in holo to save the world, and another to ask them to sacrifice even more to protect the people who hadn't.

Meanwhile, the outside territories were much more divided. Delegates from Territories 6, 7, and 11 had pledged themselves to the solution; they'd also charted the highest percentage dead. Territories 1 and 12, on the other hand, mostly unscathed by the megaquake, had pledged zero. Human selfishness at its best. Kasey committed those territories to memory. Info like this could be factored into calculations of who deserved to wake and who, for the sake of everyone else, was better left in stasis.

Granted, they'd all suffer if selfishness prevailed. The solution required a 100% participation rate or none at all. Governments would rather let their people die than fall behind. The deadline for a consensus was just a week away, and with only 57% delegates pledged despite Kasey's presentations and P2C's broader maneuvers, Kasey had no idea what else might help.

Ekaterina did. At night, she messaged again, asking if Kasey was willing to present in Territory 4 tomorrow—in person. "You wouldn't be exposed," Ekaterina was quick to mention. "But to make inroads among some of these territories, we're going to have to establish more of a human connection."

Of course, Kasey thought into her Intraface messaging app, transmitted it, then looked to the night sky beyond the polyglass.

She was in the Coles' unit, sitting on one of their chaises. As her biomonitor reminded her this morning, it was the seventh anniversary of their passing. Seven years since the day Celia had sobbed in her room, and Kasey had violated her brain by trying to cancel her pain. Correlated or not, Celia had spent the next two anniversaries alone. It was only after Kasey committed her second violation by trying to rebuild their mom that Celia stopped avoiding her. Together, they'd gone to the Coles' unit; Kasey had watched as Celia dusted off the picture of Ester, Frain, and their boy on the coffee table before filling the vase with everfiber flowers. The gesture seemed wasted on the dead, but when Celia did it, it felt right in a way Kasey couldn't emulate. So tonight, Kasey had come empty-handed. She wasn't her sister. Wasn't persuasive or likeable enough.

If Celia were here, the human connection would already be made.

Sighing, Kasey swiped through her Intraface until she came to the folder labeled CELIA. She'd let Actinium keep the physical Intraface—seeing the kernel still unnerved her—but she'd downloaded the memories to her own. Problem was, she couldn't bring herself to touch the folder icon. She tried to remind herself that memories, Celia's or not, were just code. Kasey and Actinium needed to analyze as much human behavior as possible to design their secondary barometers. But same as the first time, a force held Kasey back. It wasn't simply respect for Celia's privacy. It was dread. Because it was possible to love someone without fully understanding them. Possible to love parts of them, and not their whole. Kasey's bots had scared

Celia. Kasey feared seeing the rest of herself through her sister's eyes.

Ding! The notification from her Intraface was a welcome distraction. Two blinks, and Kasey was brought back to Ekaterina's message. Actinium had reacted to it with a checkmark. Kasey waited for his name to turn an inactive gray. When it didn't, she messaged him privately.

Have you been?

She didn't need to specify Territory 4; he'd understand the shorthand.

The speed of his reply was strangely gratifying. *Once.*

What's it like?

Cold. Dry.

Kasey waited for more. None came. *That's it?*

Patience, Mizuhara. You'll suffer it firsthand tomorrow.

A pause in the conversation. Kasey didn't know what else to say. SILVERTONGUE offered no suggestions. After it kept auto-opening during her presentations, urging her to be more engaging, Kasey had uninstalled it. She had no use for an app that didn't perceive life-saving information as engaging.

Her heart stilled as Actinium's avatar pulsed blue; he was thinking again. Seconds later:

Are you busy?

No. Kasey paused. *You? Working?* :P The emoticon slipped out of her. She considered it, deleted it, and sent the message without.

No. Actinium paused too. *Not working.*

Kasey could almost see it: the slide and latch of his gaze,

his silence a dare for her to comment on his work habits. She could, if she wanted to. She could speak her mind without fear around Actinium now that they'd built something together. They were on the same wavelength—perhaps had been as early as the all-nighter they'd pulled reviewing Celia's memories, they'd communicated via glances and gestures. They'd streamlined their communication even more since then, and now, staring at the last message from Actinium, Kasey sent him a holo hotspot on a whim. Told herself she wouldn't be disappointed if he didn't accept.

Held her breath as the air before the chaise glowed.

For a split second after Actinium holo-ed in, he seemed dazed. Kasey was too. She'd never seen his holograph before and certain details were lost in translation even after she bumped his opacity up to 100%. Like the texture of his hair. It lacked definition, the strands flat and lifeless compared to when the wind had messed it—not that Kasey should have been thinking about his hair at all. She redirected her gaze to the window, throat itchy. Must've been the particulates in the unit.

"Do you come here often?"

The pitch of his voice was unaltered, at least. "More often than before," Kasey said. "Celia used to come for the windows." It wasn't lost on her that wherever they went, whenever they talked, they couldn't escape Celia's pull. But why would they want to? She was their common denominator. Their compass, setting them on this course. "We argued about it, in the beginning. I didn't want to visit."

"Why not?" asked Actinium, sounding genuinely curious.

"It felt like trespassing."

She didn't say the owners were dead, or name them. Everyone knew who lived on stratum-100, including Actinium, who scanned the unit and said, "It's a lot of unused space."

"My dad insisted it remain uninhabited. In memoriam." If it sounded elitist, it was because it was. The one and only time David Mizuhara had violated his own principle of space-saving living. "Our families were close," Kasey felt the need to add, but that portrayed a community of elitists, living as high as their rank. How did they come across to someone like Actinium, whose unit had no fancy furniture or windows for natural light?

"You must think us strange," Kasey said as Actinium did a slow walk around the unit. "So removed from human nature."

"What if human nature is the last disease we have yet to eradicate?" Actinium returned to her. The moonlight passed through his person. He left no shadow on the ground.

"A disease," Kasey echoed as he sat at the other end of the chaise. It didn't react to his holograph, too dated to receive virtual input. To the furniture, Actinium might as well have been a ghost.

"Think about it," he said, and Kasey did. She glanced toward the polyglass and considered the sea beyond it.

"The world would be filled with people like me," she concluded, an honest assessment. "And therefore worse off."

She offered a smile at Actinium. He didn't return it. His

expression was serious, bordering on severe, and Kasey squirmed, her discomfort taking her back to their first meeting, REM misfire and all.

"Will your cat be okay?" Ekaterina hadn't mentioned how long they'd stay in Territory 4.

Actinium blinked once, slow. "Jinx will take care of him."

"And your clients?"

"None of them are as important as this."

"You won't miss it?"

"No."

"Why not?" Kasey asked, and Actinium glanced to the window.

"I've never belonged."

"Same." She couldn't decide what was more surprising—his admission or hers.

"I know." A whisper, barely audible. "Home is where the mind is," said Actinium, and Kasey froze, her body going hot and cold as she recalled staring at her bedroom ceiling, contemplating the concept of eviction. She'd ironed out the logistics, performed damage control to feel *in* control, and then none of it had mattered. She'd accepted the deal. Science became her past. Her secret. But she had another secret:

She'd almost chosen eviction instead.

People confused Kasey when they invariably violated the properties she ascribed to them. But science was different. Science didn't blindside her; it outsmarted her. It didn't try to understand her, but Kasey understood it. With science, she felt safe. But with Celia, too. Two choices and only one, Kasey had realized, would be seen as normal. For Celia, she'd tried to be normal. For Celia, she'd stayed, and it'd been the easiest and hardest decision she'd made, eleven years old now feeling like yesterday, as Kasey trembled, breath coming quick. She heard her name and glanced up, saw Actinium's gaze, across a chaise on which he did not exist, but he did to Kasey. He'd articulated a feeling Kasey had lived, and for moment, Kasey wished he were here.

Wished she could actually feel the hand he'd placed on her shoulder.

Then she shook her head. Stood. "I should go. Pack. Early start."

She wasn't sure what she was saying; Ekaterina hadn't even sent them the itinerary.

Actinium had the grace to nod and stood himself. "Until tomorrow."

He logged out, leaving Kasey alone.

She sat back down on the chaise. Breathed deep, oxygenating her blood. Her heart pummeled her chest with the strength of two; she dismissed it. This was just a part of the journey, of becoming more human as she avenged her sister.

She swiped back to Celia's memories, pushing Actinium out of her mind, and opened the folder, then the subfolder labeled xxx that she hadn't reviewed before.

It expanded to three hundred memories of all the boys Celia had loved and been loved by.

Kasey closed it, heart pounding again.

Think outside the box. There had to be a way to understand her sister's relationships without reviewing every memory manually.

She began to develop an algorithm that would match biomonitor data to memories by date, and then narrow the memories down to the ones that corresponded with oxytocin, dopamine, and endorphin spikes, the respective hormones for socialization, motivation, and goal achievement. Of the memories left, Kasey filtered for people, prioritizing recurring faces. She hit RUN. The algorithm spit out the top five results.

Her own name and face topped the list.

Strange. Stranger still was how Actinium was not in the top five, which included Leona, or the top ten, when Kasey expanded the parameters. At number twelve was Tristan. Dmitri, number seventeen. By number fifty, Kasey, perplexed, searched directly for Actinium among the netted memories.

0 RESULTS.

Kasey ran the program again. Same result—zero.

She did a face search through all of Celia's memories.

No saved ones of Actinium.

The unit suddenly felt colder, though the temperature in the corner of Kasey's gaze stayed the same. An insidious thought zapped her; she located Celia's memories of the time they'd gone to the sea. She rewatched it, laser-eyed, went as far back to the memories from their childhood, when Genevie had been alive, watched those too, pulled up the biomonitor data on the day Genevie had died, and found the neurotransmitter spike that corresponded with the adjustment she'd accepted on Celia's behalf. Her panic abated. The memories were real. The

biomonitor data was real. The facts were real and they were as
followed:

Celia had been poisoned.

She'd gone to the hospel. She'd left by sea. The evidence for
that was all there.

Then where was Actinium? The boy who'd sat across from
her on this chaise? Who'd been in this unit just moments ago?

This unit.

Time slowed. Stilled.

Reversed its march.

Actinium had holo-ed here. Via Kasey's hotspot. But a
hotspot was nothing more than a tether, allowing people to
holo to your location. It had nothing to do with access permissions, permissions being nonapplicable to public domains,
but this was private. And not Kasey's home. Had it been,
Actinium holoing in would have prompted ACCEPT GUEST
to appear in her Intraface, like it had at her party. That Kasey
hadn't been given the option meant one of two things: Either
Actinium had hacked his way in, or . . .

A chill filled Kasey's bones.

. . . or he wasn't a guest. In this unit.

This unit that belonged to the Coles.

There was only one way to confirm.

Actinium was good at hacking. But so was Kasey. Finally
free to use every trick she knew, she peeled back the layers of
Actinium, rank 0. She stripped him down to the boy behind
the identity, the same boy in the picture frame atop the coffee
table, whose face *did* exist in Celia's memories, and Kasey's,

too, but seven years had changed it, aged it, and left it utterly unrecognizable.

• • •

Ekaterina sent the itinerary at midnight. By then, Kasey was far too deep down the rabbit hole to reply.

She reviewed everything she could get her hands on. The media coverage of the copterbot crash. The report from the forensics lab. The cambot footage of the departure: Genevie, Ester, Frain, and the Coles' son, a ten-year-old boy, waving at the crowds on stratum-100 before they boarded the copterbot. Kasey studied the clip again and again, until she found it.

Actinium's secret to surviving the accident that'd killed everyone else.

Her brain, kicked into overdrive, began to shut down non-essential functions. First to go were emotions. She could get upset, or she could get answers to her questions, too many of which relied on Actinium's cooperation. Back in the Mizuhara unit, Kasey drafted several messages, deliberating over her tone. Sent none come afternoon. Departure time. She set off for P2C headquarters. She'd confront him in person. A perfectly logical plan—assuming they'd be on this trip alone.

"Meridian?" Of all the things Kasey had prepared for, this was not one. "Why are you here?" she asked, brain ejected out of autopilot mode and forced to assess this new confounding variable standing outside of P2C headquarters.

I could ask you the same, said the sour look on Meridian's face. She was clearly prepped to travel, a duffel bag slung over her shoulder. "Officer Trukhin invited me."

Ekaterina. Kasey opened the itinerary she'd been sent and read it in detail—down to the note about adding personnel that could be viewed as grassroots support by the Territory 4 locals.

"She asked if I'd be interested in presenting a variation of my solution." Meridian went on, right as the copterbot descended. "Yes, you heard right. Mine. I submitted it." At that moment, Actinium arrived. Meridian pointedly refused to look at him, reserving her glare for Kasey. Then, with a turn of her heel, she proceeded to climb into the copterbot.

You don't know what you're getting into, Kasey wished she could say. Could not, of course, or confront Actinium. Could only take the seat between the two of them. To her right was a boy who knew her, knew their true agenda, but who had hidden himself. And to her left was a girl who thought Kasey's worst crime was hogging the solution when it was so much worse. Yes, with Meridian here, Kasey finally confronted how her and Actinium's vision for the world would be viewed by outsiders—as a crime. Immoral and unforgivable.

And now she couldn't even trust the person who was supposed to be her partner.

The 3,000 km flight was too silent and too long, then too short after they touched the ground. From the copterbot they were ferried to a car—an antique driven by a live chauffeur. Heat roared from the vents to combat the outside freeze. A polar vortex had taken up permanent residence over the

258 • JOAN HE

northeastern territories after the arctic melt, and beyond the car windows laid a world stark and bleak, sun radiating in a barren sky, clouds dispatched by high concentrations of atmospheric carbon. The roadside crowds were the only sign of life, and the throngs densified as they neared the embassy.

The car pulled into park.

"Good luck," Ekaterina messaged as Kasey secured her breathing mask. It couldn't protect her from the dry-ice air, an assault on her lungs the second she stepped outside, into the blinding flash of cameras. Behind an orange barricade, reporters in the flesh pushed and shoved for the best angle. Citizens, some with masks and some without, held up signs criticizing the government's megaquake response. The expressions on their faces were somber—save for one group of men, women, and children, waving at them.

"Meiran! Meiran!"

Meridian waved back. Her relatives, Kasey realized, tensing at the sight of their unmasked faces—right before all the faces in the crowd glitched into Celia's, eyes blacked out by block letters.

IF PREMIER DU COULDN'T SAVE 1.5MIL LIVES DON'T EXPECT THE ALIENS TO SAVE YOU

The image overlays vanished by the next blink. Meridian's relatives became Meridian's relatives again, but their smiles were gone.

Meridian appeared just as stricken. "What was that?"

"An Intraface hack," Actinium answered.

Kasey checked her files. Everything was still there, including her few stored memories of Celia. The hackers must have accessed them to generate the faces.

The ache in her chest reawakened, and as the premier greeted them inside the embassy, a marble room with tall windows, her second heart pulsed. Who Actinium was didn't change what'd happened to Celia. Didn't change the amount of energy being used to warm this room, and how much more people had to pollute just to solve problems produced by pollution. "Aliens," the protestors called them. Was it because they lived in the sky? Because they'd come down to subjugate them to another way of life? *Would people ever willingly give up their freedoms for the good of others?* Kasey wondered as attendants led them to the auditorium, in which they were to present the solution. Or did their family members first have to die?

Ding. A message from Actinium. *Are you okay?* he asked, and Kasey almost flinched. As if he could claim to care.

And as if she *should* care. *Who did you see?* she wanted to ask him. *Your parents?*

A moment alone, without Meridian, was all she needed.

But for now:

Yes, she replied, before stepping onto the stage to tell more lies.

• • •

A moment alone, Kasey quickly learned, was as scarce as clean air on this trip. P2C, with their trademark efficiency, had scheduled back-to-back events. After their presentation, they

were to visit a hard-hit midland Territory 4 hospel. They would
be delivered by fueled plane; the 2,000 km flight would be the
equivalent of Kasey's carbon emissions for the last five years.

Whatever it took to appear accessible.

As they crossed into the countryside, Kasey snuck a sideways
glance at Actinium. Territory 4 was where the crash had happened. What was he thinking? Feeling? His mind grew more
unknowable to her by the minute, like the terrain below as
night crept over it. Then the plane dropped in altitude, bringing the land into grotesque focus. The midland basin, a natural
fortress since antiquity, had been transformed into a death trap.
Mountains had bulldozed over villages, trees torn out of the
ground like bones through skin, and in places, the crust itself
had fissured. Scars of hardened lava wormed through the land—
more than Kasey had ever beheld. Celia might have seen beauty.
Kasey only saw only a brutal reminder of a world untamed by
its human owners, if they even deserved the title. For all their
innovations, they were microscopic, a fact that became painfully
apparent when they landed outside the hospel.

Another misleading term.

Eco-city hospels were all like the one Kasey had stormed
into: calming sanctuaries built to maximize the human experience. This hospel, constructed to treat victims of radioaxon
poisoning from a compromised fission plant, 20 km north, was
as flimsy as a pop-up market and loud as a factory, its only
product being death. Trucks emblazoned with the Worldwide Union symbol rumbled through the dirt. Personnel—
including members of the Territory 4 defense force—rushed

down barely set tar walkways. In the eco-cities, there was one doctor for every hundred citizens. Here, whatever the ratio was, it didn't seem like enough. Medics certainly couldn't be spared for PR, and the one assigned to them was red in the face and arguing with the P2C camera crew when Meridian, Actinium, and Kasey reached her. She looked to be around Celia's age.

Like Celia, she wore no antiskin.

This wasn't the island. Wasn't shielded. A gurney rattled by them, bearing a body covered by a sheet, and Kasey's mouth dried. "Where's your antiskin?" she asked the medic.

"Ran out." Then the medic turned her attention back to the crew—"*One* tour, that's it"—but the crew's attention had swiveled to Actinium. Everyone stared as he unzipped and stepped out of his antiskin.

He placed the protective gear into the medic's hands.

The cam swung back to Kasey before she could recover. The unspoken cue lingered.

I'd never put you in danger, Actinium had promised. So had Ekaterina. *You won't be exposed*. But vows were human constructs. They died out here, in the wilderness.

Kasey should have been prepared.

She took off her antiskin, flesh crawling as it came into contact with air. Her biomonitor warned her of the toxins entering her system. Only for a little while, she told herself.

Just this once.

Meridian started to unzip hers.

Just one swim.

Her fingers, Kasey noticed, were shaking.

One more trip—

"Don't."

The boom and camera swung Kasey's way.

"We're being filmed," Meridian muttered beneath her breath. Kasey didn't care. She was well aware of the price she and Actinium would have to pay to make others do the same. But Meridian didn't have to be caught in the crosshairs, and Kasey was relieved when the medic interrupted them.

"We done here?" The medic strode down the tar walkway and shouted "Come on!" when they lagged. "I don't have all day!"

They followed the medic into the arm of a ward, the narrow path tiled with cardboard and deconstructed crates. PVC strips, held together with duct tape, formed the walls around them, rippling as they walked. The air grew acrid with the smell of waste, human and chemical, and Kasey, who'd barely survived stratum-22, was woozy by the time they reached a series of plasterboard doors set into the walls, leading presumably to patient rooms. In the back of her mind, she understood she couldn't face other humans like this. If she vomited on camera, it'd completely undo the point of the visit.

"Wait—" she started to say to the medic, and broke off at the *bang*. It came from one of the plasterboard doors as it fell down and a man burst out, a bundle in his arms.

He ran straight into the wall.

The PVC rippled, absorbing the impact. But Kasey couldn't absorb what she was seeing. She stared as the man rammed into the PVC again, as if expecting it to yield. The duct tape held.

And so he turned, and charged toward them instead.

"Don't engage!" shouted the medic.

Meridian flattened against the wall. Kasey stumbled to the side.

Actinium didn't move. His head snapped up when the man was almost upon him.

His fist cocked back.

Later, Kasey would try to sequence the memory. The initiation. The escalation. What came first—the punch that slammed into the man's face, causing the bundle to tumble from his arms, or the knife, flashing in the man's hand? But this moment, like everything else about the trip, would resist her. It followed no order but nature's disorder.

Meridian screamed. The medic cursed, and called for guards. Two ran in and tackled the man as Kasey ran to Actinium and tried to hold him back. He wrestled in her grip. She wasn't prepared for his resistance—or his elbow, the bony end bucking free and swinging into her nose.

The gush was immediate. Warm. Kasey let go. Her attention fractured to the bundle on the floor—antiskins, scattered and now splattered with red—then to the cowering crew, cameras still rolling, and through the blood pooling in her mouth, she managed to shout, "*Cut!*"

• • •

The medic wouldn't even look her in the eye when she handed Kasey gauze for her nose.

Meridian had been hysterical. "Are you *sick*?" she'd screamed at Actinium. "He was stealing some antiskins! *Big deal!*"

Actinium hadn't said anything. He looked as he did now: head bowed as he sat on the crated-bench, hair fallen out of its carefully combed style, a visor around his eyes, each hand a fist over his knees, knuckles blanched while Meridian railed.

"Meridian . . . please," Kasey had said, which provoked Meridian more.

"Oh, so *I'm* the problem now?"

She'd stormed off. Maybe Kasey should have followed her, and left Actinium alone, but something compelled her to sit beside him on the bench. She'd stayed until her nose stopped gushing five minutes later, though the silence didn't break, and she couldn't find a way to wipe the blood from his shirt so it, too, stayed. Red against white, like when he'd smashed the glass, except then, Actinium had been in perfect control. This time, she'd seen something rabid in his eyes. Had the chaos of their surroundings infected him? Or was this who he really was?

"You need to tell me the truth," she finally said. A message came from Ekaterina. She ignored it. She'd tried to be as motionless as Actinium, as if sharing his stillness could allow her to share his state of mind, but he was a black box to her. "Who are you?" she pressed when he didn't reply.

Why is it that I can trust you one moment, and be hurt by you the next?

Silence. Then, in a voice that rasped: "I think you already know. Say it," he ordered, when she did not.

Kasey swallowed. The sound boomed in her ears. "Andre Cole."

"A dead person."

"You never got on the copterbot." Kasey adopted the same pose as Actinium, her hands on her knees and eyes to the ground. Her voice dropped. "You built a bot."

The departure footage had given it away. When Ester dropped her purse before boarding the copterbot, Andre Cole hadn't moved. Not even to blink. Reactions to novel situations. The hardest bit of programming to get right. No wonder Actinium hadn't been repulsed by her violation of the Ester Act; he'd beaten her to it. Constructed his model with a degree of finesse that was admirable, even if his deception was not.

"A dead person who violated his parents' act," Actinium revised. His gaze was still hidden from her when Kasey glanced over. "Doesn't that disturb you?"

"No," she admitted. "Not as much as you not appearing in any of my sister's memories." She drew in a sharp breath. Her nose throbbed. "Why?"

Why did you lie?

For a long time, Actinium did not answer. "My intentions shouldn't matter."

Logically, they shouldn't have. Intentions, good or bad, didn't impact people. Consequences did. It was the consequences of someone's actions, well-intentioned or not, that'd killed Celia.

But Kasey wanted to know. It defied logic. Caring for Actinium, despite the high probability he'd lied to her in other ways too, defied logic. "How did this world wrong you?"

"In the same way it wronged your sister."

"The crash was an accident."

They'd shared silences before. Comfortable ones. Pained ones.

This silence was humid, a calm before the storm.

"An accident." Actinium's shoulders began to shake. Kasey tensed; she wasn't good with tears. Then he lifted his head, and she realized he hadn't been crying at all.

"That's what my parents would have wanted you to think." His lips were slashed between a laugh and a wince, his black eyes aglow with pain. "No, Mizuhara. Call it for what it was: murder."

||||| ||||| ||||| ||||| ||||| ||||| ||||| ||

DISBELIEF. GRIEF. ANGER. SHOCK. BY the time I run every emotion programmed into me, the timer on the pod is down to 191 HR 07 MIN 31 S.

How many days is that? I do the math. Easily. Mentally. My vision swims as I notice these things that make me . . . not me.

In 7.96355 days, the pod will stop functioning. Everyone will be doomed, trapped forever in stasis, but first to die will be the person I pushed. *Not my sister*, I tell myself, when I finally get to my feet and back away. Not Kay. Kay wouldn't want me to die for her. Wouldn't want to kill me, like Hero, except it's incomparable, because Hero had no awareness over his actions. No control. Kay is in perfect control—of herself, and of me. She designed me so that I would have no choice over my own life, no dignity in my own death.

Realizing that is what ultimately gives me the strength to walk away.

I leave the facility, determined and undaunted by the prospect of surfacing from the bottom of the ocean and swimming back to the island. Or so I tell myself. Because I swim too fast, like I'm scared that I might regret my decision, and the more I try to escape, the more my body numbs and the line between my consciousness and my . . . *programming* blurs and the memories slip back in even though they aren't mine; I don't want—

· · ·

Back at the dome.

· · ·

Back at the surface.

· · ·

Back at the dome, *in* the dome, standing before the stasis pod, the timer glowing on its door.

<u>164</u> HR <u>18</u> MIN <u>59</u> S

6.84651, my mind thinks, before I wrench it—and my body—away, run before both are overtaken again.

· · ·

Back at the surface.

This time I go slow. Every stroke hurts. It feels like I'm swimming through stone.

Sunrise, sunset, sunrise.

Five days left now.

I'm so tired.

So weak.

Am I hallucinating when I see land? Or—worse—am I'm really back at the dome and I can't trust the optics of my mind?

No, I'm on the shore. This grittiness—it's sand.

I collapse on it, boneless. Brainless. I could pass out. But I didn't come this far just to let my unconscious regain command.

I make myself stand.

I'm back on the island, and I've never been happier. I spot the house—and energize when I remember who's in it.

That energy curdles to unease when I enter the kitchen. Dust coats the countertops. How long has it been? I recall my excruciating swim. Two days to return to the island on my final attempt, but factor in all the time I lost in between and the time it took reach the dome in the first place and that means—

"I've been gone for five days."

"Agree," says U-me, rolling out from the living room.

Five days, Hero's been tied up.

He's conscious when I enter M.M.'s bedroom. A recent development, I pray. Even if he doesn't need food or water to survive, he doesn't *know* that, and it's not even worth asking if he's okay. Who would be, after being bound to a bed for five days? Unable to meet his eye, I focus on untying him, the task made harder because his wrists and ankles have swelled around the rope, and as I struggle, he poses the question on me instead.

"Are you okay?"

His voice is soft as ever. My fingers stop, and I make the mistake of looking at him. Under his sky-colored gaze, I feel translucent. I wonder if he can see the murderer under my skin—the girl who killed him and the girl who, in the coming days, will also kill her so-called sister.

I wonder if he would flinch away from my touch if he knew what these hands could do.

But when Hero says, "I'm guessing I tried to kill you again," I remember I'm all alone in knowing our place in the universe has forever changed. This boy is no longer the biggest threat to my existence. The truth is so much more sinister.

And my first instinct is to shield Hero from it. "No, love. You didn't do anything like that."

The lie comes easily. Have I done it before? Lied to protect someone I care about? Or would that be Celia? Who am I? Celia, or Cee?

"Then . . ." Hero trails off, trying to make sense of his circumstances.

"What did I say?" I attack the knots with newfound resolve. "I like it kinky."

I undo the final knot. The ropes fall, and Hero grimaces as he flexes his wrists. His pain pains me, and to my alarm, I find I still have tears left to cry. At my sniff, Hero glances up. "Cee?" Before he can ask me what's wrong, I silence him with a kiss. I swallow his questions, my tears, and relish the way he said my name—not as a letter, or the third iteration of some experiment. *C-E-E*, I remember spelling out for him. *Pronounced like the sea outside that window.* From the start, he said it as if I were real. I *am* real, I decide. I'm Cee. Not Celia, as much a stranger to me as Kay. I don't need either of them. I can be happy with myself. Live for myself, in service of no one else.

Or, at least, live for the people who actually care about me.

"Are you okay?" Hero asks again, breaking the kiss first—breaking it, I think, just to ask. Concern shines upon his face, held between my hands. His rise to cover mine. "What happened?"

He doesn't ask, *Why are you back?* But I hear the question anyway, and suddenly feel like I've let him down. He was rooting for me, the only one of us with memories, to succeed. Get off this island. Find my sister. Fulfill my cosmic destiny. He doesn't know, of course, that humans manufactured our fates. And he never has to know. I won't hurt him the way not-Kay hurt me. We are as real as we believe ourselves to be.

"You were right." I draw his right hand, still wrapped around mine, to me and kiss his knuckles. "There's nothing to find out there."

38

THAT COULDN'T BE RIGHT.

Murder. The copterbot had been autopiloted, its only passengers Genevie and the Coles. The destination coordinates had glitched midway through the flight. It was a malfunction—"a technical error," Kasey said to Actinium. His frigid laughter died.

He got to his feet.

Walked down the makeshift hall.

However crude, the PVC walls still offered some protection from microcinogens and radioaxons, levels of which rose as Kasey followed Actinium outside. Her biomonitor beeped, its warning consumed by the cacophony of trauma and triage around them, but even that faded as they walked onward.

They stopped at a drop-off at the edge of the hospel clearing. A silt sink suctioned away the land below.

"Human." Actinium's voice was as dark as the surrounding night. "A human error, not technical."

Kasey waited for him to explain. "What happened?" she asked when he didn't.

THE ONES WE'RE MEANT TO FIND • 273

"More or less what happened here. A megaquake. Victims, desperate for relief." He pocketed his hands. "They mistook the copterbot for a supply plane. Their hackers tried to redirect it to their village." A shrug-like pause. "Failed, evidently."

His nonchalance belied the weight of the disclosure.

How do you know? another person might have asked, but Kasey trusted his ability to hack any info he so desired, even if she couldn't trust him. The real question was: "Why doesn't the rest of the world know?"

"The event was cognicized from the minds of involved parties."

"That's not—"

"It was in their wills. My parents'. Your mother's. They knew the risks accompanying their line of work." Off his tongue, *their line of work* sounded like a euphemism for something awful instead of the philanthropy it was. "They understood any outside-territory *accident*, so to speak, would be used to impede humanitarian progress and give ammunition to political opponents of HOME."

"And the bot?" Was that a preventative measure, too? Had the principled Ester Cole flouted her own beliefs about the separation of humans and bots to protect her son from these relief trips?

"My doing," Actinium said simply. "I was trying to make a point. After the trip."

The sentence ended there. He made it sound deliberate. But Kasey heard the catch to his voice. He'd meant to go on, but couldn't. *After the trip—*

He would have shown his mother that bots were no different than humans.

Kasey didn't know what to say. She was bad at comforting people—so rarely did she understand their pain—but now she understood. Intimately. An innocent experiment, he'd conducted, with ramifications beyond his imagination. It was like Kasey's own story, except eviction didn't come close to being left, in the span of one night, as the only Cole alive. The confusion he must have felt. The paranoia and, worst of all, the helplessness.

Helplessness crushed Kasey now. "Actinium—"

He cut her off. "I don't need your pity. Just you."

You. As in Kasey.

As in, he needed Kasey.

Kasey, and not Celia.

Impossible. Unthinkable, more so than Actinium not appearing in Celia's memories, which reminded Kasey—"Celia—"

"Came to me. Asked for her Intraface to be destroyed. I never lied to you."

It couldn't be. Celia—Kasey—but—the island—*the shield.* "Leona?" Kasey sputtered, brain short-circuiting.

"What about her?"

"How do you know her, if not through Celia?"

An intake of breath. "Leona's my *aunt*, Mizuhara."

Aunt. It took Kasey a second to see. Not the resemblance—they looked nothing alike—but the pieces. How they fit into this new equation. The shield, from Actinium. The teachbot—*a gift*, Leona had said, *from my sister.* Ester Cole, whose unit

THE ONES WE'RE MEANT TO FIND • 275

Celia liked for the same reasons she liked house on the shore. The furniture was degradable. Impermanent. The floor bore scuff marks like scars. *It was loved*, Celia would've said.

Love. A funny emotion. Surely it'd have driven Leona to insist that Actinium live with her. If she knew he was alive, that was. Had he modified his face like his ID? Had he grown close to Leona under a guise, like he had with Kasey? *Why?* Kasey crossed her arms, hugging herself. *Why me?* To go through such lengths, just to approach *her*. The thought agitated her, felt like more of a betrayal than Actinium concealing his true identity.

"What did you tell Leona?" she demanded before her mind could spiral deeper.

"That I'd escaped an attempt on my life."

An accident. Not an attempt. Unintentional.

But the same could have been said for so many man-made mistakes. A pipe leak: an accident. A landfill leaching into the groundwater: unintentional. *Human*, Actinium had pegged as the root of the accident, and Kasey knew he could prove it like a theorem. Earthquake × humans mining the earth to its limits = megaquake; megaquake × human-built fission and chemical plants = public health disaster; public health disaster × human desperation = 1 copterbot hijacking. Extract the common factor.

Human.

"I convinced her it was safer for me to stay undercover," Actinium continued, and Kasey heard everything he compressed into one word. *Undercover*: an orphaned ten-year-old deciding to act incognito. "I knew what I wanted to accomplish." Not eye-for-an-eye revenge, but wide-scale change. Disasters weren't caused by individuals. "However long it took, I was resolved to walk this path alone.

"Then I came across the P2C report. On you. Your bots. You knew my secret untold," Actinium said, voice softening, and Kasey's spine tingled as she was transported back to the pier, standing beside Actinium like she did now, the storm around them inside them, too, her darkest truth shared without a spoken word.

"I wondered: What else in my mind also existed in yours? What could we achieve, if we worked together?" He glanced up to the sky even though there was nothing to see, the stars long-lost to the omnipresent smog. "Seventy-seven stratums between us, yet I felt closer to you than I had when we were but one floor apart. I hoped, if the circumstances allowed, we'd meet again. Now we have, and now you know." Actinium finally looked to her. His gaze was solemn. "All my secrets, untold and told."

The night seemed to expand. It swallowed the sound of life and death, shifted the hospel to a universe away. It absorbed Kasey's body; she was a cluster of synapses, firing her from one emotion to the next. Sympathy to suspicion to empathy to discomfort. For Actinium, gravity didn't exist on Earth. Gravity existed in *her*. It was heady. Overwhelming.

It couldn't stop her from circling back to the pity Actinium hadn't asked for.

Just as Meridian's appearance had thrown Kasey out of

orbit, so too did learning that she and Actinium weren't hurting over the same, recently opened wound. In seven years, she could be like him. Still bleeding. An actual ghost, dead as far as the world was concerned.

"Is this what you really want?" she asked.

The distance between them didn't change, but the magnetic charge did, Actinium's every emotion so similar to Kasey's that they could have physically repelled each other.

"You answer," he said, then transmitted her a file.

A classified P2C document, beyond her permission level. The text was dense but Kasey was used to skimming for key points.

The first one was already bolded in the title.

. . . Deep-sea pipe leak . . .

The rest rushed by . . . *Cleanup underway . . . minimal risk posed to populace . . . limited ocean foot traffic . . . mild adverse health outcomes for the majority . . . low chance of severe outcomes . . . avoid alarm . . . responsible party to front the costs . . .* words a whirlpool, pulling her gaze to the bottom of the document, where she saw a familiar face among a row of faces.

A familiar name.

Their entire family, residing fifty stratums below the Mizuharas.

Celia's murderers, found by Actinium.

"They're not just out here." His voice was quiet compared to Kasey's pulse. "They're among us, too, in our cities, relying on us to protect them from a world *they* ruined. And in spite of that, in spite of their ranks, they think they deserve more."

"Who?"

A voice, behind them.

Heartbeat slowing, Kasey turned.

Meridian stood several meters away, silhouetted by light from the hospel.

How much had she heard?

"Who do you think ruined the world?"

That much at least. But the situation wasn't unsalvageable. All Kasey needed—

"Those with ranks mid-five digits or more," Actinium said, and Kasey looked at him in horror. *Why?* But she knew why. It was the same reasoning behind sharing the P2C file with her. *Remember: You have a stake in this too.* "Or those who pollute," Actinium went on, airing out the words that he and Kasey had shared, in the dead of night. "Past or present tense irrelevant, since all environmental damage is permanent within our life spans."

The night seemed to hold its breath.

"Fuck you," Meridian spat at Actinium, before turning to Kasey. "Well? Say something."

Something. People were rarely literal and Kasey knew Meridian didn't actually want her to say *something*, but to refute everything. To deny that Actinium's thoughts had ever crossed her mind. To lie. It's what SILVERTONGUE would have recommended, given Kasey's minimal conflict settings back when she'd installed it. Minimal conflict was what she still wanted. Her mouth opened.

Her throat closed.

Her anger wasn't all of her, but it was a part of her, and she was tired of hiding parts of herself, however inhuman, from people.

Her silence was telling. Meridian backed away. Something dawned in her gaze, and Kasey both dreaded and embraced the accusation headed toward her. The true reason behind her and Actinium's mission, seen through. The facade dismantled—

"So that's why you never offered to help."

Kasey blinked. "Help?"

"Oh, please!" hissed Meridian. "Your mom helmed the HOME act! Your dad oversees immigration! You could have put in a word for my relatives if you wanted to!"

The thought had never occurred to Kasey. Did that make her a bad person? Or did that make her . . . Kasey? "You never asked."

"For charity?"

Well, yes. Wasn't that what it was? Asking didn't change the nature of the favor. Besides, Meridian wasn't like Kasey. She was vocal about her opinions and needs.

But when would Kasey ever learn that humans were complex and full of contradictions?

"I always do things for *you* without being asked!" said Meridian, and Kasey was stunned to hear her resentment. "Meanwhile, you? You ignored all of my messages in the last week." It wasn't personal; David could have messaged to say he was moving to the moon and Kasey would have ignored him, too. "Next thing I know, you're friends with *him*." Meridian jabbed a finger in Actinium's direction. "Where was *he* when no one wanted to sit with you?" On stratum-22, but that wasn't the answer Meridian wanted, nor was it the answer Kasey wanted to give: *She* hadn't needed anyone.

Meridian breathed hard, then went on. "You know what he is? The privileged-as-hell kind. The kind who takes off his antiskin and hands it to a medic because he's oh-so-heroic, who probably travels outside for an *immersive* experience."

The privileged-as-hell kind.

Takes off their antiskin.

Travels outside for an immersive experience.

"What can you tell *him* but not *me*?" Meridian asked, and Kasey thought she might actually be sick, especially when Actinium joined in.

"Go on, Mizuhara." His tone was impossibly sleek and cool, and when Kasey met his eye, she knew she was exactly where he wanted her: cornered. *Choose*, he was saying to her. *Me or her. Justice or complacency. Yourself, or everyone else.* "Tell her the truth. Tell her who killed—"

Crack.

Actinium's hand rose.

Kasey closed hers.

If she squeezed her fingers tightly enough, she could erase the stinging of her right palm. But she couldn't erase the mark on his face, already reddening.

It was all she could think to do, to stop him. The public could speculate as much as they wanted about Celia's death, simplify a girl to her name and picture and color her in with their conjectures. But the truth was Celia's to tell. And Kasey would protect it—protect Celia—no matter the personal cost. She could alienate the world, if she had to.

She could estrange both sides.

"I don't know who you are anymore," said Meridian, staring at Kasey. "You're like . . . a different person."

No, Kasey imagined saying. *I'm just not who you want me to be.* She'd say it to Meridian *and* Actinium.

She'd walk away from the two of them.

But she wasn't who she wanted to be, either, and it was Meridian who walked away from her first, then Actinium. They left her alone.

Kasey told herself she preferred it.

|||| |||| |||| |||| |||| ||||
|||| ||||

LAST NIGHT, I TRIED TO leave the house. The gouges in the door are proof. They're the first things my eyes focus on once I blink away the sleep, on my feet and standing before the five long streaks of peeled-away varnish, one for each of the throbbing fingers on my right hand. You know what I have fewer than five of?

Days to find Kay.

If I change my mind.

I won't. I can't. Not only would it be the end of me, but of Hero, too, I'm guessing, probably also programmed to terminate to satisfy human ethics. And I can't end Hero, who's passed out on the couch just one room over. I was too, before I sleepwalked to the door and tried to tear it down. We're both exhausted—him from fussing over me yesterday, and me from keeping up my devastated I-couldn't-find-my-sister act. It wasn't hard. My heart pumped out a steady flow of guilt. But then the dreams came at night, my unconscious mind trying

to get me to do Kay's bidding like it's designed, and now a bitter taste fills my mouth. I won't be manipulated like this.

Even if I remember all of our trips to the sea.

Even if I remember how I hurt Kay after Mom's death.

Even if I remember the day I almost lost her completely.

I rub at my eyes. The nail marks don't go away.

U-me rolls over to me. Together, we consider the door.

"I tried to break it."

"Agree."

How many things have I done that I'm unaware of? Better
yet, how many things has *Hero* done that he's unaware of? He
doesn't remember trying to kill me. But what if there's more?

A suspicion worms under my skin. I glance down at U-me.
"Hero untied the rope that day on the ridge."

"Neutral."

If she was with me, she probably didn't see.

But she wasn't with me on the morning I woke up in the
ocean. She was right here, on this island with Hero while I
was busy drowning, time unaccounted for, between me passing out and me waking up to find Leona gone.

I bite my lip. "Hero got rid of Leona."

"Agree."

"You let him."

"Agree."

Betrayed by my own bot. "But *why?*" I'm not angry. How
could I be? My whole mission to build a boat and leave this
island was fabricated. It's *good* that Hero dumped Leona into

the sea, even if he didn't do it intentionally. It's just . . . I remember my panic. The gritty bite of despair, like sand in places I cannot reach. The pain of losing Leona after losing Hubert . . . all for nothing.

"Why?" I ask again.

U-me whirs.

I turn my direct question into a statement. "You wanted me to stay."

"Strongly agree."

My chest tightens. "I'm staying," I say, first to U-me, earning myself a "strongly agree." Then I say it to this house. "I'm staying," I say for a third time, to myself.

I'm not going anywhere.

A tug in my gut.

This is my home.

The tug turns into sharp, stabbing pain.

My family.

I double over, teeth gritted, one hand pressed against my stomach as if to hold in my innards, the other scrabbling at the doorknob.

The next thing I know, I've gotten it open. I'm sprinting over the sand. I'm jerking to a stop short of the surf, my muscles twitching against what *I* want and what my body's been tricked into wanting. I fall to my hands and knees, gridlocked. The day's a windy one. Dry sand peppers the bottoms of my bare feet. When the tide rushes in, the foam nearly meets my fingertips.

Find me.

I scramble back and claw my broken fingernails into the sand. This can't be the rest of my life. It just can't. I try to remember what Kay explained to me, how my happiness levels determine whether the "Find me" command is released. I think back to all the suffering I've endured on this island.

The pain in my gut fades.

I think of Hero. Of U-me. Of simple joys, like watching a sunset or eating a taro biscuit. I think of the moments and memories I've made that can truly be called my own, and the pain reignites. The false memories bleed into the real ones.

How sick—that my happiness should be the meterstick. But I can adapt. I switch between recalling suffering and joy until my body adjusts to the seesawing physical reactions. I can't stop the pain, but I can stop myself from bending to its will.

I'm sweaty and hollowed out by the time I feel ready to return to the house. I crawl back onto the couch, where Hero's still sleeping, and curl beside him, letting the rhythm of his breathing be a metronome to my own.

Please, I think as I shut my heavy eyelids and tuck my aching hands into my elbows. *Let me sleep without dreaming.*

And thankfully, I do.

When I wake, I'm still on the couch. The space beside me is empty. The blanket is tucked up to my chin, slipping off as I pull myself up. A broken fingernail catches on a carpet fiber and I wince—then sniff the air.

Something's cooking.

I pad into the kitchen and am greeted by the sight of pots and pans bubbling on the stove, an array of taros on the

286 • JOAN HE

chopping board, and Hero wearing a slate-blue V-neck sweater and a rooster-print apron, hopping around U-me with a pot in one hand.

"Morning," he says when he sees me by the doorway. "Or should I say, 'Evening.'"

I stick out my tongue, then wave a hand at all the dishes on the table. "What gives?"

"It's—no, U-me!"

U-me knocks into a pot handle, and soup pours like lava from the stove to the ground.

"I got it," says Hero, righting the overturned pot and placing it into the sink while throwing a towel over the mess. "Sit. It's your welcome-back meal."

Welcome-back meal. Hero pulls out a chair for me. I sink in. Smile, despite the tinny, mocking voice in the back of my mind. *Welcome back to the island! Your life is a lie! And now you're deceiving the only other person who deserves to know! Hooray!* "You didn't have to, love."

"I wanted to." Hero passes over a bowl of mashed taro, and again, a memory of eating fancy mashed potatoes with Kay resurfaces—except now I remember we did it in holo. The food was as fake as these recollections. And this food before me might as well be fake too. I don't need to eat it to survive. In fact, I bet if I stopped eating and "starved," then my wired need to find Kay would abate. *Conditions no longer habitable: Cancel command.*

But what sort of life is that? I don't want to concede pieces of my humanity just to preserve it. And I don't want to live forever in Kay's shadow, either. This island is the problem: I'm only a two-day swim from Kay, plus a billion bodies in the sea. That image kills the rest of my appetite.

"I was thinking . . ." I clear the mucus from my throat. "I was thinking we could leave the island."

Silence.

"You said there was nothing out there," Hero says slowly. Gently.

Still.

Shit.

"If we sail long enough, we might be able to find something," I say, trying to cover my slip. If the *bulk* of Celia's memories can be trusted, then there should be other lands out there with shelters ready for the humans when they reemerge. "And I thought . . ." I moisten my lips. "Well, I thought we could try finding my sister together."

I hate this. Hate this hate this hate this.

I have to do this. Saying I don't care anymore is too suspicious.

Hero frowns. "But what about food?"

And back we circle, to the original reason why I couldn't take him with me. "We can stockpile."

Hero glances to the spread on the table. It's practically all the possible taro recipes under the sky and, more importantly, all the taro. "Sorry. I wouldn't have—"

"It's fine. It's no rush."

No rush.

My guilt congeals, clotting my heart. *Four more days.* I can do it. Four. Short. Days. I'll lock the door every night and make U-me stand guard if I have to. In four days, this indecision will pass, because there will be nothing to decide. I just have to hold out until then . . . after the pod fails . . . after she, Kay—no, not-Kay—

"Cee?"

My name draws me out of my thoughts, into the present moment, where my fingers are bleached white around the fork handle and Hero's half risen out of his seat.

I shovel a forkful of taro into my mouth before he can come over. "Mmm. Delicious."

Slowly, Hero sits back down. I scrunch my face dramatically. "But it's missing something . . ."

"What?" he asks, warily, not 100% buying my act.

I'm committed to it. "Butter, I think."

Hero takes a careful mouthful. Chews, and decides to humor me. "I think garlic."

"Yuck."

"Yuck?" He sounds as offended as I was, when he rejected my names. "What's wrong with garlic?"

"Garlic breath, that's what."

"Who cares about that?"

"I would, if you had it," I say, raising my brows meaningfully.

It's endearing, how he can still flush. "That's why you'd have to eat it too."

"Nope."

"You wouldn't even know, if I snuck it in."

"You wouldn't dare," I claim. The look on Hero's face says

otherwise. "That's it. You're banned from the kitchen. I'm taking over as chef."

"No, please. Garlic-free it is," says Hero, much too quickly, to my genuine offense. I rise from my seat and he holds up his fork as if to defend himself, his eyes alight with laughter. Then his face stiffens. His body spasms.

The fork falls out of his hand.

40

DING. A MESSAGE FROM EKATERINA.

Ding. The clip of Actinium fighting the Territory 4 man had leaked and was trending.

Ding. Delegates were rescinding their support from Operation Reset.

Ding. The plane was about to leave.

Ding. Where was Kasey?

Currently? Sitting on the ground outside the hospel, her back to the PVC wall. Didn't particularly want to be here, didn't belong elsewhere, so she stayed, watching from the sidelines as shouted orders went unheeded, victims arrived on gurneys and departed in body bags. Supplies rolled into the makeshift wards and came out in metal drums of biohazardous waste. Medics ran back and forth, carrying things, dropping things.

Thunk. Kasey flinched as a container landed and tipped over, centimeters from her toes.

"Argh!" The medic crouched down, gathering the spilled toximeters. Kasey crawled over to help. As they refilled the container, the numbers on the toximeters caught Kasey's eye. The levels for both radioaxons and microcinogens did not match the readings in her biomonitor.

She turned to the medic. "They're broken."

"I know," said the medic. She shoveled the last of the toximeters into the container, hoisted it into her arms, and stood.

Kasey stood too, concern growing at the medic's lack thereof. "They're not safe to use."

The medic gave her a look. "I know."

In front of the hospel, a ring of Worldwide Union trucks had been parked, each designated for a different job. Kasey followed the medic to the trash truck, and stared as all of the toximeters were dumped in. Stared some more as the medic, after dusting off her hands, withdrew a small rectangular box from the breast pocket of her hazard suit and shook out a cylindrical filament. She struck the filament to flame and inserted it between her lips, sucking in deep, exhaling a plume of gray. It wasn't odorless, like the hallucinogenics popular in the eco-cities, and it irritated Kasey's lungs.

"Not a local, are you?" asked the medic as Kasey coughed.

"No."

"Let me guess. VR-city?"

E-city, Celia had called their home. Same thing, Kasey supposed, and nodded.

"Figures," said the medic, inhaling more air pollution. "Live here long enough, and you'd know better than to trust everything." She nodded at the toximeters that'd joined the pile of used surgical gowns and shriveled IV bags. "Half the gov-issued ones are tampered with. The levels only go so high. 'Anti-panic measure,' they say." One last inhale, and she dropped the filament onto the ground, where it glowed, a spark in the dark, before disappearing under the medic's shoe.

"You should put on an antiskin," she said to Kasey, grinding her heel. "Your organs rotting? Now that shit's real."

Then she made for the hospel, leaving Kasey by the truck with her smoke and her words.

She reopened the P2C file Actinium had sent her. Reread it, properly, as she would have done sooner or later. It just happened to be sooner, thanks to this one exchange, that she found the data she was looking for. The date of the leak.

It fell before, not after, the day she and Celia had gone to the sea.

A full two weeks prior.

The ocean had already been poisoned.

Despite Kasey checking the water with a P2C issued toximeter.

Despite the reading: **SAFE FOR SKIN CONTACT**.

120 bpm. 130 bpm. 140 bpm. ALERT! From her biomonitor. Her heart rate reached the anaerobic zone. Someone was talking to Kasey. Shouting her name again and again. *Go away*, Kasey thought. Said. Out loud. The sound of her voice brought her back into the world and she saw that it was a P2C copterbot. Not here one second ago (or had it been minutes, or hours?), but here now, hovering in front of Kasey and making a scene.

MIZUHARA, KASEY, please board. MIZUHARA, KASEY, please board.

Kasey boarded.

And smashed her fist into the window.

Pain splintered down her arm.

140 bpm. 150 bpm. 160 bpm.

Was this how Actinium felt? Learning that his family had died without him, because he'd boarded as a bot? Because all Kasey could think was Celia had died because Kasey had been sheltered. Protected. From head to toe, wrapped so neatly in her antiskin and goggles that her biomonitor hadn't gone off in the water. The poisoned water. She'd used the toximeter. Relied on its numbers. Her mistake wasn't trusting the tech.

It was trusting the humans the tech served.

As the copterbot flew, taking her back to the embassy like it'd been ordered to do, Kasey geolocated David Mizuhara.

For once, he was at home.

She opened the holo app in her Intraface and pressed LOG IN.

No stasis pod detected. Continue?

YES

Warning! Free-holoing, without stasis support, increases risk of cardiac arrest.

CANCEL

I am aware of the risks and accept.

I ACCEPT

||||| ||||| ||||| ||||| ||||| ||||| ||||| ||||| |

HE CRUMPLES LIKE A BODY without a spirit, head dropping into his hands. The fork is still ringing on the floor when I rush to his side and kneel. "What's wrong?" I reach for his arm.

"Get back."

"But—"

"*Get back.*"

My hand retracts. I watch, helpless, as he lifts his head spinal disc by spinal disc, eyes glazed over with pain. The veins in his hands stiffen, followed by the veins in his neck.

The spell passes the way it came: without warning. He sags in the chair, panting. Shakes his head as if to clear it.

"What hurts?" I demand.

"It's nothing," says Hero. I glare, and he amends, "Just a headache."

Something tells me it's not the first time this has happened. He doesn't seem surprised enough, and was able to speak to me through the pain. "When did you start getting them?" I ask.

Hero doesn't say anything.

"Since I came back?"

After a moment, he nods.

Since I smashed an oar into your head. I slide my hand over his forehead and push up his bangs. Everything looks healed from the surface, but it's what's underneath that worries me. He could have a concussion—*if* we have the equivalent of brains. If we don't, and it's just wires and hardware inside our skulls, then I could have broken something that will never heal on its own.

How do I ask without giving our true natures away? "Besides the pain . . . do you feel any different, mentally?"

"As in, do I have memories?"

I nod.

Hero's gaze drops to the fork on the ground. He shakes his head, and picks the fork up.

"Hero . . ." He's keeping secrets from me. I know it. And I'm in no position to judge him for that, but I could help, if I knew his truth. If he knew *mine*, he'd never be able to return to the life he has now. Kay stole my world from me. I won't do the same to him.

"Tell me what's wrong," I say quietly.

His honest nature wins out in the end. "I've been hearing voices."

My blood slows as I recall Kay's. *Find me.* "What do they say?" I venture.

"Stop her." He swallows. "And in my dreams, I . . . now see a face." His fingers twitch, as if itching to mold the face out of

clay. We have no clay, so I hand him the next best thing: the butter knife.

Hero hesitates. "It'll ruin the table."

"Screw the table," I say, and at last he digs the knife tip into the wood.

A man's face emerges. Now, I like an angular face, but this one is *too* angular, skeletal almost, and I find the austerity to the man's expression disturbing. The other disturbing thing? How good Hero's crude line drawing is. Is his programming the source of his many talents? What was he made for? *Stop her.* Is it too self-centered of me to think I'm the *her*? Why would anyone want to stop me? I look back to the table. Maybe Hero is also disconcerted by his own drawing skills, because he doesn't say a thing. We stare at the face in silence.

I break it. "Who is it?"

Hero sets the knife down. "I don't know."

"But then how can you draw it?"

"I don't know."

"So you don't remember them? Or someone like them? Someone from your past?" *False* past, but maybe there are answers there.

"No. Cee . . ." Hero looks pale. He rocks onto the hind legs of his chair. "What if I don't *have* a past? *What if?*" he repeats, already sensing my resistance. "Just consider this: What if I never had a name?"

That's impossible, I would have said before. *Everyone has a name.* Now I realize I took so much for granted. Things I thought everyone deserved—a name, a past—are not guaranteed to us. And when they are given, it's for a reason. Memories are how Kay controlled me. They bolstered me when I considered giving up. They reminded me of who I was and who I am and who I could be. I am the vehicle; they are the gasoline. They drive me to "find Kay" on top of my explicit programming, because even if my happiness levels failed to trigger the command, my memories would have held me hostage to the idea of a lost sister.

Meanwhile, maybe what Hero's meant to do doesn't *require* memories. Or his creator simply couldn't be bothered to build in a fail-safe. Anger boils up my throat at the thought—that who we are is determined by how others intend to use us. *It's not fair*, I think, especially when Hero says, horror hushing his voice, "I've wondered it this whole time. If you didn't ask me for my name, I wouldn't have realized I was missing one. Some days . . . I can't even remember how I used to act or talk."

No memories . . . and no personality. I recall how Hero shifted from jumpy to skeptical to glum when I first met him. His considerate nature has always been a constant, but the rest, I now see, was never quite stable.

He rocks the chair back to a steeper angle. "I'm sorry," he says out of the blue.

"Why?" His apology only enrages me more. We're at no fault.

Even our faults are built into us.

"Sometimes . . ." Hero starts. "I think about all of this from your point of view. Three years on an island, alone. You must have been so happy the day when I washed ashore." He smiles, rueful. "Then it turns out I have nothing to offer. No goals of my own, no past to share."

"Hero . . ."

"It's hard to live for myself if I don't even know myself. But I do know you. You were there the moment I woke up, driven and strong. You made me *want* to live for you. And for you, I wish . . ." He looks away, as if holding my gaze pains him. "I wish I were everything you had hoped for and more."

My anger grows icy. *I'm not strong. And you think I have goals of my own? A past of my own? Well, sorry to break it to you, but it's all a lie. And I've been lying to you. I'm sorry about that, too.*

Then the ice melts. And I just feel . . . sad. For me. For us. We deserve joy. We deserve to live without the guilt of letting anyone down.

To live without guilt, period.

I move, sliding myself between the table's end and his knees—then *onto* his knees. The chair comes down on all four legs with a jolt.

I straddle him, looping my arms over his neck so he has nowhere to look but me. "I was never hoping for anyone or anything," I say. "Not once in these three years. Joules, I didn't even realize how lonely I was until you showed up." I rest my forehead against his. There may be lies between us, but right now it's only the searing truth. "I want *you*, not everything and more."

Thunder rumbles outside.

As I wait for a reaction, a lock of hair slips free from my ear. Slowly, Hero reaches up and tucks it back. The brush of his knuckles against my cheek causes memories to resurface, of other boys doing the same thing.

But I'm not Celia. And Hero's not just some other boy. His fingers are careful but certain. They skim down my sides and stop at my hips.

He pulls me in closer as our lips lock, his grip hardening. I shift—wickedly deliberate—and the nape of his neck heats up under my palm, but he doesn't break the kiss.

Hooking a leg around the back of the chair for leverage, I move in until we're practically flush, the negative space between us slimming as we rid ourselves of our sweaters and reveal our true shapes.

"Wait." He breaks us apart.

"What's there to wait for?" My fingers are already working on the knotted drawstring to his cargos.

He tries to stop me. "A dance under the stars."

I bat his hand away. "Cliché."

"A midnight row on the sea."

"Cheesy."

He catches my wrist. "My *name* is cheesy."

"You sure?" I don't think *cheesy* is the word that comes to mind when I lean in and whisper it—along with all the other things I want—into his ear.

I pull back, satisfied to see the pink in his cheeks and the fluster in his gaze. Then his eyes narrow. In one smooth motion he stands, sweeping me up, his footing sure against the hardwood floor.

We're nearly at the bedroom before we both remember

the mattress is gone. At least we still have the blanket, back to being a carpet, and a door for privacy. Hero presses it shut and sets me down on the ground as it begins to rain. Droplets run down the windowpane as we fumble, hands on fabric, hands on skin. Memories rise with goose bumps in the wake of Hero's palms—of other palms, other boys. But they belong to Celia.

This is my first.

Our first.

And even if Hero doesn't have any memories of his own, he's still asking if this is okay, if I'm okay, if we need protection—all the responsible things normal humans would ask. His innocence makes me ache, and before that ache turns into guilt, I hush him with my mouth and roll over on top.

We sink. Onto, into, subsumed like waves, muscle tendon sinew pulled taut, slickening with each clutch of breath.

Afterward, we lie on the carpeted floor, the rain outside slowing down with the beat of our hearts. The sweat on my shoulders cools. I shiver, and Hero pulls me in. I tuck my head under his chin. The ends of his hair tickle my right cheek, then my own tears. They eek out silently, sliding over the bridge of my nose and pooling in the shell of my left ear. They're not sad tears. Not happy tears. Just . . . tears. Warm as the ache between my legs. Real as the ribs beneath my skin. And for a breath, I forget. Everything. I'm just a body nestled against another's. We're nothing as timeless as stars in orbit. More like two grains of sand before the tide rushes in. Here, then not. Human.

42

THEY SHARED 50% OF THE same DNA. The same phenotypic expressions—attached earlobes, flat feet, fingernails that ended barely after they began. They had the same personality traits, too, such as an inability to connect with other people and below-average tact.

But when Kasey saw her dad, she wished she shared nothing with him at all.

It was morning in the eco-city. Tuesday, with scheduled rain. David Mizuhara was in his room, sitting at the foot of his and Genevie's bed. It took up far more functional space than it needed to. All the furniture did; her dad, Kasey knew, could have lived off much less.

She strode in front of him, thinking she might cast him in her shadow, forgetting that as a holograph, she had no consequence in this world. Even if she did, she doubted he would have noticed her.

"You knew."

As if coming out of a dream, David glanced up. "Kasey?"

She projected the classified P2C file and swiped it to him. "You knew their pipes were leaking."

"Where did you get this?"

She was the one asking the questions, not him. "Why go through such pains to cover it up for them?"

David frowned. For a second, she thought he might push back. Then he sighed with the weariness of someone who'd defended his position many times. "They were among the inaugural admittees under the update to HOME. The leak was brought to our attention after the fact. Given the stakeholder scrutiny, we thought it best—"

"*You* thought it best."

". . . to contain it," David finished, seemingly unbothered by Kasey's outburst.

HOME. *HOME.* Kasey could have punched something again. Again, all for Genevie's HOME.

Did you know? She'd rehearsed the words in her head. *We went down to stratum-0. We swam in the sea. The toximeters said it was clean.*

Did you know?

You didn't. How could you have?

I killed her, because I was safe.

You killed her so that everyone else would be safe.

Yet when she reached for anger to fuel her delivery, she found a vacancy instead, similar to what was reflected back at her in David's eyes.

"What if their leak led to someone's death?" she asked.

"What?"

"*What if?*" Kasey insisted, and David pushed up his glasses.

"More people are dying because of rank exclusion to sanctuary."

The skies let loose on schedule, according to Kasey's Intraface. She couldn't tell in this room, boxed in by four windowless walls, trapped with her dad. Except it wasn't her dad. Not the one she'd known as a child. An architect concerned only with his blueprints. Apathetic toward policy and people, working from home while their mom jettisoned around, from galas to talks in every eco-city and territory, promoting HOME, following her calling as David followed his.

What had changed?

One day. That's all they'd needed, whether they knew it or not, for David Mizuhara to find them sneaking to the sea, to stop them, do more than send a simple message warning them away from stratum-0. To be present.

To care.

What had changed, Kasey realized, was that after their mom had died, their dad had committed himself to her work. He kept her dreams alive while he wasted away as a person, a proxy for their mom. Kasey couldn't hate him if she tried—and she tried. Tried to think of one last cutting remark. Gave up.

Logged out.

Her consciousness returned to her body in the copter-bot. Her breath came fast. Her mind's eye was cluttered with biomonitor alerts. Her heart rate had peaked to a critical level. Two more minutes, and that level might have flattened to zero.

The foolishness of her actions sank in. She could have died.

Died.

Like her dad had died. And Actinium. The boy he'd been, killed in the crash. His entire existence devoted to rejecting the ideals that'd led to his parents' deaths. His rage was a fire, yes, but it only burned bright in the darkness of his self-made coffin.

Kasey's vision blurred; she found tears in her eyes. They weren't for Celia. Kasey didn't cry for what couldn't be changed. She cried for the people who were still alive, biologically, physically, alive, but who were casualties, too. They let the dead live inside them. Their actions were not their own. They were bots, albeit flesh and blood, with beliefs and behaviors rewritten into them like code.

As for Kasey? This rage wasn't hers. She didn't need revenge to fuel her. Didn't need fuel at all. Was that such a detriment? There were plenty of full-fledged humans in this world. An overpopulation, if anything, of desperation and elation, of love and the violent ends it drove people to. There was enough pleasure, and enough pain. The planet was a plenty chaotic place. Kasey didn't have to contribute to it.

She could choose herself.

Choose the cold, clear sensation on her cheeks as her tears dried.

Choose her version of life.

||||| ||||| ||||| ||||| ||||| ||||| ||||| ||||| |||

"STILL UP?"

I ask from the doorway. Moonlight slants through the crack I've made, illuminating part of the bed, but not Kay's face. Her "yes" floats through the dark. I wade through it, climbing onto the bed. She's lying on her side. I mirror her position, facing her, find her open eyes.

"Can't sleep?"

Kay nods.

"Me neither." Every time I try, I see the bots she made. My immediate reaction was horror, visceral and primal. Then that horror turned inward. I never knew Kay was working on these. How did we drift so far apart?

Kay is speaking now. Her voice pulls me out of my thoughts. "We can still stay in touch. Through messages, or holo."

"What are you talking about?"

"My eviction."

She doesn't pad the statement. She says it as it is. Without fear. She's accepted it, and I remember why it was so hard, after Mom's *death, to be around her. Seeing her so self-sufficient only made me feel more broken. I'm used to being the one people rely on and I hated the way Kay exposed me for who I really was: a girl shattered by vaporous things. Like Mom's love. I hadn't lost it so much as I'd lost my ability to earn it, to be a daughter worth her notice in a world competing for it.*

Still. What I said to Kay in that moment, when I saw her dry, uncrying face, was unforgivable, and if we've drifted, that's on me. It's easier to lose myself in other people than it is to see Kay and know that even if I apologize again and again, it'd be only to comfort myself. She won't recognize ever being hurt when she has been—hurt enough, apparently, to linger on my words and build a bot version of Mom. And that makes me feel extra shitty. I've taken back what I said, but I wish I could do more. "You're not going to be evicted," *I say now.*

"It's the law."

"The law serves the people." *Kay doesn't reply.* "Kay. Listen to me. You belong here, you hear that?" *Her eyes shut, and I pull her close.* "You belong here," *I say, cupping the back of her skull in my hand. It feels small. There's so much brilliance in there, but at the end of the day, she's just an eleven-year-old kid. When she needed me, I wasn't here for her.*

That changes now. From this point onward, I'm going to be a better sister.

I wait until she falls asleep, then shimmy off the bed, careful not to wake her.

Dad's not in his room. I go into mine, step into my stasis pod, and holo to P2C headquarters. There, I find him still at his desk. Its surface glows with all of Mom's legislation. I used to think of his determination to finish it as noble. Now I only feel disgust. We, his flesh-and-blood children, were left behind too, and I doubt he's even aware of the trouble Kay's in when I grab his chair by the back and spin it around.

"What—Celia?"

"You have to help her," I say.

"Wake up," I say.

I grip the arms of his chair and shake it. "Do you want to lose her, too?"

• • •

Sunlight streams past the curtains, burning away the dream like mist over the sea. But it doesn't burn away the lump in my throat—or the tears on my face. Fresh ones, already cooling as I lie on the floor of M.M.'s bedroom, among the isles of clothing we shed last night. The skin dries tight.

Right. Happiness leads to memories.

At least I'm still in the house. To think I used to be scared of waking up in the ocean. Now I'm scared I'll find her in my sleep—physically, and figuratively. I'm scared of seeing her eyes whenever I close mine. Scared I made the wrong choice—that despite everything, she *is* my Kay and I'm not Cee, but Celia. My hand can still feel the curve of Kay's skull. The silk of her hair. My heart takes to the false memories like a sponge, absorbing them until it feels like I might burst, and I'd bolt to the sea right then and there if not for Hero's arm, a weight around my waist, and the weave of our legs.

I wiggle around to face him, the boy who anchors me. His bangs cover his right eye. His lips are parted slightly in his sleep. I run a fingertip over the bottom one, smile when I remember the way I judged his face, the first I'd seen in three years. Then my smile fades.

I must have been made to look like Celia. Was Hero modeled after someone too?

So what if he is? If he *isn't*? His face belongs to him. He gives it life, not the other way around, and it's grown on me, becoming as beautiful as his voice. I drink in its sight for a minute, then disentangle myself, grabbing a bathroom towel and wearing it like a strapless dress as I head into the kitchen, where I brew some dandelion-leaf tea. I drink it as if it's served in a china cup. The hot ceramic against my knuckles borders on painful, but even pain is sensation. I can't imagine ever being without. To not be able to feel the steam on my face, or the sea wind, brisk when I open the door to a bright blue sky, stitched with white seagulls.

My days of seeing in black-and-white feel like a strange dream. Maybe this unease in my gut will too, along with the guilt of lying to Hero, once it no longer matters if we're human or not. We'll be the only ones in the world.

The only ones in the world.

The tea I just swallowed rises back up my throat. I shut the door, brew a new mug, and set it down on the bedroom floor as I kneel by Hero.

"Hey." I place a hand on his shoulder. "Rise and shine."

He doesn't wake. I envy him. No nightmares. No walking to the sea. But that's the way it should be. The way it *will* be, if I can hold out three more days. One, really, if it takes me two to swim to the dome.

One.

Day.

Left.

Smart of Hero to sleep off the time. I'll leave him to it. I start to rise.

A hand closes around my ankle.

Hero lets out a pained *oof* as I fall backward and onto him.

"Serves you right," I say, rolling off to see his watering eyes.

"Stay."

"Make me."

He cocks his head to the side. Then, before I can do a thing, he rolls me over so that I'm flat on my back and he's leaning over me on locked elbows.

He undoes my towel. My skin puckers from the sudden onslaught of air, and my arms move to cover myself.

He stops me. Unfolds me, carefully, tenderly, reverently, like I'm an origami bird and he's learning the sequence of how I came to be. I feel every spot his gaze lands, and flush. Celia's used to impassioned meetings in the dark, like yesterday's. But today the sky is clear and the sun is up, rays from the window baring us anew.

Light ripples over Hero's shoulders as he leans in.

He presses a kiss to the hollow between my collarbones.

He draws the fuse down, from throat to sternum to navel. Past my navel, to a point where his lips linger, and I think he might stop there and come back up for air.

He doesn't stop.

• • •

The dizziness starts in the morning and worsens by night. Horrible timing. It's Tabitha's eighteenth birthday, and I pulled out all the stops to get our party of fourteen into πthons, one of the few clubs that still exist outside of holo. Just coming here will cause our ranks to go up by a tenth of a decimal. But you only turn legal once, and when Tabitha insisted on staying with me by the bar, I told her to forget about it.

In the end, it took recruiting Rach as my designated babysitter to get Tabitha out onto the club floor. "Thanks," I now say to Rach. We're sitting at the bar as everyone else dances, the antigrav and fog machine making it appear as if they're floating on clouds. "I owe you one."

"My shoes were killing me anyway," Rach says with a shrug, then asks if I want a detox, or if I'm up for more.

They assume I'm drunk. In reality, it's been almost a year since I overdid the Allegro shots. Ever since repairing my relationship with Kay, I've tried not to worry her. She doesn't like it when I come home wasted, or stay out too late. Which is why I've snuck out tonight.

"Detox sounds good," I say. Can't hurt. Might even help. I've been feeling shitty all week. Night sweats, cold hands, flailing in

yoga—you name it. Now, I rub my fingertips. They tingle, numb. Maybe it's time I reinstall my biomonitor. Reinstall notifications, that is. As annoying as the alerts are, I'm not trying to cancel my eco-city healthcare plan by deleting the app entirely.

"One detox for her, and one galaxy for me," Rach says to the bartender while I glance to the club floor to see if Tabitha is having fun. I can't spot her at first. Buzz is talking to Joelle. Zane, Ursa, Denise, and Logan are competing in some sort of dance-off that's completely off the beat. Aliona has clambered onto the stage and seized the mic, and Rae is busy seducing one of the DJs. Then there's Lou and Perry and . . . Tristan. With Tabitha.

He's got an arm around her waist. She giggles at something he says.

"She was going to tell you but kept freaking the fuck out," Rach murmurs into my ear.

"Yeah?" I rub my hands; they've become as numb as my fingertips.

"Yeah. So I told her I'd tell you instead. But then I forgot."

"Of course you did," I tease. Rach has a terrible memory. The rest of us are convinced they forget something every time they walk through a doorway.

"Yeah, yeah. But you're not upset, right?" I shake my head and Rach nods in affirmation. "Who needs Tristan when you can get any fish you want in the sea?"

The bartender slides over our drinks and winks at me. I smile, then glance back to Tabitha and Tristan.

Tristan might look like he's all brawn and no brains, but he's actually really passionate about nutrient synthesis. And Tabitha is super into coding virtual culinary experiences. They'll be a perfect pair. Plus, I was the one who broke up with Tristan amicably. I shouldn't be upset. I'm not, I tell myself, deciding to order a galaxy as well. Rach grins and raises their matching drink once mine comes. "To graduating."

"To graduating." I grin past my anxiety. I still don't know what I want to do or what I'm good at. Ester once told Mom that I had the compassion to be a doctor, but neither of them lived to see me almost flunk out of chemistry. I'm not as smart as Kay, or as driven as Mom. I don't have a calling to improve the world, and as much as I like helping people, I don't think I could handle having lives on the line.

I guess I still have time to figure things out, *I think, and down the drink.*

The world is spinning minutes later. What a lightweight I've become. I tell Rach I have to go to the bathroom, and barely make it into a stall before vomiting into the toilet bowl.

That's it. Biomonitor, you win. *I reinstall notifications. The app's been off for so long it needs to update. As it does, I rinse out my mouth at the sink, and catch sight of my face in the mirror above it. Frowning, I touch the bruise at the corner of my lip. Not sure how I missed that. I pull out my concealer from my clutch and pause.*

The girl in the mirror looks sad. Maybe clubs are no longer my thing. The music tires me out more than it invigorates me. I much prefer the sound of the sea.

"Celia?" Voice, from the bathroom entrance. I look, see that it's Tabitha.

"Is everything okay?" she asks.

"Never been better." I untwist my concealer. Swipe, blend, re-cap. Take that, bruise.

"Is that Zika Tu I hear?" I ask, going to Tabitha, looping my arm through hers, and cajoling her out the doorway.

She hesitates. I get it. She shared a moment with Tristan, then saw me run to the bathroom. Hard not to jump to conclusions there, especially if she was, in Rach's words, "freaking the fuck out" about liking my ex.

But really, we're cool. I squeeze her shoulder. "I'm happy for you, Tabby." I know she'll understand what's implied, and after a moment, she smiles, tentative. I smile back; hers grows more confident.

I live for this. Seeing the people around me thrive.

Enough with the moping. Despite my dizziness, I join everyone on the club floor and dance my heart out. Keep on dancing even when my biomonitor finishes updating and floods my mind's eye with warnings, hospel summons, and a prognosis that answers the question of my after-high-school future. If anything, I dance harder. In two months, my friends will be off at college, innotech firms, and making something out of their lives.

And I'll be dead.

• • •

We live—shamelessly. We talk, we laugh, we breathe, and we do all the things that steal away speech, laughter, and breath, and when the hour beckons, we dress each other in the most ridiculous of M.M.'s sweaters and put on pants. We tend to the taros, tidy up the house, and sketch out a design for a real boat. Celia, I realize, would have envied us. This is what she craved: purpose and meaning, the simple act of creating something with her hands. It's the perfect day.

And it doesn't last.

The tug starts at sunset. I ignore it at first, just like I ignore the stream of memories, and continue to sweep the porch alongside Hero. But the pull in my gut intensifies. Black splotches eat at my vision. My heart feels too big and my lungs too small; there's not enough space inside me for blood *and* air *and* memories to circulate.

I tell Hero I'll be back, then rush to the pier and empty out my stomach. The waves whisk the worst bits of me out of sight. No one will know that I, Cee, puked up my guts in the sea. And no one will know that somewhere in the deep, a girl named Kay is dying in a pod.

Her stunned gaze rears in my mind again. It's always this moment I can't get past. The moment she forgot I wasn't her sister. The moment I remembered.

You never saw her die, I said. Her, not me. Celia, not Cee.

Because *I* am Cee. I'm alive, and Celia is dead. *I'm Cee*, I think fiercely, shedding off the last of my denial. Not Celia. Not . . . human. That's the paradox: To believe in myself, I must also accept who I am. *What* I am.

A bot.

As a bot, maybe I don't deserve to live as much as a human.

No. I won't think that. The sun will set. The moon will rise. And then it'll be the sun's turn to rise, and it'll be over. It'll all be over, I think, trembling in equal parts apprehension and anticipation, nauseated at the enormity of what will happen— must happen—and so lost in my thoughts that I don't hear him approach. Arms slide around my waist, and my heart jumps, then slows, beating in tandem with his.

"You're shivering."

"Just cold," I say, and Hero hugs me tighter. Together we stand, listening to the sea around us and beneath us, licking at the pier planks. The sky ripens, brilliantly orange.

"What are you thinking about?" I murmur.

"You," he says. I place my hands over his. "And how it feels like I might still lose you."

To? But the answer lies before us. The pier is a peninsula between two worlds, and I know exactly which one Hero is referring to. My grip tightens over his knuckles. "She's not out there."

He doesn't say anything to that.

"Tell me this is stupid."

No reply.

"Say it!" I spin around and pound a fist against his chest. He lets me. "Say it, dammit!"

"She'll always be out there," Hero finally says, exactly the *opposite* of what I needed to hear. "As long as you exist, your hope will, too."

Hope? I've got dread and panic and guilt and fear, but no hope. None whatsoever. Hero wouldn't know, though. He still thinks I *want* to find Kay. He doesn't know that finding Kay would mean losing myself. Now, I don't think my life is worth a billion, but unlike Celia, I don't *care* what the masses think. Don't need to please my friends. I've survived three years marooned on an abandoned island, for fuck's sake. I have me. U-me.

And him. I lift my fist from Hero's chest, lift my gaze next. "What do *you* want?" Hero doesn't answer. "Do you want me to go?"

He sucks in a breath. "Don't ask me that."

"Too late. I already have."

A shadow passes over his eyes. "I want you to stay," he finally admits. "I want to *make* you stay, in every way I can. But—" I wince at the word, even though I saw it coming. "I don't want to be the thing keeping you on this island." He takes a step back from me. "I know it's not much, but principles are all I have."

And he doesn't need more. How do I tell him? That he's no less of a human being than me just because he doesn't have memories, a past, or other people? "Look, love—"

I break off as Hero suddenly stiffens. His jaw flexes.

His hand shoots for my throat.

I dodge—barely. I retreat and Hero whirls on me, his back to the sea, and I stumble, adrenaline coursing through my veins, but not fear. He's not actually trying to kill me. And I can't even die. It's fine, it's fine, it's—

"What—" Hero chokes off as his hand surges again. His nails scratch my neck, and the pain focuses my gaze, fixing it on his face—

His face, misshapen with horror and confusion.

The bottom of my stomach falls out. He's trying to kill me, just like the other times. But unlike the other times, he's 100% aware of it.

"Hero—"

He jerks out of my reach, pinning down his twitching right arm with his left one. It's like there are two people warring in his body, and it's terrifying to watch. When he finally gets his limbs under control, mine are petrified with dread.

"What was that?" he gasps, a sheen of sweat on his brow.

The lie springs to the tip of my tongue. I'll tell him I've never seen this happen before, then gather him close and hold him until the incident fades from his mind and mine.

But his expression is so haunted, and I no longer have the heart to keep on lying to him.

So I tell him the truth.

44

"YOU."

An accusation. A question. He hadn't expected to see her. Why would he have? Since returning to the eco-city four days ago, their stay in Territory 4 truncated as delegates withdrew and the failure of Operation Reset seemed all but imminent, they hadn't spoken or come face-to-face. The hand mark on Actinium's cheek had faded, but the pain Kasey had inflicted was real.

He'd hurt her, too. First with lies, then with the truth. They were even.

Too bad for Actinium, Kasey played to win.

"I'm here for a tattoo," she said. In the background, GRAPHYC was abuzz. The world might have been ending, but body modifications still needed to be done. Jinx yelled at one of the employees to quit spying, and Kasey heard the curtain behind her fall. It divided the front of the shop from the back, the back being where Actinium's office was. He stood in the doorway now, making no move to let her through. *Is this a joke?* his expression asked.

Kasey wished. To an onlooker, it would appear that they'd left things unresolved. But she knew exactly how Actinium had taken their last interaction. He'd poured his heart out to her and she'd balked. She'd asked him if this was what he wanted when really, she was asking herself, and he'd sniffed that out. He'd pushed her to the edge to test her; she'd hesitated, unable to jump. Her true choice, whatever it was, was not his.

As a team, they were finished.

But Kasey still had unfinished business with Actinium. "I found your hours," she said. "I know you're working." She took a step forward. He stood his ground. No matter; there was enough space for her to squeeze in and he stiffened as their shoulders brushed, before turning to face her.

"I design them." His voice was pure ice.

"My design is simple."

"I don't ink."

"Don't, or don't know how?" Kasey challenged.

Actinium answered as she thought he might: by closing the door. A click, and suddenly the tiny space grew even tinier. It contained a green recliner, a stool, filing cabinets, and two large monitors atop a desk. Undecorated and utilitarian, like his unit, with the exception of the rabbit. A gray one, stretched out and dozing on the keyboard.

Not a cat, Kasey noted.

Just one of the many things she'd misled herself on.

A holograph floated before her nose, interrupting her study of the mammal. "Sign the waiver," said Actinium, and Kasey did, waiving her ability to hold GRAPHYC accountable for any post-procedure complications. "Payment upfront."

She transferred the amount. That gave Actinium pause. She'd said this wasn't a joke, but he didn't believe her. How far was she willing to go? "So what will it be?" he asked, sardonic.

What will you choose?

She told him. His lips thinned, but he kept his opinion to himself. He had her sit down, then snapped on a pair of black gloves before taking the stool. He positioned an armrest between them. The rabbit on the desk continued to sleep.

"Your wrist."

Kasey held out her right. Actinium placed it, vein-side up, on the rest.

The next few minutes passed procedurally. The swabbing of disinfectant, then some sort of numbing cream, a reminder that this would hurt. The handheld machine buzzed as Actinium switched it on; the hairs on Kasey's arm rose, followed by goose bumps at the light pressure of his hand on her wrist. He lowered his head and waited, allowing her one final chance to back out.

"Start," Kasey ordered, and so came the sting that quickly heated to a burn.

You know all of my secrets, untold and told.

Kasey watched as the ink appeared in her skin, becoming one with her cells. Why, she'd wondered before, would anyone ever want to alter their flesh bodies when less permanent options existed in holo? In her case, she'd needed a valid excuse to be here in person. A guaranteed amount of Actinium's time, just paid for. A reason to sit in this chair, as Celia had, to confirm his final secret, untold.

"You knew she was going to die."

With his head bent so close, she could almost see straight through his skull. He would have recognized Celia—if not on sight, then by transaction tracking when she paid. He would have extracted her Intraface as requested, and destroyed it under Celia's eye. But between those steps, he would've also figured out why she'd come. It'd be easy enough; a quick hack into her biomonitor. Kasey would have done the same. Top-stratum girl, asking for Intraface removal? The mystery would have been too enticing to resist.

"You knew she was sick, and still you let her walk out those doors."

I hoped we would meet again, Actinium had said, *if the circumstances allowed*. As if circumstances couldn't be engineered. What better way to reenter Kasey's life than with the pretext of a shared loss? Sister. Lover. Celia dying to a man-made error in a perfect mirror of his own parents' death would have been the cherry on top.

"You wanted us to have this bond," Kasey went on, voice remarkably steady, just like Actinium's hand as he continued to ink. The dark line grew around Kasey's wrist.

He stopped. "She chose this."

That's what Kasey had said when she'd learned of Celia's disease. The second heart in her chest was but a seed then, and her anger—at Celia for giving up on Kasey—was inaccessible. Actinium had unlocked it. Now, she'd seen what could be done in the name of anger and love, and understood why most people couldn't control how they responded. It was biological. Lose a limb, and you bleed. Pain was directly proportional to the value of what was lost.

To Kasey, Celia wasn't an organ or limb. She was light that Kasey, as a human and not a plant, didn't need to survive. Still, her warmth was missed. Her death had left Kasey's sky without a sun.

"I don't care what she chose," she said to Actinium. Her voice rasped. "You knew what she meant to me."

The needle stopped.

"And you?" Actinium's head finally lifted; his gaze burned into hers. Close, but when Kasey measured the distance between their eyes with her Intraface, still too far. "Do you know how much you meant to her? When I say she chose this, I mean she chose *you*. She chose to leave and accept her fate because she knew you'd try to convince her out of it. She didn't want you to pod yourself." Kasey couldn't follow. *What do you mean?*—but Actinium had already *tsk*ed in exasperation. "You refuse to see it. I debated on how to explain my stake in finding Celia's truth to you, but then you showed up, so ready to believe I loved her without evidence or proof. For someone so analytical, you assumed."

So? Everyone had an exception to their rules. Celia was Kasey's. "You led me on."

A muscle tensed in Actinium's jaw. Was it regret Kasey saw in his eyes, or a trick of light? The needle returned to her skin before she could decide, and she winced at the increased pressure.

"I planned on telling you when the time was right." His voice dropped to a mutter. "Clearly, I was justified. You learned too much too soon, and look where we've ended up."

The buzz filled the silence. The sleeping rabbit twitched its nose.

"No," Kasey said quietly. She tracked the movements of Actinium's hand. Stroke, lift, blot. "This was always to be our end." Stroke, lift, blot. "Your truth showed me I must live mine."

"And what is that? This?" Stroke. "Even now you chain yourself to her." Lift. No blot. The excess ink feathered on Kasey's skin. "You think you're inferior to her, but you're not. Look at me," he said, and Kasey did—with an imperceptible forward lean this time.

One. Two. Three seconds, at the requisite distance.

"You're brilliant," Actinium said, in perfect harmony with the completion jingle that rang in Kasey's head. A pop-up appeared in her mind's eye.

SCAN COMPLETE

She had what she needed. She'd chosen, as had he. His vengeance wasn't hers.

It was time to let him go.

But that would mean giving up on the boy who'd, in his

own twisted way, been there for her as she came to terms with Celia's death. The boy who'd built a shield around the island to protect his loved ones, and given his antiskin without second thought to a frontline medic. His beliefs may have outgrown his parents', but Kasey still saw a glimmer of the child in the photograph, standing between Ester and Frain, raised by the ethics of medicine, named after the scientist who'd discovered elemental actinium, the key to curing cancers of old. He was the dark-eyed boy, always hiding, whom Kasey had hidden from too. They'd been similar from the start, determined to be strangers if only to resist the socialization attempts of their moms.

If she was going to leave, she had to offer him the same way out.

"We could be free from them," she said. *From the dead.*

"Freedom is running away."

"Choose science with me."

"Science." Actinium scoffed. "Every cure enables the creation of another disease."

"So we cure them."

"*People* are the disease, Mizuhara."

Kasey fell silent. She would miss debating with him, no topic too sensitive to broach. Miss . . . this. This common language they had, even if it was based on lies.

Actinium must've felt it too. When he returned to inking, his hand shook against her skin. "I thought you'd understand." His voice sounded younger. "You, of all people."

Yes, Kasey the anomaly. The one with the mechanical mind,

who'd built bots just like him. The only person who knew all of him.

And consequently, the only person who could stop him.

"I know, you know," said Actinium, gaze still down, and Kasey's breath momentarily froze. "You won't forgive me. Your logic ends with her."

And yours, with your parents. Logic ended where love began.

If Kasey loved Actinium, she'd excise his parents from his memory. Others would see it as cruel; she saw it as kind. He'd be able to live his life free of theirs. But Actinium was right. She would never forgive him, and therefore never love him. Following her heart meant following logic, leaving no room for random acts of kindness. Logic told her this:

Eventually, humanity would need Operation Reset, and as long as Actinium was out there, privy to its inner workings, he would hijack it, make it serve his own motives. Kasey wouldn't excise his motivation, but she could remove the fuel she'd added to it.

She checked the tattoo. It wasn't finished yet.

Incomplete it'd have to be, then.

"I'm sorry," said Kasey, before hacking into Actinium's bio-monitor with the retina info she'd scanned, just like she'd once hacked Celia's. Given the number of times they'd discussed their plan, in a variety of settings, it would have taken her too long to set the parameters. So Kasey did the more foolproof thing.

As the rabbit on the desk woke, she cognicized Actinium's every memory of her.

卌 卌 卌 卌 卌 卌 卌 卌 卌

I TELL HIM EVERYTHING. ABOUT Kay. About me. About the facility in the sea. Time does not stop for my confession, and the orange of the sky rots to russet. The clouds become bruises. The sea bleeds around the horizon, the sun puncturing its navy skin. Our shadows grow long over the pier planks, and Hero's touches my toes by the time I finish.

Finally, he speaks. "How many times have I tried to kill you?"

One time on the beach. Possibly one time on the ridge. One time on Genevie, and one time just now.

"Two?" Hero asks as I say, "Three."

Silence.

"Maybe four," I add, my voice quiet.

The last of the sun sinks. The air cools. The tide rises, blue-black, washing over the planks and sloshing at our feet as Hero begins to pace back and forth.

He comes to a sudden stop. He covers his face with both hands before pushing them through his hair, then turns to face me. "Why didn't you tell me?"

Because I wanted to protect you, and because it doesn't matter. We're real. But every reason sounds like an excuse. By lying to him, I chose *for* him, just like Kay chose for me. I took away his autonomy.

"I'm sorry," I whisper, the words paltry.

His breathing accelerates. I had a whole dive to the bottom of the sea to show me that I wasn't human. He's getting this all at once.

"Hero . . ." I start, but he's already shouldering past me. He strides down the pier. *"Hero!"* I turn after him, but don't chase him. I don't deserve to; he needs space and time.

He doesn't come back to the house that night.

Around midnight, I search for him along the shore and at the cove. No luck. The wind picks up. U-me greets me on the porch as I return, but I don't have the energy to entertain her. I sit on the couch, legs to my chest, arms crossed atop my kneecaps, and bury my face in the nest of limbs. Eventually, my mind goes dark like my vision. This time, I dream my old dreams. The touchstone images—of cherry ice pops that melt too quickly, a sequined dress that fits my body like a second skin, and Kay's hand, reaching for mine as I climb down a white ladder to join her in the sea—are almost comforting, even if I still wake up with tears on my face. I wipe them off before heading to the kitchen, brew tea like it's a part of some normal routine. My hands shake.

Final day.

The kitchen door opens as I'm filling a mug—or trying to. I can't seem to aim and most of the tea has spilled onto the countertop. I glance up from my mess to find Hero in the doorway, in the same clothes as yesterday, hair windswept.

"Where did you—"

His mouth's on mine before I can finish. I start to kiss him back; he breaks away to lift me.

We end up at the counter—on it, against it, clothes half on, half off. Our rhythm is serrated, like the shards of sound we don't manage to swallow. The countertop drives into my tailbone, and my nails dig into his shoulders as we come apart.

"Are you okay?" It's the first thing Hero asks after he finds the air for words. His breath is ragged, and he rests his forehead against my shoulder to catch the rest of it.

"Better than okay," I gasp back.

We clutch each other like we're breakable. But we're not. We may be breathless right now, but we'll never be permanently without breath.

"How can it be?" Hero whispers into my shoulder. He lifts his head to look at me, and the confusion in his gaze blisters me like a flame. "You and I . . . we both feel so real."

"We *are* real, Hero."

"But so are the people—"

I press a finger to his lips. "Don't think about them."

"But I have to." He pulls my hand away. "Because if you decide to wake them, I might stop you. I might kill you. The worst is that I don't *know* what I might do, Cee." He begins to tremble. "I just don't know."

"Shhh." I take his head into my hands and draw him to my chest. His tears run warm over my breast and down my ribs.

"It's okay," I say, even as my own heart clenches around my false memories of Kay. We are the same, Hero and me. All we can do is live and feel as much as we can, to rebel against the life and feelings we can't control. "It's okay, love."

"Strongly agree," comes U-me's voice from the doorway leading to the living room, and I glare at her. But then Hero coughs out a wet laugh. A real one. This is our normal. Voyeuristic androids and tears shed over our overlords.

Slowly, we separate ourselves. Even more slowly, we get dressed, prolonging the present. As I tighten the drawstring to my cargos, Hero pauses, sweater caught around his elbows. His gaze drifts.

"Hero?"

Eyes refocusing, he shrugs his head through the neck opening. It leaves his hair going every which way. "Will you come with me somewhere?"

Honestly, I was looking to stay in. In this house, I feel protected. Kept at a distance—however slight—from the sea. Justified in defending my home and life.

But Hero looks like he needs air, so I open the kitchen door and say, "Lead the way."

Hero does, pausing only when U-me follows us down the porch. "U-me, mind if it's just us?"

U-me whirs.

"She doesn't do questions," I explain to Hero, then to U-me: "Stay, U-me."

U-me blinks, unhappy with the order, but honoring it and letting me and Hero go.

We trek past the rocks behind the house, over the squidgy mud and then the shale scape. The fog is thick today, reducing visibility to mere meters, but Hero moves as if he took this path not too long ago.

"Why do you think I was made?" he asks casually, some minutes into our walk.

I try to give an equally casual answer. "I don't know."

"You were made to wake your sister."

"Sure."

"Who's supposed to wake the entire population. And I'm supposed to end you." *You don't know that*—but I guess there's no one else on this island for him to kill. "Why?" asks Hero.

The topic feels morbid, but I should be glad Hero is comfortable enough to talk about it. "Dunno. Maybe the person who made you didn't want the entire population waking up."

"Sounds like an asshole."

"We don't know what the world . . ." I trail off, searching for the right verb tense. "*Was* like. Maybe everyone turned evil, and whoever made you was trying to do good."

"You don't have to make me feel better, Cee."

His voice, while quiet, holds a rare edge. My mouth opens and closes, fishing for words.

"Sorry." We speak at the same time, break off, and try again. "I just—"

I smile. "Joules, are we a mess."

Hero shakes his head. "*I'm* a mess. I'm not even programmed with the right language."

"Right language?"

"Yeah. You say words I don't understand, like 'Joules.'"

"How do you know Joules isn't my secret lover?" I tease as we walk around a shelf of shale.

Hero doesn't say anything for a second. "Do you? Have a secret lover."

"*Did*," I correct. "And I—" I correct myself. "*Celia* . . . well, she knew a lot of boys."

"And here I thought I had no competition."

"Consider yourself lucky we met on this island," I say, and Hero laughs, but silence descends as we come to the ridge.

On a day like this, I can't see the top. It's just an ombre of gray fog and stone, the neon-orange rope the only thing breaking up the monochrome. I catch myself wondering if the ridge was always a ridge, or if it once served some practical purpose. It couldn't have been a mountain—it's too narrow in width— but maybe it was a—

Levee. The thought comes abruptly. *And the shrines on the other side used to be houses. People lived in them, 989 years ago.*

Eerie. I run my tongue over the backs of my teeth, noticing the build-up of plaque. "Want to turn back?"

"If you want to," says Hero.

Something in his voice makes me hesitate. "What do you want?"

Don't ask me that, he said last night, when I posed the same question.

But today, he says, "To climb."

"For fun?"

"Why not? If beach yoga is your thing, rock-climbing can be mine."

Add extreme sports to our list of common hobbies, then. "Okay," I say, grabbing the rope. "But I want a shoulder massage afterward."

"Can do," says Hero, taking a hold of the leftover rope behind me.

I've been away from the ridge long enough that my muscles are stiff. Maybe a normal human can't even make this climb without dying, and as I near the top, I recall Kay's words.

We designed you to be mechanically hardier than a real human.

How many times did I fall in the beginning? More than I care to remember, that's for sure. I've had more than my fair share of broken bones. But I always heal. And then there've been the handful of *really* bad falls—too high up, the ground too far—where I've blacked out. Did I die? Have I been revived, like Hero? Would death leave a physical mark on my body, at least?

I realize I don't know the answer to that, and when Hero reaches the top behind me, I turn to him and clasp his face between my hands. I've checked his forehead before, but now I check again, searching for a scar and finding none. His wound has healed over completely. I should be troubled, because that means I might have lost scars myself, but I'm just relieved I don't see a single trace of my killing blow. I start to quiver, my breathing becoming rapid.

"Hey." Hero holds my wrists. "It's okay. I'm okay."

"No. No, you're not." Am I hyperventilating? Definitely.

Why now, though? I've faced scarier things. But nothing beats realizing our bodies are not ours, and even if Kay ceases to exist, her control over us remains indestructible as long as we do too.

"Cee, really, I'm oka—"

"I cracked your head open with an *oar*."

Hero blinks. "The oar I made?"

I nod, bottom lip trembling.

"So I died, and came back . . ." *to life* ". . . hours later," he finishes, skipping the words we both know.

Again, I nod.

I didn't cry, not then.

I cry now, hands still cupped around his face.

Hero thumbs away my tears, brushing them from my lips. Then, slowly, so different from the rush of before, he angles his head. His mouth replaces his fingertips.

He kisses me, featherlight, and I'm the one who presses in. He lets me, before backing toward the edge. Rocks tumble down the ridge.

I start to tell him to be careful, before I realize he has been this entire time. This walk was carefully planned. This climb. This kiss, as carefully planted as a first.

Or a last.

"I wanted to give you the space to decide," Hero says, and my mind pinwheels. What did he just ask me to confirm? *So I died. Came back hours later.* "The time. Without my inter-ference, mental or physical. And this"—he glances over the edge—"is the only way I know how."

No—

334 • JOAN HE

I scramble for him, and almost reach him, but falter when he says, "Don't, Cee." His voice is soft. Fearless. His eyes, though—I think I see fear there, but the wind covers them with his hair, and his lips smile. "Don't choose me, or her. Choose yourself."

Then he jumps.

46

THE DEATH OF OPERATION RESET came quietly on deadline day. Only 29% of delegates had pledged. The world had failed to come together. Behind the scenes, the solution's two masterminds had suffered their own bitter break. But unlike a megaquake, there were no reverberations to be felt. Not in the eco-cities, at least; business as usual on this Sunday afternoon. In eco-city 3, residents milled through stratum-25's emporium, going from vendor to vendor as they did their shopping for the odd essential. Few noticed the P2C symbol materialize in midair, at the center of the piazza.

But they did notice the girl that appeared moments later.

Her holograph spawned like a game avatar in the middle of not just stratum-25, but of every stratum, in every eco-city. She wore a black school blazer. Her hair was bobbed, her bangs combed straight. Her face had last been seen blurred and bloodied in a viral clip. Now it was clean and fresh, as far as the crowds could tell.

Only her mind was obscured from them.

It was better that way, for a tempest still raged in Kasey's brain. Everyone lived at the expense of someone else. Those who refused to admit that, who'd rejected the solution because they could *afford* to, because it *inconvenienced* them . . . well, maybe Actinium was right and they didn't deserve saving in this finite, material world, where more for someone meant less for someone else.

But science was infinite. Science knew no revenge. No emotion. It was above the gnarly questions of who ought to live and who ought to die for infringing on another's right to life. Science was what made Kasey feel alive.

And after a five-year ban, it was hers again.

Kasey breathed in. In another timeline, she read the lines scripted for her by P2C. It'd be wise to; they almost hadn't permitted her this postmortem speech after the Territory 4 debacle.

In yet another timeline, she condemned the territories that'd rejected Operation Reset, and revealed the name of the company that'd killed Celia while she was at it. She stoked the fire.

In this timeline, Kasey chose neither. "This is for my sister."

In a house on Landmass-660, her face was a projection in Leona's living room.

"Four months ago, you died."

In a Territory 4 relief shelter, she glowed from an old-school monitor.

"Everyone has their own theory about what happened."

In units all around the eight eco-cities, her words echoed directly in people's heads, brought to them by their Intrafaces.

In a body shop on stratum-22, a dark-eyed, dark-haired boy paused his work to listen.

"The truth is you died to this world. You were poisoned by it. Like so many are being poisoned now."

Kasey didn't reveal their visits to the boat rental, or to the island. Some secrets were best left at sea, between sisters.

She brought a hand to her chest and felt her simulated heartbeat. Would the people behind the pipe leak have been evicted if David Mizuhara hadn't covered up their tracks? Did they deserve that, and what ripple effects might their eviction have had on others relying on HOME as their one means of admission to the eco-cities, such as Meridian's extended family? Again, Kasey didn't know. She wasn't Genevie or the Coles, wasn't well-versed enough in *human* to forecast people's irrational prejudices or discriminations. But she did know this:

"None of us live without consequence. Our personal preferences are not truly personal. One person's needs will deny another's. Our privileges can harm ourselves and others."

When she looked to the faces staring at her from stratum-25's emporium, she saw Celia's among them. This wasn't the side effect of secondhand, virtually rendered hallucinogenic smoke, or a hacker messing with her visual overlays, but a mirage of the mind, as real as Kasey wanted it to be real.

And in this moment, she wanted it with her whole heart. "You were a victim of someone else's livelihood," she said to her sister. "Your life paid for their living. Yet you shared their belief, and the belief of so many others in this world, that the freedom to live as we choose is a right."

Kasey's hand fisted over her heart, until she could no longer feel its beat. "I disagree," she said directly to Celia's face, and despite the fear that her sister would react with horror, she went on. "In our time, freedom is a privilege. Life is a right. We must protect life, first and foremost. Together, we pay this price.

"But down the line, we may be able to create the world you dreamed of. Where neither life nor freedom has to be rationed. You always believed it was possible." At that, Celia smiled, and Kasey's throat fogged. "I will, too."

Then she logged out, returning to her stasis pod in the Mizuhara unit. Her eyes opened to the readings of her vitals, all in the normal range.

Now to begin again.

I THOUGHT I'D FACE MY end at sea.

But it's here, on the ridge, staring at the spot Hero stood heartbeats ago, that I realize no matter what I choose, I will lose a part of me. There is no winning.

Fuck everything, then. Fuck my tears, which blind me, and my lungs, spasming as I try to make the climb down. The rocks hurt my knees even though the pain is just part of my programming, and I curse, curse Hero, who, considerate to the end, even thought to jump off on the meadow side, as if to give me the option of bypassing his body completely on my way home.

Well, too bad. Whatever I decide, I'm not leaving him. I grit my teeth and continue my descent. The fog thins, and I start to make out the rubble meters below me, and—

Blood.

Blood on skin. Blood on bone.

Blood on something white but decidedly not bone.

Spindly tubules tear out from his torso, where his rib cage

340 • JOAN HE

should be. They flex and dance like spider legs across his body, a body already on the mend.

I fling my gaze skyward, suddenly weak in the limbs. The denial surges again, and I think, *That can't be him.* We ache and cry and gasp with so much *life.* But when I try to continue my descent, I find that I can't. Death should be silent, but Hero's body clicks and clacks as it puts itself back together. The uncanny sounds nauseate me. Bile sears my throat.

I wanted to give you the space to decide. The time.

"Stupid stupid stupid." And yet, so well-thought-out. He can't come after me while he's dead. He can't hold me and tell me that he wants me to stay, either. From now until he's revived, it's truly just me and my decision.

The rope bites into my hands as I hang, unmoving. Minutes pass. Or hours. Time always seemed distorted on this island. Now it vanishes all together as a dimension.

Numbly, I begin the climb back up.

I reach the top. *I'm sorry.* Without giving my muscles the chance to recover, I descend down the other side, hardly able to see through my tears.

I'm sorry.

I hope my arms will give out. I hope to fall, break, and wake with Hero.

I decided, I'd lie to him. *I decided to stay.*

But I don't fall. Don't break down. My legs bring me all the way back to the house before they give. I clutch to the kitchen countertop for support, sobs spuming from my chest.

I can't do this alone.

"What do I do, U-me?" I gasp as U-me rolls into the kitchen, drawn by the sounds. "What do I do?"

U-me doesn't answer. She's not programmed to process questions, or make life-and-death decisions.

But I am.

I'm not alone. A team of people built my brain—built the memories in it, and even built the ability for me to generate my own. *So go on, then*, I think, stumbling into the bathroom. *Give me your best shot. Convince me.* I climb into the tub, fully clothed, and run the tap. Water bulges against the rim, then spills over onto the tiled floor. I let it submerge me.

I choose to drown.

• • •

"I'll take this one."

The boy stands in the doorway of the operating room. An employee, by the looks of his apron. His voice, more precise than any of the scalpels laid out, sends a shiver down my spine.

For a second, the bodyworker with the puffer fish tattoo doesn't speak. Then she shrugs. "Less work for me. Though I have to say, I didn't take you for the type."

The type of boy, I know she means, who'd be drawn to a pretty girl. But he should know I won't be much for conversation. I can already feel the effects of whatever was in the flask, making everything hazy.

The bodyworker leaves, and the boy sits down before me, and through the haze I see that he's not really someone I'd be attracted to. His hair is dark, yes, as are his eyes, which I like, but there's a laser-sharp focus to them and an energy radiating off him that feels . . . intense.

"An Intraface extraction," he says, and I nod, mouth dry, and that's all I remember before the drug takes over, the world fades to dark, and when the lights come back on, I'm still sitting in the chair but the clip-on sheet around my neck is gone, and on a tray table before me is my Intraface. Extracted.

"You don't have to die."

I crane my neck to see the boy standing behind my chair. "There may not be a treatment in this lifetime," he continues, "but they can pod you and save you in another."

It's obvious once I process it. "You looked."

"I did." He doesn't even sound the least bit contrite. If he looked, then he knows—"Celia Mizuhara."

My teeth click. So much for anonymity. "What do you want?" I demand.

"To protect your sister."

That throws me for a loop and for a second, I forget to be angry. I blink twice at him, and receive an error message when his rank refuses to display. Of course—anonymity is GRAPHYC's very selling point. But then he must do something on his end because his ID appears over his head.

ACTINIUM

Rank: 0

Yeah, right. Kay, incident with the bots aside, is the most law-abiding person I know. She'd see a hacked ID and stay six feet away from the boy.

But then he says, "I know we weren't close, despite the machinations of our moms."

Moms? He doesn't offer any other words, just his gaze. His unsmiling, dark gaze, something familiar about the shape of his eyes. Then I see it—and can't stop seeing it even though it doesn't make any sense. The resemblance to Ester Cole has to be a coincidence. Even when the boy introduces himself as Andre Cole, I'm thinking, Impossible. *I must still be recovering from the neuron-damper.*

"You died," *I say.*

"*I should have," says the boy calmly. "But I sent a bot in my place. A prank, you could call it." He comes around to the front of my chair. "So now you understand." Pulls up a stool. "How I know what your sister's been through." He sits down, and faces me. "For her, live."*

The info is rapid-fire. Bots. Kay. A dead boy—Andre Cole— who understands her. My brain struggles to piece it all together, then gives up. It focuses on what really matters.

For her, live.

He makes it sound simple. It's not. To start, it's not exactly "living" if you're unconscious in a pod, frozen for who knows how long, basically dead in any era previous to ours. Plus, Kay doesn't even know. Doesn't know I was sneaking out to swim in the sea because I didn't want to worry her. Clearly that's *backfired. It's my fault, and my fault only. Kay was always reminding me of the risks, and I didn't listen to her. I chose to live the way I wanted to live. And now I alone should bear the consequences.*

"Is there something so wrong about choosing a natural death?"

I ask the boy. His eyes say yes. The option to freeze myself is there, so why not take it? It's the rational choice, and it's what Kay would tell me to do. "She'd convince me to change my mind," I now say to the boy. "She'd even offer to pod herself with me." And be twice as hurt if I stood by my choice, without knowing the truth: that I would pod myself in a heartbeat if I could wake up with Kay still beside me. But, as I explain to the boy, "She belongs here, in the now. If you care for her, you'd agree with me. So let me go out the way I want. It's one of the few freedoms I have left."

The boy—Andre—doesn't reply. In silence, he stares at me, until I'm convinced he's seen everything. How I shake at night. How I almost lost the courage, before coming here, to go through with this on my own. I want to tell Kay. Want her to tell me it's okay, that the world will be still waiting for us—me and her— when we return eighty, a hundred, or a million years later.

I want to, but more than anything, I want her to make her choices independently of mine.

"Destroy it," I say, nodding at the Intraface. "I'm not leaving until you do."

Slowly, the boy stands. He retrieves a glass boxlike machine, and drops the Intraface into it. I've never used mine much, compared to other people, but there's still something about seeing the kernel turn into a white powder that feels painful. All those memories, gone.

But Kay will always be with me, in my mind.

"Thank you," I say to the boy when it's done.

He nods once. Then, quietly: "I'm sorry."

He says it so sincerely, like he's personally sorry the ocean poisoned me, that I can't help but laugh. And once I laugh, I suddenly feel lighter. "If you run into her," I tell him, "remind her for me, will you? Tell her if there's anyone who can move the world, it's her."

Then Celia rises out of the chair. Celia—not me. I'm still sitting as she stands, cleaving from me like an exorcised soul. I rise behind her, and watch as she walks, hair longer than mine, swishing with every stride out of the operating room, through the body shop. Even terminally ill, her brain jacked up on pills, she walks with a confidence that causes the conscious clientele to turn and look at her.

It's the walk of someone who knows their place in the world.

And for once, she really does. I know, as Celia leaves GRAPHYC, that the last of her fear has vanished. This is her choice—to spend her final days under the open sky, breathing the air billions before her and billions after her will breathe, carried away by the amniotic blue. Living this lifetime to the fullest, even at the very end, in hopes Kay can live hers.

• • •

I sit in the tub until the water goes cold.

All this time, I thought it was about Kay. Her life versus mine. But now, with this final memory—one so clearly manufactured by my brain, nonexistent on Celia's original Intraface—I realize Kay is not my choice.

I step out of the tub, and peer into the mirror upon the

sink. I see her face. The girl I was built to look like. She stole my freedom of mind. I should hate her. But I can't hate someone I understand. And I understand her, better than anyone. Better than even her sister.

I wish I could speak to her. I know *she* thinks she's shallow, growing up with a mom like Genevie and a sibling like Kay, one a leader in the outside world, the other able to think up entire universes. Compared to them, Celia thinks of her seemingly outsized life as frivolous. I wish I could tell her she's wrong. She's brave. Strong. Her empathy is a well so deep it knows no bottom. Her grit is inexhaustible. Before I had a part of her name, I had her strength to crawl out of the water. I have her capacity for love, and I haven't wasted it. I love U-me. I love Hubert. I love M.M. I'd love Hero too, given more time. I love the tang of sea wind on my face and the damp of the sand between my toes. I even love this island, believe it or not, and I love the idea someone else did too, a thousand years ago.

I'd love my sister, if I had one.

I don't.

I may never know if Kay deserves to live more than me.

But I know this: No one enters this world by choice. If we're lucky, we can choose how we leave.

I saw how Celia chose. I bore witness to how she used her final moments to be true to herself. A protector. She protected her sister, and now she's not here to do it again, and it's my turn, and I choose her. The one person who didn't receive all of Celia's unconditional love, who was here for me, through these last three years, before U-me and before Hero. A girl dead to the world, but she lives on in my brain and heart. She was looking for meaning. For something bigger than her. I can give that to her. I can find her. A girl lost at sea.

Not anymore.

48

KASEY CROUCHED AT THE END of the starting platform, waiting for the beep.

On your mark—

**卌 卌 卌 卌 卌 卌
卌 卌 卌 ////**

I STAND AT THE END of the sunken pier, watching the waves ripple into the fog. U-me rolls beside me. I smile at her. "Stay, U-me."

50

BEEP.

||||| ||||| ||||| ||||| ||||| |||||
||||| ||||| ||||| ||||| |

WITH U-ME TO BEAR WITNESS, I step off the planks, into the water.

52

BUT KASEY DIDN'T JUMP.

As the mock swim meet went on without her, she stared at the approaching person, her face a haze like it'd been at Kasey's party.

Yvone Yorkwell.

"Hey," said the girl as she neared, in a swimskin like Kasey. "Bad timing, I know, but I'm pretty sure this is the only period we share and—"

"Less chitchatting, more swimming!" called their gym instructor from across the pool.

"—I just wanted to say, I watched your speech."

Kasey felt her toes curl against the pebbled rubber of the starting platform.

"And it really resonated," Yvone rushed to say. "So, let me know if there's anything I can do. To contribute to the effort."

Their gym instructor started walking over.

"There is no effort." None Kasey was still a part of. P2C wouldn't be expecting her return as a junior officer; she'd served her time, making a mockery of their trust on the international stage during it. Meridian and Kasey hadn't spoken since that day in Territory 4, and as for Actinium, Kasey had deleted him as a contact while leaving GRAPHYC. She hadn't looked back. That didn't mean she didn't regret her path. It'd been easy to refuse him in the moment, but harder to convince herself now—back in school, her environment mostly unchanged, surrounded by peers who didn't understand her— that she was brave enough, human enough, simply *enough* to impact a world she, herself, often felt so distant from.

"There is no effort," Kasey repeated when Yvone didn't leave. Then, before their instructor could tell them again: "I have to swim."

She jumped. The world roared, then went silent.

The water closed over Kasey's head.

|||| |||| |||| |||| |||| ||||
|||| |||| |||| |||| |||

I SWIM.

54

KASEY DIDN'T SWIM.

She sank to the bottom and curled into the fetal position.

Actinium had claimed she was running away. The opposite: Her life had come to a standstill in the weeks since, and with no one to hide behind, or to take the reins for her, she'd been forced to face herself—her thoughts, choices, and mistakes.

She'd made so many mistakes.

But underwater, she could just *be*.

Thoughtless.

Formless.

When she opened her eyes, the colors were muted but still complex. She carried Celia's heartbeat with her, yes, but also her own. It was a strong heartbeat, amplified by the pool. Efficient, like her mind. Too efficient, perhaps. A flaw, by the standards of humanity, and also evidence of it. A machine would have been perfectly designed. A creature with no self-awareness would have known no insecurity. This nagging sense of incompletion, like a puzzle piece misplaced, had to be the immeasurable quality Celia was talking about, its shape and size different for everyone but its existence—this absence— uniting them. All of them.

Even her and Yvone.

Kasey located the classified P2C file in her Intraface and stared at it, just like she'd stared at the folder containing Celia's memories this morning before school. After a while, she'd taken the memories out of her brain. Loaded them onto an external chip. Waited for the sacrilegious feeling to settle, then placed the chip in her pocket.

Celia was dead.

Other people were still alive.

Kasey might never relate to them.

But science served the living, not the dead. It didn't care that it was Yvone's face at the bottom of the P2C file. Yorkwell Companies, family-owned and headquartered in Territory 3, had caused the leak while shutting down their outdated deep-sea mines as a part of their immigration deal into the eco-city. Involuntary manslaughter, you could call it. Well-intentioned, not that intentions should matter.

But consequences couldn't be changed. Only prevented.

Kasey closed the file. Deleted it. Felt bad for a moment, for not feeling more affected. Maybe she was forgiving Yvone too easily. Maybe she was betraying Celia's memory. Then she reminded herself of her choice—to live, as herself, for herself.

She was no lesser for feeling less.

She freed the pressure mounting in her chest. Carbon

dioxide bubbled from her nose, drifting to the surface where it belonged. Where she did, too. With or without a team behind her, she'd make good on her final promise to Celia. It'd start here, with emerging into a world that needed her every bit as much as it'd needed her sister.

SIX YEARS LATER

"*I THOUGHT I MIGHT FIND* you here."

Over the waves. Over the wind. A ghostlike voice that, for a nanosecond, made Kasey forget who she was and where.

Then she remembered.

· · ·

TWENTY MINUTES EARLIER

"You're certain?"

Kasey asked from Leona's porch, where she stood after turning down tea inside. In T-minus twenty-nine hours, Operation Reset would go into effect en masse. Before then, she had thirty-some things to do, and double-checking that Leona didn't want reconstruction bots installed on this island wasn't one of them.

"I have the shield," Leona said, and Kasey felt her face harden.

"It won't last." Her voice, over the years, had deepened. People didn't listen to reason but rather authority, even if that authority was as superficial as putting on a steely persona and a white coat. "It might self-maintain for a century." Two, maximum. "But then it'll deteriorate." And though the island wouldn't disappear, like so many others during the arctic melt, it wouldn't be spared by the elements. "Nothing will look the same," Kasey insisted, doing her best to drive the point home for Leona.

"We'll rebuild."

"It'll be difficult." A *ding* from her Intraface, notifying her of an impending meeting. Kasey blinked it away. "You might not have any aid."

"I'm not afraid," Leona said with her own hint of steel.

Kasey's mouth opened. And shut.

They were no longer talking about this island, but the person who haunted it.

Actinium was gone by the time Kasey returned to GRAPHYC, six months after her last visit. The unit at the top of the stairs had been stripped bare, like his brain with regard to memories of Kasey and their solution. But he did not forget his ways. A year and a half later, he would assassinate the premier of Territory 2, coincidentally (or not) the territory that'd pledged the fewest number of delegates during their PR circuit. Since then, a string of murders—from CEOs in unsustainable industries to average citizens with below-average ranks—had all been linked to him. The Worldwide Union had assembled a task force to catch him, and when intel traced Actinium visiting the island, the whole of it and its residents had fallen under surveillance.

Through it all, Leona's brown hair seemed to gray before Kasey's eyes. Still, the woman refused to heed Kasey's warnings— that Actinium wasn't just a menace to society, but to Leona as well. If she believed she could rehabilitate him, just like this island, then she was gravely mistaken.

But what use was logic? It ended where love began.

"Any contact with him must be reported," Kasey now reminded Leona, the words made trite by repetition.

Leona replied by taking a hold of Kasey's hand. Kasey stiffened. She was surrounded by people at any given moment, but everyone—her lab included—was held at a respectable arm's length.

"You've worked hard, Kasey."

As a servant of science, she'd only done what it had asked of her.

"We're all very grateful."

She was as numb to gratitude as she was to death threats. It came with the job.

"Without you," Leona continued, "so many wouldn't have this second chance."

"Too many already won't." After dropping out of school, it'd taken Kasey nearly a year to find an innotech company willing to sponsor her, then another year to convince the Worldwide Union and P2C to trust her once more. Three years to secure global commitment to Operation Reset, one to devise a system to enforce universal participation. Total time elapsed: six years. Disasters suffered: two more megaquakes, three tsunamis, and countless category five hurricanes. Dead: 760

million. Eco-cities had opened their doors to refugees on a rank-blind basis, but the corrective action came too late, and at a cost. Physiological illnesses, once eradicated by the Coles, spiked again with population density, and mental health declined when holo requirements exceeded the recommended maximum in an effort to reduce overcrowding.

If only consensus had been reached sooner; opportunity cost calculations performed faster. But Kasey had come to accept inefficiency as a symptom of the human condition, and the frustration in her chest was an ember of its former self, dying out as Leona squeezed her hand.

"You did the best you could do. Celia wouldn't want you to blame yourself."

Celia. After Operation Reset's failure, Kasey had come to the island, alone. She and Leona had traveled past the levee to watch Francis John Jr. repair the boat. What Kasey remembered of those days: summer, sunlight green through the trees, the screams of the O'Shea twins nearby as they played in Francis's pool. Then came fall. The boat was finished, and something in Kasey finally healed. She knew this because hearing Celia's name no longer brought a lump to her throat.

"I have to go," she now said to Leona. She eased her hand free. Headed down the porch. A copterbot awaited her on the beach. *Ding*—the meeting had begun without her. That was fine. It'd been low-priority anyway, thought Kasey, then stopped short of the copterbot.

Maybe she did have time to spare.

One minute, she told herself, allowing her feet to choose

her destination. They brought her to the pier. A peaceful place to soak in the sea and wind, except it was hard to soak in anything when her Intraface chimed with constant notifications—messages from her lab, from P2C, interview requests, and more. She answered the urgent ones, flagged others, then checked the feeds out of habit. Meridian Lan's talk show was trending. Kasey caught the tail end to a clip.

"—polluted Earth. But what about privilege?" Meridian sat on a scarlet couch, opposite her cohost. "Those who industrialized first set rules for others. Territories behind the curve were expected to adopt clean energy *and* advance their societies after centuries of exploitation."

"And can you *really* even call yourself clean if you're just moving manufacturing out of your own backyard and into Territory Four's?" added the cohost.

"Took the words right out of my own mouth."

"Now here's a name the world knows: Kasey Mizuhara, CSO of Operation Reset. Would you say she's an example of the privileged?"

"Absolutely," said Meridian. "And I think she's playing at savior."

It wasn't untrue. Example of a "savior" thing Kasey had done: Before moving out of the Mizuhara unit and severing contact with David, she'd forwarded him the Lans' relocation application, reminding him that she could reveal P2C's cover-up of Yorkwell Companies at will. She had no intentions of actually following through—couldn't, seeing as she no longer had the file—and she also had no intentions of telling Meridian.

They'd never restored their friendship. Correspondence. Relationship. Whatever you called it. In retrospect, Kasey saw its one-sidedness—saw it even back then, but hadn't spoken up. Like so many areas of her life, she'd been content to let others set the terms. Was she at fault? Was Meridian? Kasey didn't think so. In that lunchroom eleven years ago, they'd been children still. They'd grown out of each other and into themselves. Into science, for Kasey, and punditry for Meridian. Kasey felt no ill will toward her. Not all molecules were meant to bond.

She closed the feed and took one last look at the scenery around her. The minute was up. If Leona didn't agree to reconstruction bots, then the pier would surely sink. So be it. It served no practical purpose, and besides, it was here that Kasey was reminded most of the foolish girl she'd been, so unsure of herself, she'd borrowed the emotions of someone else. Here, that she could still hear his voice, over the waves—

A voice. Right now.

It came over the waves.

What were the chances? High enough for Kasey to turn, but low enough for her to wonder if she was hallucinating. Or if she'd been hacked.

The probabilities of either, unfortunately, were even lower. As a public figure, her biomonitor filled her bloodstream at any given moment with nanobots to fight off bio-terrors. Her retina, brain, and DNA down to her skin cells were protected by anti-hack technology. She was a fortress. Opaque, in every sense of the word.

Unlike Actinium. Standing at the end of the pier, his holograph half transparent. Kasey tried tracing a lead to his physical body. No luck. Her teeth gritted, temples tensing, the words he'd said echoing through her head.

I thought I might find you here.

"It was a good trick," he said, approaching. In addition to growing more secure over the years, holographs had advanced visually. Actinium's managed to capture the way the wind moved through his hair—longer now, grown out of its part, bangs in disarray. He was thinner, his features gaunt. His black trench coat hung off him, the front open to a white T-shirt that clung to his ribs. A five o'clock shadow darkened his jaw, but his eyes hadn't changed. When they hit Kasey, she felt like she was looking into a mirror, and even though he wasn't real, she found herself taking a step back right as he said, "But everyone knows to back up their files."

What files? But Kasey didn't need to ask.

For six years, she'd operated under the assumption that whatever Actinium did, it was without his memories of her. Of them. Now, to know he hadn't forgotten—he'd only let her think so—

"What a waste of space," Kasey deadpanned. So she'd failed. Actinium? He'd just given up his advantage by revealing that fact. She still had the edge. Operation Reset would still go into effect. This turmoil inside of her—these feelings of resentment, joy, humiliation, relief—were perverse and overblown, like all emotions.

He was one soul, compared to the billions relying on her.

"Still playing down your self-worth," said Actinium, walking ever closer.

"I know my worth without you saying so."

"Then you've changed."

And he hadn't. Mentally, certainly, and physically when compared to the latest Wanted ad—not that Kasey would ever admit to looking at them. "What are you here for? To gloat over my oversight?" she asked, taking a step back.

"Partly." He stopped exactly 3.128 meters away, according to her Intraface. "Mostly to tell you that you'll fail."

Impossible. Kasey's mind ran through the scenarios. The stasis pods were guarded around the clock; their original plan of engineering them with a permanent lock, triggered by rank, was no longer feasible. There was the barometer technology, but even if Actinium could replicate it, manipulate it to wake him before everyone else, then what? The population's pods were unbreachable without Kasey, as re-habitator zero, and Kasey's pod would only open upon being found by her bot, programmed to take her out of stasis regardless of Act—

"I've developed bots that know exactly how to stop yours."

So? Kasey almost asked. *You don't get to choose who wakes and who doesn't. Only I can.* Without Kasey, in fact, no one would wake—

No one would wake.

Stop her, stop her bot from waking her, and everyone would stay in stasis.

It'd be a world without people.

"You can't stop my bots." Kasey was glad for her naturally monotone voice; it gave nothing away, none of her horror or disgust or shame. She was wrong. He *had* changed—from a monster to something worse. "Kill them, and they'll just regenerate."

"There are other ways to sway a person from their course," said Actinium.

"Are you speaking from personal experience? Because I don't think I swayed you from yours."

At that, he grinned. The nerve! He took another step forward, and Kasey instinctively reacted with another backward one. Except there was no more pier behind her.

Just sea.

Her center of gravity tipped. The sky spun overhead—and stilled as something caught her around the waist.

"Others might believe there's power in a single step," murmured Actinium, the cadence of his breath brushing Kasey's ear. Her eyes widened. His warmth was real. So was the brace of his arm. The press of his chest. "But most choices are made before you reach the edge."

He released her, and stepped back. As he did, his figure shimmered. His opacity increased to 100% as he turned off the illusion filter he'd set upon himself. He had calibrated it to match Kasey's Intraface presets perfectly, tricking her, fair and square, into thinking that he'd come as a holograph when really, he was here. Physically here.

In the flesh.

She could kill him. He could kill *her*. This close, he could have shot her point-blank.

Why hadn't he?

"I know your mind as well as you know mine," he said, but did she? Why would he give up the element of surprise? Where was the benefit to offset the risk? Surely, any moment now, he would reveal his true hand.

But as Kasey's brain fired through the possibilities, all Actinium did was turn away.

"We'll see who wins, in a millennium," he said, walking back down the pier. Something shimmered at the end of it, concealed by the same illusion tech Actinium had used on himself.

A copterbot.

The sight of it restarted Kasey. She whipped out the REM she always carried with her and fired.

Missed.

Her next shot hit the copter, denting it, but the paralysis effect was negated on the inanimate object. Actinium dove in and the copterbot rose.

It vanished with a wink.

• • •

Back in her unit, Kasey stood in her airshower. After a few minutes, she switched to aqua-mode.

It was one of the few luxuries she allowed herself. Celia had been right; air didn't come close to the cleansing effect of water. At the end of a long day, sometimes a hot shower was what Kasey needed to feel reborn.

But today, no matter how scalding the temperature, she

368 • JOAN HE

couldn't seem to sanitize her skin. It only reddened, and her blood heated with it.

If she'd realized he was real from the start, Actinium would be captured by now. If she'd been faster, sharper. If she'd had better aim—

Most choices are made before you reach the edge.

Without toweling off, Kasey sat at the foot of her stasis pod, rubbing the *C* tattooed around her right wrist as she deliberated.

The average person in her position, with conventional morals, would notify the Worldwide Union of Actinium's newfound—or rather, never-forgotten—intel. Having devoted the last few years of her life to studying them, Kasey was capable of average human behaviors. She could lay bare her past relationship with Actinium, if asked, even if it meant losing her authority as Chief Science Officer. That wasn't the reason for her reservation.

Wasn't the reason why the doubt seeped in.

People are the disease, Mizuhara.

Just as Kasey knew typical human behaviors inside and out, she also knew the typical pitfalls. The logical fallacies. The bias for certainty. Introduce any possibility of the solution being compromised, and Operation Reset would be canceled at worst, stalled at best. The suffering would be protracted for who knew how long while the world redoubled its efforts to catch Actinium. He'd win at his own game simply by eluding capture.

What a nuisance. He ought to have just killed her. *Why didn't you?* Kasey thought.

Her own brain conjured Actinium's response. *For the same reason you didn't kill me.*

Jaw tensing, Kasey stood up and faced the interior of her stasis pod. Its high-shine finish reflected a woman who'd successfully convinced her species to follow her to the depths of the sea.

But she wasn't one of them. And unlike the girl she'd been, she'd stopped wishing to be. This was who she was.

She had her worldview, as did he.

She had her bots. He had his.

It would be his hypothesis versus hers.

Let the experiment run, she could almost hear him say. *If you trust yourself.*

And not tell the rest of the world? It'd been seen as gambling with lives. But not all gambles were reckless. Her labs had put her bots through every simulation imaginable, for a success rate of 98.2%. The average population might not have been able to tolerate a 1.8% chance of failure, but Kasey could. Probability was on her side.

It hadn't always been. The first bots had deviated from their programming one in five times to choose their own freedom. Not everyone was as socially driven as Kasey had assumed. It took a certain kind of person to carry out the mission to termination, a person powered by the need to be needed, who took shelter not in a house but in a heart. Celia was that person, Kasey realized, when she ran the chip of her sister's memories through the simulation generator. She'd accepted her terminal prognosis, in part to avoid condemning herself to a lifetime in a pod and in part to prevent Kasey from podding herself as well. To this day, Kasey disagreed with the decision. Found it extreme and rooted in Celia's own biases. But her sister was only human, as prone to harmful beliefs as much as the next person. It'd taken Kasey a while to come to terms with that—that Celia's fear of letting her loved ones down could be considered a flaw. She had her own insecurities, just like Kasey, and a million facets that Kasey, too blinded by the brightest ones, only saw after her sister was gone.

But better late than never. Once Kasey accepted that she and her sister were equals, she knew what she had to do. With her blessing, her lab had abandoned programming the bots with generic memories and used Celia's directly. It was the logical choice, eliminating replication errors, and even provided Kasey a bit of illogical comfort. She trusted Celia. They might not have been "joined at the hip," to use the language of normal people, but their bond could bridge any distance of minds or millenniums.

Yes, Kasey now thought to Actinium. She believed in herself. Believed in the perfection of her design.

Like everything else, though, it'd taken time, and the last six years had exacted their toll. Had Celia been alive, she would have been horrified to see the state of Kasey's hair, buzzed to save on the upkeep, and her living space, spartan as a space station, and her nonexistent social life. But Celia also would have been proud. As Kasey came to understand her sister's every side, she realized Celia had never been scared of her bots. She was scared that she'd failed Kasey, been absent when Kasey, unaware of it herself, had needed a sister most.

Celia shouldn't have worried. These days, Kasey needed very little. The things she *did* need—her bots, her labs—were dispensable. Not Celia.

The only place Kasey still found Celia was in her dreams. Her sister would be waiting every night, no matter how long it took for Kasey's mind to release her. Together they would go down to the sea on a ladder. They would float for days under the sun, never pruning, and Kasey would reel up the words from the bottom of her heart:

I love you.
And even if you failed me,
I'd never replace you.

ACKNOWLEDGMENTS

While I first drafted this story in 2017, I was revising it through 2020. It was a strange experience, to say the least, working on a plotline centering on a global disaster as one unfolded in real life. But even in an isolation not so different from Kasey's, not a day went by without me thinking about people—specifically, the ones who made this book possible.

To Leigh (again) and Krystal: You believed in this story before I did. When I was facing a dead end, your words gave me the courage to hit SEND.

To John, who took on the torch of belief and pitched this one fiercely to all the right people, and to Folio, Kim Yau, Ruta Rimas, and Sarah McCabe as well: I will always cherish your reads.

To Jen Besser, who made me feel calm and at ease during our first call (a huge feat, for anyone who knows me): You helped me turn this story into something I could believe in myself. Thank you from the bottom of my heart.

To the entire team at Macmillan, not limited to but including: Luisa Beguiristaín, Kelsey Marrujo, Mary Van Akin, Kristen Luby, Johanna Allen, Teresa Ferraiolo, Kathryn Little, Bianca Johnson, Allyson Floridia, and Lisa Huang. Thank you to Brenna Franzitta, and an extra big thank-you to Aurora Parlagreco, not only for the design but also for the hand-lettered title.

On the topic of art, my unending gratitude goes to Aykut Aydoğdu for the cover, Paulina Klime, and Eduardo Vargas for the gorgeous endpaper illustrations. Thank you for gracing this story with your gifts.

To the entire team at Books Forward, especially Chelsea Apple, Ellen Whitfield, and Marissa DeCuir. Thank you for pitching Kasey and Celia so passionately.

To Marie Lu, for replying to that one email many years ago and for the kind words that have given me one of those rare, full-circle moments in this career.

One more time, to everyone involved in *Descendant of the Crane*. Eliza, you helped me grow immeasurably as a writer, and I will be thanking you with every book. Jamie, Lyndsi, Onyoo, Marisa, and Jordy, thank you for staying by this hermit in the most hermit-y year yet.

To Indigo for the staff pick of the month; Liberty Hardy for Book of the Month; Daphne Tonge for Illumicrate; Emily May, Chaima, and Vickie Cai for the reviews that introduced the book to so many new readers; and the bloggers, librarians, and booksellers who helped *Descendant of the Crane* find its footing. Last but certainly not least, thank you to all of Hesina's Imperial Court, with special shout-outs to several members of the old guard: Shealea Iral, Mike Lasagna, Vicky Chen, Samantha Tan, Adrienne McNellis, Mingshu Dong, Bree of Polish & Paperbacks, Megan Manosh, Harker DeFilippis, Shenwei Chang, Jaime Chan, Sara Conway, Felicia Mathews, Lexie Cenni, Hannah Kamerman, Julith Perry, Sophie Schmidt, Emily Cantrell, Kristi Housman, Aradhna Kaur, Avery Khuan, Nathalie DeFelice, Justine May, Rebecca Bernard, Lauren M. Crown, Noelle Marasheski, Maria, Angela Zhang, Rita Canavarro, Heather (Young at Heart Reader), Lili, Stella NBFD, Davianna Nieto, Auburn Nenno, Jocelyne Iyare, Maddi Clark, Danielle Cueco, Zaira Patricia SA, Lauren Chamberlin, Kris Mauna, Sarah Lefkowitz, AJ Eversole, Michelle (magical reads), Anthony G., and Ashley Shuttleworth.

To Michella, Jamie, Kat—first friends and fans. To June and Marina (fact: Umami Girls is the best chat, and I can't wait to see all our books on shelves one day). To Hafsah, most wise and wondrous goat with the best taste and keenest eye: I don't know what I'd do without you.

To Heather: This rewrite exists thanks to you. More stories of mine will likely exist thanks to you. Much love, friend. I hope we get to do this again and again and again.

To my parents, always. Thank you for keeping me alive all these years.

And finally, to William. I saved the cheese just for you. Through thick and thin, proximity and distance, you are the one I was meant to find.